Bolan slammed the M-16 across his adversary's gun hand

The crack of breaking bone was audible above the driving rain. Ryan roared in agony. He lifted his hand and stared at the split flesh.

"Bastard!" he screamed.

He saw Bolan staring at him, his own battered, bloody face glistening with rain. The look in the man's eyes unnerved him. They were cold, devoid of compassion.

"Lessons are over, Ryan. This is for keeps."

For the first time in his life Ryan really knew how it felt to look death in the eyes and understand what it meant.

He turned to run, but there was nowhere to go.

Don Pendleton's Mack
Bolan®

Zero Option

A GOLD EAGLE BOOK FROM
W✦RLDWIDE®

TORONTO • NEW YORK • LONDON
AMSTERDAM • PARIS • SYDNEY • HAMBURG
STOCKHOLM • ATHENS • TOKYO • MILAN
MADRID • WARSAW • BUDAPEST • AUCKLAND

First edition July 2004

ISBN 0-373-61497-7

Special thanks and acknowledgment to
Mike Linaker for his contribution to this work.

ZERO OPTION

Printed in U.S.A.

Justice is the constant and perpetual wish to render to every one his due.

—Emperor Justinian, c.482–565

When individuals believe they are above the law or beyond justice, they deserve a harsh lesson in reality.

—Mack Bolan

PROLOGUE

Zero Platform One, Earth orbit

Zero Platform One moved on its slow orbit against a background of star-dappled darkness, silent and seemingly dead. The exterior was composed of aluminum and titanium steel, the burnished surface dotted with antennae, signal and scanning dishes, targeting probes. Rings of sensors crisscrossed the platform.

The upper section had a row of observational windows that ran the circumference of the dome. The lower, much larger dome could rotate on an internal rail system and held long-range missiles in multiple banks that jutted from the surface like so many metal blisters. Directly above the missile clusters were laser and particle-beam weapons. On the central ring of the platform sat a series of smaller missile pods. These were for the protection of the platform itself. The pods were linked to some of the sensor arrays, which in turn incorporated long distance radar scanners. Picking up the approach of any object, the platform's own defense system would analyze and determine any possible threat. Once confirmed, a series of both verbal and electronic warning signals would be transmitted, giving the object ample time to identify itself. If the object ignored the warnings, it would be destroyed without further delay. A correctly received reply would generate an order to retreat. If that was acknowledged and the appropriate action taken the matter would be concluded. If Zero didn't receive the expected response, it was programmed to take full punitive action. In essence nothing was allowed to get within one-quarter mile of Zero without being challenged.

Although Zero appeared dormant to the casual observer, that was far from reality.

Zero Platform was in a state of hibernation. Within the outer shell the electronic heart of Zero lay in standby mode. Its main functions were in electronic slumber, waiting. But in its half-life Zero carried out useful functions. Its information gathering probes scanned Earth activity. It was locked into a ring of roving satellites, code-named Slingshot, that had a defense capability, but that also fed intelligence data into Zero's data banks. Sound and vision were picked up on a global scale. Zero assessed, collated and fed the information back to Zero's collecting station. That was a minor part of Zero's function, but until the platform was placed on full operational status it was a useful adjunct.

Zero's potential lay in wait. In the ice-cold emptiness

of space, endlessly orbiting Earth, Zero had more to offer than simple eavesdropping. It had the capability to become the U.S.A.'s most potent defensive-offensive weapon. That power would remain dormant until Zero was activated by the one man who would have the platform under his control. Until that time came, Zero would stay silent. Waiting patiently as only a machine could...waiting for its partner...

New Mexico

HE WAS ALONE, hurt, running for his life from an unseen enemy.

Major Doug Buchanan, United States Air Force, was in his early forties, a physically impressive figure in or out of uniform. He wasn't a man to back away from confrontations, violent or otherwise. He'd flown combat missions in the Gulf War, and had six confirmed kills to his credit. He was a quiet man, proud of his service career and dedicated to his country's defense.

On this particular night he was running for his life, unsure who the enemy was but knowing full well that if he stayed near the base he was going to die. He had already seen many of his friends and colleagues shot down without hesitation by the strike team that had breached the base perimeter. Whatever their identity, the intruders were well versed in the activities of the project. They had moved swiftly, efficiently, seeking out the main defense points and taking out the armed U.S. Air

Force security detachment before moving into the base proper, where they had used autofire and grenades to deal with the base personnel, both civilian and military.

The normally peaceful area had become an inferno of gunfire, detonations and the screams and cries of hurt and dying people. The intruders moved with trained precision from section to section, firing as they went, then set off explosive packs that reduced the base to rubble. Powerful incendiary devices were also used, sending intense fire in among the shattered buildings, where it devoured equipment and any of the people trapped there.

Buchanan had escaped by a simple fluke, physically blown out a window by the force of one of the explosions. He landed in shadow at the base of a wall, stunned but unhurt. He remained on the ground for long seconds, hearing the sound of mayhem all around, and realized that he had a chance to escape if he took it immediately.

He crawled along the dusty ground, moving beneath parked vehicles until he reached the perimeter fence. He dragged himself under the wire, following the natural contours of the ground until he was two hundred yards from the fence, and rolled down the slope of a dry wash, where he lay in the tangled scrub until the sounds of destruction quieted.

When he peered over the lip of the slope, he saw that the base was engulfed by raging fires, minor explosions occasionally sending showers of sparks into the

soft dark of the New Mexican night. He could still see
the intruders, dark shapes silhouetted against the
brighter glare of the flames as they moved back and
forth, checking and rechecking, weapons firing when
they discovered a survivor.

As Buchanan watched, he heard the sounds of helicopter rotors beating the air. Flame and smoke swirled
in the rotor wash as three dark choppers rode the night
sky over the base, then settled. They were on the ground
only long enough to pick up the attack force, then they
lifted off and rose into the darkness, the sound of their
engines fading quickly as they angled off across the
empty desert terrain.

Buchanan stayed where he was for a while longer,
checking in case anyone had been left behind to make
a final sweep for survivors. He crouched in the dust,
studying the base, his mind trying to make sense of it
all. *Nothing* made any sense. He thought about going
to see if any of the base personnel had survived, but
he knew the answer. No one could have lived through
that attack. It had been too thorough. Too professional.
His own survival had been due to pure good luck. His
duty now was to inform his superiors back in Washington about what had happened at the base. The only
way he could do that was by reaching the nearest
highway, flagging down a ride and getting to a secure
telephone.

He checked his position by the stars, pushed to his
feet and headed cross-country in the direction of the

main highway. It lay some ten miles west, and it would take some time to reach it.

He glanced at his watch and saw that it was way past the time for his medication, which meant that he was going to start feeling uncomfortable in a while. His exertions would only aggravate the situation, but there was nothing he could do about that. He had to inform Washington. It didn't matter that he would be in pain. It wouldn't be the first time. All he knew was that since he had undergone the final implant surgery, he needed his medication to stave off the discomfort and the pain of those damned *things* inside his body. The implant team back at the base had explained that it would take time for his system to accept the implants, and as long as he continued with his medication it wouldn't be a problem. Now those people were gone. Dead, and his medication was lost. So he was going to have to keep going under his own steam.

The first real twinges started to make themselves known after the first hour. Deep-seated discomfort that became nagging aches radiated throughout his body. Buchanan kept moving, trying to ignore the sensations that were alien and scary. This was the first time he had really felt the implants. Up until this night the medication had kept the discomfort under control, deadening the feel of implants. It began to feel as if he had living things inside him and they were waking from a long slumber. They made the skin of his arms and hands itch where some of the implants lay just below the surface.

It was almost like experiencing tiny electric shocks, and he imagined the implants bursting through his skin and exposing themselves. The thought unsettled him. It was only now, in his current position, that he gave thought to what he had allowed to be done to him. And he *had* allowed it, volunteered to be the first to undergo the radical surgery that was vital to the project. He had been chosen as much for his service skills as for the inescapable fact that he had advanced cancer. The Air Force doctors had given him no more than eighteen months before the disease took him. They had then given him an option—the Zero Option—a way that he might live longer while still being a useful member of the Air Force. Buchanan had been intrigued, and had asked to know more.

When it had all been explained, they gave him time to digest it all. It meant time alone, sitting in his lounger, staring out the window at the spread of the country beyond his house and letting the information seep slowly into his mind. He went over it again and again, at first finding it almost impossible to believe what he had been told.

Reason had made its plea and Buchanan, never one to deny what was staring him in the face, took the decision that would—if everything worked out according to his briefing—alter his life in a number of ways. Acceptance of the program would deny the cancer its victory, but Buchanan's existence would take on a new form. True, he would be alive, but he would be bound, both physically and mentally, to the machines that gave him that life. Buchanan chose his path because he wanted to stay alive per se, and he was also curious to experience this radical technology. He was, if nothing else, a romantic in that he viewed the future with open eyes and a willing heart. The thought of space travel and the machines that would take man there fascinated him. And this opportunity he had been presented with would allow him to be one of the first to taste this innovative technology. If it worked for him, it could later be adapted for deep-space exploration. A way of overcoming long-distance travel for future generations.

If it worked.

Buchanan had been given the downside of the project. It wasn't guaranteed to be one hundred percent infallible. His participation was as a guinea pig. He would be monitored on a 24/7 basis. Every breath, every movement would be recorded, discussed, analyzed, until there was a definitive answer one way or the other. His private life would be near nonexistent, and even when he slept his vital signs would still be monitored. There would be nothing he would say or do that would go unrecorded in some way. There would also be discomfort during the initial stages. It would take time for him to become used to the implants as they slowly integrated with his own system, remaining dormant until the time he took up his position within the project itself and became as one with the machine that would assimilate him.

The concept scared the hell out of Buchanan at first, and he had some sleepless nights. But he was man full of curiosity and he threw himself into the Zero program. As well as his innate need to know more, his being part of the project meant he had little time to dwell on his developing cancer. The mass of information he needed to absorb took over his waking hours. The project medical team also had him on a course of drugs designed to hold back the pain of his disease, so the weeks following his acceptance of the offer were extremely busy ones, allowing no time out for self-pity or periods of reflection on what might have been.

The weeks passed in a blur, leaving Buchanan little time to think about anything else. Much of his waking time was spent with Dr. Saul Kaplan, the man who had both created and helped direct the entire project. Kaplan was a man of many talents, one of them being his ability to be able to both sympathize and to stimulate Buchanan when the strictures of his disease and the effects of the Zero treatment became overwhelming. The two men had become good friends. Buchanan had looked on Kaplan as his mentor, his adviser, and he was both shocked and dismayed when he was informed that Kaplan had withdrawn from the project. Something had made the creator of Zero step back and analyze what he was doing. For whatever personal reasons Kaplan had gone, leaving no indication of where he had gone, or why, or whether he would be back.

Buchanan had felt betrayed. Lost. His only contact

with reality had deserted him. He spent a few days in contemplation of his future before his natural optimism returned and he had, for want of no other avenue, thrown himself back into the project. Gradually things had returned to normal, or whatever passed for normal in Doug Buchanan's new world. With his implant surgery behind him, Buchanan allowed himself to be immersed in the next stage of the project, spending hours connected to the computer database as it filled his head with information and instructions, the neural net inside his body drawing in the streams of data and filing them away for when they would be needed.

And then the attack had come. One quiet night, when even Buchanan was relaxing.

As with most surprise attacks it came suddenly, shockingly, the New Mexico night ripped apart by explosions and autofire. The crackle of guns and the blast of explosions. Now he hoped he could stay alive long enough to alert his superiors.

The temperature had dropped considerably, the desert air chilling him. He tried to keep on the move, knowing that if he stopped too often, for too long, he might not be able to resume his walk. With his medication long overdue, Buchanan's pain had become extreme. It was, he assumed, like drug withdrawal. His body cried out for relief and he was alternately hot, then cold, his joints aching where the implants were blending with his own living tissue, the neural network beginning its slow, agonizing transformation.

When he checked his watch he saw he had been on the move for three hours. He wasn't sure just where he was, but after a position check he knew he was walking in the right direction. The highway was dead ahead. It had to be. Doug Buchanan was no beginner when it came to search-and-locate procedures. It was something the Air Force drilled into its pilots from the start of their training. How to walk out of enemy territory with the minimum, or total lack, of any guidance equipment. They learned the location of stars in the night sky, the way to insure they were on course without the aid of a map or compass. So no matter how hurt he might be, as long as Buchanan could use his eyes and determine his position, he *would* locate the highway.

If he had been in prime physical and mental condition, Buchanan would have heard and seen the old red Dodge truck coming. He had just come across a dusty, tire-marked dirt road, when his dulled senses warned him of danger.

It was a shade too late.

The instincts that had walked him across trackless miles of empty desert failed him at the last moment. Maybe he was tired. Weary from fighting off the effects of the change taking place inside his aching body, he didn't see the pickup truck. It came barreling out of a dip in the trail, tires throwing up clouds of dust as it crested the rise only yards from him.

The unexpected glare of the headlights engulfed Buchanan, pinning him against the desert backdrop like a butterfly to a collector's board. He half turned, throwing up his hands to shield his eyes from the light. All he saw was the wall of light, then he picked up the roar of the engine as the driver stood on the brakes. The pickup dipped and rose like a bucking mustang. The rear slid from side to side, then it was on him. Buchanan put out his hands to ward it off, making a desperate lunge to get out of the way. He didn't make it. The front of the truck caught him a glancing blow, not hard enough to kill him, but forceful enough to lift him off his feet and throw him in the air. He came down on the side of the track, hitting hard, coming to rest against a jutting outcrop.

Stunned, his body in agony, Buchanan picked up the sound of the truck coming to a stop. Doors banged. It seemed a long way off, and then he heard voices. They were faint, and spoke in a language he couldn't understand. The voices closed in on him. He felt hands touch him. He tried to resist.

And that was all he remembered…

CHAPTER ONE

Nassau, Bahamas

Jack Grimaldi pushed through the hangar door and made his way to the office on the far side. He could see Jess Buchanan through the glass partition. The young woman was bent over a high desk, working on a flight plan for an upcoming charter flight.

The Stony Man pilot had known the young woman for some months, ever since she had been caught up in a mission involving Able Team. Grimaldi had stepped in when Jess had been threatened, dealing with the perpetrators. Since then he had visited her on Nassau whenever he could. The pair had a natural camaraderie that allowed them to enjoy each other's company. This particular visit had added interest. Grimaldi had persuaded Mack Bolan to fly across to Nassau. The Executioner had taken one of his infrequent R&R breaks, and Grimaldi had gained a deal of satisfaction when

Bolan had agreed to join him. The soldier had met Jess once before, so they were all anticipating a quiet few days. For Bolan and Grimaldi it would be a welcome break from the ongoing visits to the war zones and the ongoing struggles against the evil that ravaged the world.

Jess glanced up as Grimaldi neared the office, waving a hand behind the glass. As usual when working, she wore coveralls and a long-peaked baseball cap over her blond hair.

"Hey, Tex, how's the Alamo?" she asked.

Grimaldi smiled. The remark was a throwback to the first time they had met. Grimaldi had been using a cover ID that had him as a Texan. She sometimes teased him by recalling the cover name, just to catch him off guard.

"Ha, ha, ha," he said.

As he drew near, he slipped an arm around her slim waist and kissed her on the cheek. Buchanan turned her head to eye him.

"Is that the best you can do?"

"During office hours. You never know when the boss might be around."

"I am the boss. Remember?"

"Hell, so you are," Grimaldi said and completed his greeting.

"Now that's more like it, Tex."

For a moment the woman drifted away, her mind occupied by something else.

"Still thinking about that phone message?"

"Sorry, Jack. I know it's crazy but I get the feeling there was more to it. I know I haven't seen Uncle Doug for some time, but he sounded strange. Like he wasn't sure about things. Damn, it's hard to explain."

"You know him better than me."

"I hope he calls again. Last time I saw him was when we buried Dad. He calls and I'm out. And what did he mean about keeping quiet about his call? Not talking to strangers? Jesus, Jack, I missed his call."

"No way you could have known he was going to get in touch, Jess. Likely he'll call again. Don't give yourself a hard time."

She nodded.

"So what's on the agenda today?" Grimaldi asked.

"The choice is yours."

Grimaldi glanced at his watch. "Lunch. Then waste time till Mike arrives. Figure we work something out."

"I'll need to tidy up. Get into some clean clothes. Can you wait while I do that?"

"I can do better. How about I come and help?"

Buchanan laughed, pushing him away.

"If I let you do that, we'll be eating at midnight."

"Romantic meal under the stars sounds good," Grimaldi said.

Before she could respond, the sound of the hangar door being slammed open caught her attention. Through the office window she and Grimaldi were able to see a group of five men. They paused to locate themselves, then started across the hangar floor, one hanging back to cover the entrance door.

"Who are they, Jess?" Grimaldi asked.

She shook her head. "I've never seen any of them before."

"Do they look like potential customers to you?"

"Not impossible, but I somehow don't think so. They look more like FBI. Or IRS."

Buchanan moved to the door and stepped through into the main hangar, followed by Grimaldi.

For some reason he felt himself growing tense. There was something almost *official* about the group. Not just the uniform way they were dressed, but more in the way they handled themselves, how they walked, checking out their surroundings, one of them hanging back to cover the door, slightly turning so he could see out across the strip. He kept his right hand close to the fastened button on his suit jacket. Just so he could quickly get to the shoulder-holstered handgun he was carrying. Grimaldi had already spotted the slight bulge under every jacket. It was so slight that it would be missed by the average citizen.

But Grimaldi was no average citizen, and there was no way these people were customers. His suspicions made him step forward, slightly in front, blocking Buchanan from the men. His stance, outwardly easy, told them he was on the alert, watching for any problems.

At the forefront of Grimaldi's mind was the telephone message from Jess's uncle.

Don't talk to strangers.

"What can I do for you?" Grimaldi asked.

The lead man, his white-blond hair cut short, body solid under the loose folds of his suit, turned his head slightly so he could see Buchanan over Grimaldi's shoulder—but he spoke directly at Grimaldi.

"Are you Jess Buchanan, mister?"

"No."

"Then I don't have business with you, and you are interfering in mine."

Buchanan touched Grimaldi's arm, moving to stand beside him. "I'm Jess Buchanan. What do you want?"

"We need you to come with us. No arguments. No questions. You just do it."

"Just like that? You walk into my place and I do exactly what you want?"

The man smiled as if he were calming an unruly puppy. "Now there's a good girl. You see. No fuss. No bother." Then his manner changed in an instant, the smile turning cold as Grimaldi tensed and put out a warning hand. "I already gave you an order, mister."

"Order? Where do you think you are, friend? This isn't a military base and you're no damned squad leader."

"No?"

Grimaldi caught movement off to his left. One of the suits lunged, his move fast and smooth as he arced in at Grimaldi. His left hand, previously at his side, rose to show the dark configuration of a hard-looking compact shotgun. The guy brought up the weapon, securing it with his right hand, and he was already into his swing as he stepped around the lead man. Grimaldi brought up an arm to ward off the blow. The solid steel barrel cracked against his forearm, the blow delivered with maximum force. The impact drew a pained grunt from Grimaldi, and he swiveled hard, his right hand catching Buchanan's shoulder, pushing her aside as the lead man went for her.

As she stumbled out of the immediate area, Grimaldi swung his right hand and caught the lead man across the side of the face. The blow stung and the man's head rocked. He stepped back, anger showing in his cold eyes as the shotgunner closed in, swinging the weapon again, slamming the butt into Grimaldi's side, a savage blow that cracked ribs and drove the breath from the Stony Man pilot's lungs. The others were moving in now, dark shapes converging on Grimaldi. He was no slouch when it came to defending himself, and he used his moment of freedom to set himself, gritting his teeth against the swell of pain from his broken ribs. The pain was sharp, sweat popping across his face as Grimaldi forced himself to fight back.

He got in a few telling blows, had the satisfaction of seeing bloodied faces before the overwhelming odds closed around him and he went down under a deluge of blows from weapons and feet. He struggled to push himself upright, the continuing blows starting to wear away his resistance. His face was dripping blood. He tasted it in his mouth. A savage kick drove in over his left eye, splitting flesh to the bone. He felt the hot gush of blood, which washed downward and blinded his vision. Somewhere out of the blur of movement and sound he heard Jess. She was yelling, fighting hard. Through the swirl of dark coats he caught a glimpse of her.

She was struggling in the grip of the lead man. He held her with little effort, a crooked grin on his tight face. She reached out and took hold of his short blond hair, yanking hard. He jerked away, then suddenly, cruelly, punched her hard in the face. The last thing Grimaldi saw was Jess going limp, her mouth bloody, eyes starting to glaze over from the blow. He tried to yell to her but he was choking on his own blood. Someone stamped down hard on his left hand, breaking several fingers. Grimaldi felt himself being hauled up off the floor, pinned against the bench as more blows landed on his body. He made a vain attempt at resisting. His attempts were brushed aside. As his body began to shut down, oblivious to the continuing beating, all Grimaldi could recall was the final expression in Jess's eyes…it had been one of pure terror. And then he went under.

MACK BOLAN STOOD as the white-coated doctor came into the waiting room. The medic held out a hand, gripping Bolan's firmly.

"How is he?" Bolan asked.

"When you called you said you were family. I don't see a resemblance."

Bolan smiled. "Maybe I should have added that I'm

all the family Jack has, Doc. We work together. Right now my friend is in trouble, and I want to know how he is."

"All right, Mr. Belasko. Let's sit down. I'm tired. It's been a long day."

When they were seated, the doctor took a moment to collect his thoughts.

"Jack Grimaldi was brought in about five hours ago. He had taken one hell of a beating. We have three broken ribs on his left side. Came close to puncturing his lung. He also has three broken fingers in his left hand. In addition his upper torso, arms and face are showing severe bruising associated with the beating he took. He has a slight fracture in his right cheekbone, and it looks like someone kicked him above the right eye. Left a deep gash. His eye has swollen so he won't be able to see for a while. In nontechnical terms your friend has been well and truly worked over."

"Are any of the injuries life threatening?"

"No, but he's going to be out of action for a while."

"Is he awake?"

The doctor sighed; he knew what was coming.

"You want to see him?"

"I understand he needs rest. I'm not going to be there long, and I'm not about to put him under any kind of stress. I just need to see him for a couple of minutes. Then I'm gone."

The doctor stood and beckoned for Bolan to follow him.

"If I say no, you'll just keep pestering me. Am I right?"

"You got it."

"I've already sent the police away when they wanted to question him. So why am I letting you in?"

"Did the police ask as nicely as I did?"

The doctor shook his head and chuckled.

Bolan followed the medic down the hall and to the private room where he could see Grimaldi's prone shape on the bed through the window.

"I'll be outside," the doctor said. "And I'll be watching. Any signs of distress, and I'm hauling you straight out. He's been sedated to ease the pain, so he might not be fully awake."

"Understood. And thanks."

Bolan eased into the room. The lights were low and the room was silent except for Grimaldi's slightly harsh breathing. As the soldier stood beside the bed, looking down at his friend, Grimaldi's good eye opened and he stared up at his visitor.

"Hey, Sarge, thanks for showing up."

"I'm going to make this quick," Bolan said. "Your doc's got his eye on me."

"Sarge, they took her. They took Jess."

"Who were they?"

"I don't know. But they looked like they had military training at some time. The guy in charge had close-cropped white-blond hair. I got one in on his left cheek before they put me down."

Grimaldi was talking slowly so as not to increase any pain he was suffering. It still had to have hurt, Bolan realized, seeing the strain on his friend's face.

"Any idea why they wanted Jess?"

"The only thing I can tell you is she told me she'd had a call from her late father's brother. Jess was out at the time, and he left a message on her answering machine. She hadn't had contact with him for some time. He's in the Air Force, Sarge, and his name is Doug Buchanan. The call came out of the blue. Jess said he sounded like he was under some strain. He warned her not to talk to anyone about hearing from him and to watch out for strangers. Coincidence?" Grimaldi fell silent for a moment. "What could they want from her, Mack?"

Bolan rested a gentle hand on Grimaldi's shoulder. "Let me worry about that. One way or the other, I'll find out."

Grimaldi nodded, satisfied. He knew Mack Bolan well enough to accept those few words as a promise.

"You rest easy."

Bolan turned to leave. At the door he paused as he heard Grimaldi's whispered thanks. When he turned to look back, the Stony Man pilot had drifted into a tranquilized sleep.

Back in the corridor Bolan thanked the doctor and made his way outside. He stood in the warm afternoon sun, considering his next move. There was, he realized, only a single option open to him. Bolan walked to the street and picked up a cab. He told the driver his destination, then settled back and watched the tourists going about their business, a wry smile tugging at his lips. Taking time out to be a tourist had been the reason Bolan had come to Nassau. He had finally accepted Grimaldi's invitation to join him and Jess on the island for a few days, and had been looking forward to the brief R&R. A break from the battlegrounds that dominated his life. Bolan might have dedicated himself to a life of struggle against the forces of evil, but he wasn't so immersed that he failed to realize the need for a moment of respite. Endless missions took their toll. Time out had been called—but even that looked as if it was about to be canceled.

THE CAB DROPPED Bolan at the entrance to the charter airstrip next to Nassau International Airport. He paid the driver and crossed to the security hut. The soldier had spoken to the uniformed man earlier when he had arrived. Earl was in his late fifties, quiet spoken.

"How's Jack?" he asked.

"He'll pull through," Bolan said. "That beating he took is going to keep him in hospital for a while."

"Damned shame. I like Jack. Him and Miss Jess made a nice couple. I know he couldn't get over here to see her as often as he wanted, but when he did they always had a good time. Miss Jess got real excited every time he called to say he was coming in."

The Stony Man flier had that effect on people. His

outgoing personality reached out to embrace anyone he met. Bolan didn't fail to notice the way the security man talked about him. *Jack*—not Mr. Grimaldi.

"After it happened were the police told?"

Earl nodded. "They sent an officer after I called. He took my statement and had a look around. Thing was, the place was pretty quiet when it happened. Hardly anyone around. The cop who came, well, he didn't put much effort into things. Problem is, the police are down on manpower. They didn't even send down an experienced officer. He looked like he just got out of training school. He was a kid. Hardly knew the right questions to ask. Listen, Mr. Belasko, I know you're a friend of Jack and all. I just wonder what's going to happen to Miss Jess. Where is she? What did those people want with her?"

"I don't know. But I want to find out. Earl, you mind if I go in and take a look around?"

"You take all the time you need. I got a phone in my booth. Anybody shows up I'll make a call to Miss Jess's office."

Bolan made his way along the strip, crossing the concrete apron that took him by other charter companies until he was able to spot Jess Buchanan's place.

He walked through the open hangar, making his way to Jess's office. He hadn't expected to find anything visible to offer any information. Bolan went directly to the telephone and checked the number. He took out his cell phone and speed-dialed Stony Man. The call was bounced off the satellite link and rerouted through a series of cutouts to the Farm. Bolan's call was answered by Barbara Price herself. Bolan identified himself and told her what he wanted.

"I'll get Aaron on it. How's Jack?"

"Not at his best right now. He's going to need some time to recover."

"Listen, Mack, we'll make sure he's looked after. What do you need?"

"For now that check on all recent incoming calls to Jess Buchanan's number. The only connection with her disappearance seems to be this out-of-the-blue call from her uncle. Doug Buchanan didn't want Jess to say anything about his contacting her. Sounds like he was expecting problems."

"You think maybe he's in trouble with the Air Force?"

"Right now I don't have any idea. Look into his background. See what you can find. If he was in trouble with his own people, I can't see them handling it the way it happened. You going to have any problems getting information from the Air Force?"

"Let me worry about that. I'll call the minute we have anything." Price paused. "You take care."

"You worrying about me?"

"Nothing in the manual that says I can't."

"Then I'll be fine."

He broke the connection and put the cell phone away. Bolan spent a few more minutes going over the office. As before, he didn't expect to find anything, but it never did any harm to check things out thoroughly.

When he stepped outside again, he took a slow look around the immediate area. He almost missed the security camera set on a corner of one of the adjacent buildings. Bolan took a walk across the concrete apron until he was standing under the camera. Turning to look back, he saw that as it panned from left to right and back again it would scan the frontage of Jess Buchanan's building.

Bolan made his way back to the security hut.

"Earl, when the cop was here, did he ask about the security camera that overlooks Jess's building?"

Earl thought for a moment, then shook his head.

"Matter of fact he didn't. Like I told you before, he was nothing but a damned rookie. To be honest, Mr. Belasko, I didn't give it much thought myself. This whole thing got me so I'm forgetting things myself. I'm getting too old for this kind of work. They should have a younger man here, but they won't pay the money."

Earl beckoned for Bolan to step inside. At the far end of the hut was a monitoring setup that contained a master and four smaller TV screens. They showed black-and-white images from the cameras located along the charter strip. To one side were four VCR machines in a stacked bank, each machine numbered to correspond with one of the cameras. Bolan studied the setup until he located the camera he had seen near Jess Buchanan's building. He watched the camera pan slowly back and forth. At one point it covered the frontage of the Buchanan outfit.

"Earl, tell me you still have the tape that was in the machine when Jack and Jess were attacked."

The security man cleared his throat.

"Should have if the night man hasn't reused it," he said lamely. "I'm going to feel bad if it's been wiped."

He moved to a shelving unit fastened to the wall and began to sort through the cassettes stacked there. Bolan could hear him muttering to himself, his guilt over his lack of foresight obviously bothering him. In his nervous state he fumbled with the tapes, knocking a couple onto the floor.

"Earl, take it easy," Bolan said.

Earl took a deep breath, then started to look again. He gave a grunt of excitement when he finally found what he was looking for. He turned back to Bolan, holding up a cassette.

"I got it."

He crossed to the monitoring desk and sat. There was a fifth VCR unit under the large monitor. Earl slid the tape in and punched the play button. When the image came on-screen there were date and time indicators in the bottom right of the screen.

"Give me a minute," Earl said, pushing the fast-forward key. The on-screen image sped by, Earl watching closely. He stopped the tape and pointed a finger at the monitor. "There's Jack arriving."

Bolan watched as Grimaldi's lean figure walked across to the entrance of the Buchanan hangar. He pushed open the door and went inside.

"Wasn't much else happening that afternoon," Earl said. He leaned across the desk and pushed the fast-forward key, sending the on-screen image into overdrive. He stopped it when a light-colored car rolled to a stop outside the hangar. "Not long after Jack arrived," he said. "Come to think of it, I don't recall seeing that car come in. Wait, I remember, 'bout that time I went across to the admin building. I got a call from one of the payroll clerks. They messed up my paycheck the previous week, and he wanted to talk to me about it. I locked the hut and went over. Guess I would have been away maybe twenty minutes is all."

Bolan was watching the on-screen activity. Five men emerged from the car. They were all dressed alike in dark suits and moving like a squad of soldiers.

Score one for Jack's assessment, Bolan thought. Somewhere along the line these men had received military training. There was no mistaking the precise, controlled movements, the way they carried themselves as they walked to the entrance door, opened it and went inside.

"Damn," Earl muttered. "If I hadn't been called across to the admin, I might have seen these people come in."

"And you might have ended up like Jack. Or worse," Bolan reminded him. "Move it on."

Earl sped up the tape until the moment the men emerged from the building. One of them crossed directly to the parked car and opened the rear door. Bolan heard Earl let go a gasp of dismay when he recognized Jess Buchanan being led out to the car. She appeared dazed, having to be supported between two of the men. She was maneuvered inside, the rest of the group quickly following. The last man drew Bolan's close attention as he took his time to look around before climbing into the car...

White-blond hair, cut short. Taut features, one hand reaching up to touch the left cheek where a dark bruise was visible, cold eyes staring straight ahead. A dangerous man, angry at being resisted, liable to react violently.

Bolan studied the face, stored it away for future reference. Here was a man the Executioner wouldn't forget, and he also knew that sooner or later he was going to come face-to-face with him.

"Earl, can we see the license plate?"

Earl paused the tape, then used the remote to edge it forward, the car advancing into full frame, allowing them to study the rear end.

"I need to run down that number to see if I can locate that car."

"I can tell you where it comes from," Earl said. "Local rental agency. I recognize the number sequence. They have special plates for rental cars. Makes them easy to trace if they get stolen. We get a lot of tourists driving in for flights."

Earl wrote on a sheet of paper and handed it to Bolan. He had recorded the license number and also the location of the rental agency.

"Thanks for this," Bolan said. "Earl, if I don't get to call back, I appreciate what you've done."

"Wish it could have been more. I'll drop by the hospital some time. Have a few minutes with Jack."

Bolan stepped outside. There was a cabstand a few yards along the road. Behind him he heard the security hut door open.

"Mr. Belsako, you going to bring Miss Jess home?"

"I'll give it my best shot."

Bolan picked up a cab and had it take him back to town and his hotel. As he sank back in the seat, he thought.

It had been a long time since Bolan had dealt with something on such a personal level. Whatever the reasoning behind Jess Buchanan's abduction, enough in itself, Jack Grimaldi was also involved. Badly hurt and unable to find out what had happened to Jess, Grimaldi was about to learn the meaning of true friendship. As far as Bolan was concerned, he would step in and deal with the matter on Grimaldi's behalf. It would have been no different if the roles had been reversed. Bolan and Grimaldi went back a long way. Perhaps too far. But there were no questions that needed to be asked once the chips fell.

BACK IN HIS ROOM Bolan took time to freshen up before he put in a call to Stony Man farm. This time he spoke to Hal Brognola.

"You find anything useful?" the big Fed asked. There was a distinct weariness in Brognola's tone. Bolan picked up on it the moment he heard his friend's voice.

"There something wrong? You sound like you need a break."

"Some hopes," Brognola answered. "I've got Phoenix somewhere in the Middle East. Able chasing rebels in Central America. And you ready to go ballistic in Nassau. And there I'm thinking it might be a good weekend to go fishing."

Bolan smiled at that. "Hal, you'd go crazy trying to land a salmon."

"Yeah? I'd gamble a few gray cells just to give it a damned try."

"Anything come through on the information I gave to Barbara?"

"I was afraid you were going to ask that."

"Complications?"

"We've run Doug Buchanan's name through the military computer banks, and all we come up with is a blank. It's like he never existed. And Aaron detected some kind of a trace string. It tried to get into his system, but he blocked it."

"Meaning someone got interested when he flagged up Buchanan's name?"

"Aaron is trying to follow the trace back to its source. In the meantime the rest of the cyber team is doing what it can to find something about Doug Buchanan from other data banks."

Bolan filed the information away. Interest in Doug Buchanan seemed to be the flavor of the day.

"Anything on the incoming call from Buchanan?"

"Not yet, but we won't give up on it."

"Okay."

"You find anything at your end?" Brognola asked.

"Picked up something on the people who attacked Jack and took Jess Buchanan. I need a little more time down here before I come home."

"Striker, are you seeing more than a simple abduction here?"

"Let's say I'm starting to become curious. I'll be in touch."

Bolan cut the connection. He moved to stare out the window at the passing traffic, raising his gaze to the sunlight sparkling on the water of Nassau Harbour.

He took the sheet of paper from his pocket and checked the address of the car-rental agency Earl had written down for him. Using the room phone, Bolan spoke to the desk and asked for directions to the rental company. The desk clerk told him it was no more than a few minutes' walk from the hotel.

Bolan slipped on his jacket and picked up his key-card. He left the room, took the elevator to the lobby and left the hotel. It was early evening. The sun was warm. A breeze drifting in off the harbor made the day comfortable. Bolan eased into the crowds thronging Bay Street, which ran parallel with the harbor. The crowds were from the great cruise ships that called in at Nassau, disgorging their souvenir-hungry passengers. The vacationers surged up and down the thoroughfare, eager to spend their money and stare at the pink-and-white buildings that were part of Nassau's appeal.

If Bolan had been so inclined, he might have been envious of the simple needs of the crowds. He simply wished them well and moved on, his agenda somewhat deeper than which gaudy trinket was the best bargain.

The crowds began to thin around the time Bolan found his side street. It took him away from the harbor front, up a slight incline, then a spot where the street widened and he found himself confronted by the rental agency. The logo above the entrance also bore the telephone number Earl had written on the paper. To the left of the building was a lot where the rental vehicles were parked. Farther back was a medium-sized workshop. Bolan crossed over and took a cursory glance at the half-dozen parked cars, spotting the one he had seen on the security video.

Bolan stepped into the office. The woman behind the counter glanced up as he entered. She was dark skinned, her black hair worn in a short style that accented her striking features. Pinned to the front of her pale blue blouse was a name badge. Karen.

"May I help, sir?"

"Well, that depends," Bolan said, keeping his tone friendly. "I need some information about a recent rental."

The woman frowned. "I'm not sure I understand."

"I'm an agent with the U.S. Customs Service," Bolan said. "Agent Mike Belasko. Right now I'm working undercover, tracking a group of people we believe are committing crimes around the islands. They were in

Florida before they moved here. A few days ago they rented a car from you."

The woman continued to stare at Bolan, her eyes wide with surprise.

"Sorry to drop it on you like this," Bolan said. "The problem with working undercover is I don't get much time to warn people I'm coming. Right now I'm under pressure to keep up with this group. They could move on at any time."

"We only rent out cars," the woman said. "I don't know anything about these people."

Bolan smiled, reassuring her. "I understand that. I'm just trying to pick up some information."

"Shouldn't I ask to see some identification? I mean, how do I know you're who you say you are?"

"I don't carry anything because I'm working undercover. But I can give you a number you can call. My base in the U.S. They'll confirm anything you want to ask. If there's a problem, I can come back with some paperwork. The trouble is, it takes time and by then these people will have moved on. Look, I don't want to make a fuss. I need your help, Karen. I really do."

The woman bit at her lip. She studied Bolan. He maintained his casual attitude, his eyes fixed on her.

"What is it you want to know?"

"Any details they might have put on their rental form. I'm just trying to get hold of something we can use to track them. They rented that car." Bolan pointed to the vehicle.

Karen made a decision. She turned and went to a metal cabinet. Opening a drawer, she riffled through the files and pulled out a sheet of paper that she placed on the counter in front of Bolan. He slid the sheet toward him, checking the details.

Bolan scanned the information. He took a pen from his pocket, then used the sheet of paper Earl had given him to copy down some of the details. Once he had what he needed, he slid the rental form back to the woman. As she reached for it, Bolan laid his big hand over her slim one, putting on a little pressure.

"I appreciate this, Karen. You've been a great help."

"I hope you catch them."

"If I do, it'll be because of you."

Bolan left the office and turned toward the harbor front. He needed to get back in touch with Stony Man. From the rental form he had picked up two items that might provide some information on the people who had taken Jess Buchanan and attacked Jack Grimaldi: driver's license and credit card details.

If they had anything to offer, Kurtzman and his team would drag it to light. It was time to leave Nassau and get back to Stony Man. Bolan needed input before he moved any further on this.

Back in his hotel room he packed his few belongings, then called the desk to ask if someone could book him a seat on the next available flight back to the U.S. He made it clear he didn't mind the type of flight. The desk called him back less than ten minutes later to say he could take a charter flight leaving in two hours. It was a tourist economy flight, which meant no frills. Bolan told the clerk to book it and have his room bill ready.

CHAPTER TWO

Bolan's plane touched down in Washington, D.C., in the early hours. A quick call to Stony Man had Barbara Price on the line.

"You back on home ground?" she asked without preamble.

"Just got in. I need a ride to base."

"On its way to the usual pickup spot," she said. "I thought of coming out myself."

"That would have been nice."

Price laughed. "Then I figured you probably wouldn't have time to buy me a meal, so I decided to wait here for you."

"So it comes down to me being just a meal ticket?"

"Girl has to look after the priorities."

"You're a hard woman."

"Really? I always thought of myself as pretty accommodating."

"Some day we'll have to define your interpretation of 'accommodating.'"

"I'll talk to you later," Price told him, a smile in her voice.

Bolan ended the call and left the terminal. As he slid the cell phone into his pocket and turned toward the rendezvous area, he felt the prod of a gun muzzle against his spine.

"I don't give a damn if you die now, or in a couple of hours, Belasko. I'd prefer you stayed alive long enough to answer some questions, but just give me the option."

Bolan remained still. He calculated the odds and decided he needed to wait. The carry-on slung from his shoulder would hamper his movements, so any action against the gunman would have to come later. For the time being the Executioner did what he was told.

"A car is going to stop right here," the gunman said. "We climb in. You keep both hands where I can see them. Bag on your lap."

The car rolled into view, a Dodge Intrepid, swinging in to pull up directly in front of Bolan. The insistent prod of the gun warned the Executioner that his captor meant business. Bolan opened the rear door and slid inside the car, moving across to sit directly behind the dark bulk of the driver. The man with the gun moved quickly, crowding in against Bolan, pulling the door shut with his free hand.

"Let's go," he said to the driver.

The car eased away from the pickup point and pulled

into the lane of traffic heading away from the airport. The soldier felt an experienced hand move over his body, checking for weapons. The gunman found nothing. The cell phone Bolan carried was plucked from his pocket and tossed to the floor of the car. Satisfied, the gunman pulled back from his captive, making space between them. He kept the muzzle of his pistol, a .45-caliber Glock 21, pointed in Bolan's direction.

"You make yourself hard to find, Mr. Belasko," the gunman remarked. "Almost missed you back there. Makes me figure this isn't something new to you."

Bolan didn't reply. He decided to let the other man do the talking if that was what he wanted.

"I prefer to deal with professionals," the man went on. "Get yourself a damned civilian, and they're likely to fall apart once you show them a gun. You know what I mean? Hell, sure you do."

Still no response from Bolan. The Executioner was making an evaluation. Making sense of the armed pickup. His mind clicked through the elements of the situation. This had been done professionally. Quick, clean, with little chance for even Bolan to react. The transition to the car had been timed to the second, making these men something more than street hoods. No, these guys were... Bolan recalled something Jack Grimaldi had said about the men who had confronted him and Jess Buchanan, something about their having military training. Precise, practiced execution of their maneuver. Even in his injured condition the Stony Man flier had been able to recall the way his attackers had operated, and Bolan accepted Grimaldi's assessment. The man was too much of a professional himself to have made a mistake.

"Don't say much, do you, friend? Suit yourself. There'll be time to talk once we hit base. Plenty of time. And incentives." The gunman chuckled to himself. "Like whether you want to stay alive."

Bolan fixed his gaze on the back of the driver's head. The man had a close haircut. Near to the skull. Even from where he was sitting Bolan could see enough of the driver's neck and shoulders to know he was looking at a big man. The guy was into weight training and body development with a vengeance. He sat behind the wheel as if he were at attention. Bolan realized why the military imagery kept coming to mind.

The car swung around a vehicle ahead, the driver having decided to speed up.

"Hey, ease off the gas pedal, Buchinsky. Remember what the man said. Low profile. Don't attract attention. Remember? Piss off the enemy in this town and the mothers give you a speeding ticket and ask all kinds of questions."

"And the answers would have to be pretty damned good to explain asshole back there."

"No need to insult our guest," the gunman said. "He could turn out to be important."

"Looks like a shit nobody to me," Buchinsky said. "Give you odds he won't have a thing to tell us. Waste of time picking him up. We should dump him in the Potomac right now."

"Just do what I tell you, Buchinsky."

Buchinsky muttered to himself, flexing his massive shoulders.

Bolan watched the city slip by. He wasn't certain where they were. Buchinsky was ducking and diving, moving about the road system with ease. Taking side roads and sometimes seeming to double back on himself. The trip lasted almost twenty minutes. Then Buchinsky slowed and rolled the car down a ramp that led to a basement parking area beneath a large office building that displayed For Rent signs on the outside. As the car cruised across the parking area, Bolan glanced out the side window. The place was deserted except for a couple of cars standing near an access door at the far end. Buchinsky parked near the other vehicles.

The gunman climbed out and walked around to Bolan's side. He opened the door and indicated for him to get out. The soldier dropped his bag on the seat and stepped out.

"Stay here and keep an eye out. We don't want any surprises," the gunman said to the driver.

"Suits me," Buchinsky said.

The gunman guided Bolan to the access door. They went through and found themselves confronted by stairs and an elevator door.

"Elevator," the gunman said.

Bolan pushed the button and heard the elevator start its descent. The door opened and he stepped in with the gunman close behind. Once they were inside, the soldier was instructed to push the button for the eighth floor.

THE LARGE OFFICE SUITE held a desk and a few plastic chairs. Three men stood at the room's wide windows, looking out through the glass at the rainy night. They turned as Bolan and his escort entered the office.

"This him?"

Bolan had already identified the speaker. He was exactly as Grimaldi had described, from his physical size down to the bruise on his left cheek. He moved away from the others, his gaze fixed on Bolan, checking him out and making a swift assessment of the Executioner.

"He say anything?"

The gunman shook his head. He stood a few feet back from Bolan, the handgun held steady, making no concessions even though they were no longer alone.

The blond man paused in front of Bolan, his hands clasped at his back.

"You know why you're here, Belasko?"

"Maybe you'd better tell me."

"Questions. You've been asking questions. At the charter strip. Talking to the gate man. Then the car-rental agency. Now why would you want to do that?"

"I don't know. Why would I?"

"Maybe you're looking for someone. Same as us. Douglas Buchanan? Or maybe you know where he is and your job is looking out for him."

"Sounds more likely," one of the other men said.

Bolan glanced across at him. He had a cut lip that looked very sore. Jack again.

"Ask him if he knows where Buchanan is."

"Fair question."

Bolan remained silent.

"So what's the answer?"

The blond man's lips tightened against his teeth. He sucked in his breath, glancing over his shoulder at the gunman who had brought Bolan in. The Executioner picked up the sound of rustling clothing, heard the gunman grunt and knew that a blow was being aimed at him from behind.

Bolan held for the briefest of moments, then bent at the waist, felt the rush of air as the gunman's swing passed over his shoulder, then lunged upright. He saw the gunman's arm blur into view as it passed harmlessly over his shoulder. He made a grab for it, twisting and jerking down so that the arm was brought across the top of his shoulder. Pushing to his full height, Bolan snatched the Glock from his adversary's fingers, then yanked down hard on the man's arm with enough force to break the bone. The gunman's scream of agony was cut off abruptly when the muzzle of the Glock was jabbed against his chest and a .45 round drilled through his heart. The moment he pulled the trigger, Bolan dropped to a crouch, the Glock tracking in on his next target.

A lean guy, sporting a blue sport coat over a tan shirt, hauled a handgun from a hip holster. He raised the weapon in a two-handed grip, seeking Bolan, but the Executioner had already changed position and his newly acquired pistol fired first. The .45 slug caught Blue Coat in the throat, taking away a large chunk of flesh. The wounded gunner flopped backward, striking the window behind him. The glass bowed slightly under the impact, then threw the dying man facedown on the carpet.

Bolan had already located his next target, seeing Blue Coat's partner clawing for his own weapon. He placed two .45 slugs in the guy's lower torso, driving him to the floor in a spray of blood and a lot of pain. A third shot to the head put him out of his misery.

The blond man had already moved, turning, ducking as he lunged for the door. He went through a fraction of a second before Bolan could track and fire, and by the time the Executioner cleared the door the corridor beyond was empty.

Bolan made for the door that gained him entrance to the stairs. He went down fast, conscious of his partial exposure, yet knowing he had to get clear of the building before possible reinforcements showed up. He had no way of knowing if the blond man had additional backup, and he didn't want to find out.

He hit the fourth-floor landing. As he turned to take the next flight of stairs, the access door was banged open and a pair of armed men rushed onto the landing. Bolan knew he couldn't take the stairs without catching a bullet in the back. He spun, reaching out with his left hand. He put his palm over the closest face and pushed hard, ramming the guy's skull against the concrete wall. The man gave a grunt of pain, slumping to his knees, gun falling from his hand. The second guy eyed Bolan, then made the mistake of checking out his partner. The soldier saw the guy's hesitation, as slight as it was, and took his chance. It was, as always, seizing the moment, and turning it to *his* advantage. He turned fast, coming around from the right. Bolan's forearm struck the guy's gun hand, knocking it up and back. Maintaining his sweep, Bolan stiff armed his left fist into the guy's throat, hard, feeling flesh and cartilage cave in. As the guy began to choke, Bolan grabbed his gun arm and twisted, until the joint snapped. The guy screamed, a harsh, ugly sound due to his crushed throat, and dropped his gun, which fell into Bolan's waiting hand.

The other gunner had started to climb to his feet, clawing his fallen weapon from the floor. His eyes were searching the area immediately behind him as he completed his stand. The last thing he saw was the raised gun in Bolan's fist, then the world blew up in his face as the weapon was triggered twice, putting both slugs into the guy's head. The impact knocked him back against the wall and he hung for a moment, surprise etched across his face. Then he slid down the wall, leaving behind a trail of bloody debris. As he hit the floor he gently toppled face forward.

Bolan bent over the corpse and picked up the fallen

handgun—another Glock 21. He slipped it into a pocket, then frisked the guy for any extra magazines he carried. He also located the guy's wallet and pocketed it for future reference.

The other man was on his knees, close to unconscious, his shattered arm hanging limply at his side. He was making harsh choking sounds as he struggled for air. He offered no resistance when Bolan searched him for spare magazines for the Glock. Two more went into the soldier's pocket.

Before he moved on Bolan ejected the magazine from the pistol he was using and snapped in a fresh one, making sure the weapon was ready to go.

Bolan took the final flights of stairs until he reached the basement level. He eased the door open a fraction and peered through.

The Intrepid was in the same place, with Buchinsky waiting beside it. The man was upright, taking his job seriously, his pistol in his right hand, held against the side of his leg, out of sight but ready for use. Bolan scanned the surrounding area. There was no cover between the doorway and the Intrepid. Bolan doublechecked, then shoved the door wide open so that it swung back against the wall with a hard bang.

Buchinsky snapped his head around at the noise, his right hand bringing his weapon up as he dropped to a shooter's stance, left hand following to brace the butt of the Glock.

Bolan had stepped immediately to the right of the

door, his own weapon tracking his intended target. The moment he had the guy in his sights, the soldier pulled the trigger twice, and put both slugs over Buchinsky's heart. The enemy gunner took a faltering step forward, losing coordination, and slumped to his knees. He leaned sideways, the Intrepid's fender holding him upright. The gun dropped from his hand, clattering onto the concrete. Bolan had closed the gap by this time, and he stepped up to where the man lay. He went through Buchinsky's pockets until he located the vehicle's keys.

He opened the rear door and retrieved his bag, then the cell phone from the floor of the car. Sliding in behind the wheel, Bolan inserted the key and fired up the powerful engine. He released the brake and shifted into reverse, spinning the wheel so that the Intrepid moved in a wide circle. As the car moved, Buchinsky toppled facedown on the concrete, a thin trail of blood trickling from the corner of his mouth.

Bolan drove out of the basement and onto the street, memorizing the name of the building's rental agent before he drove away.

It took him a few minutes to establish his whereabouts. Bolan swung the car across the street and made a U-turn, then picked up the signs that would lead him to the main highway out of D.C. and back to Stony Man. He made a quick call to Price to cancel his ride.

His only immediate regret was the blond man's escape. There was a strong connection between the man, Jess Buchanan and her uncle. Bolan was about to make it his business to find out just what that connection was. He would have questions when he got back to the Farm.

"HE GOT AWAY, Colonel. There's no other way of saying it. He took out my guys and got away. I only got away myself by a hair. Sorry, sir, I let you down."

"These things happen, Ryan, so don't get paranoid over it."

"What next, Colonel?"

"Get yourself organized. I'll arrange cleanup for the casualties. It might be necessary for you to call in and see Senator Stahl. He could have some information for you."

"On my way, sir."

Colonel Orin Stengard replaced the receiver and took a breath, collecting his thoughts.

He crossed the room, staring out through the window, watching the rain falling from a slate-gray sky. The weather suited his mood at that moment. He wasn't angry, rather more disappointed that the capture of the man from Nassau had failed. Stengard didn't like surprises and the way this stranger had appeared on the scene, checking out what had happened at the Buchanan charter company and then going to the car-rental agency, suggested he was more than just an acquaintance of the Buchanan woman. The way he had handled himself when taken by Ryan's men seemed to confirm he knew what he was doing.

Stengard crossed to his desk and picked up the phone. He punched in a number, hearing it click its way through a series of distant secure lines before it rang at the other end. He heard six rings before it was picked up.

"Yes?"

"It's me."

"Problems?"

"Nothing that's about to wipe us out. I need you to do some checking. My people have identified an individual asking questions in Nassau. We picked him up when he touched down at Dulles. He was taken for questioning but he got away, taking out the snatch team in the process."

"Security agent? FBI?"

"It's why I'm calling. We don't know. All we have is a name. Mike Belasko. See what you can find out and get back to me. I need to know if this man has backup. The last thing I need at this point are agents crawling all over us."

"I'll do what I can."

Stengard made a second call.

"Eric, have you had any more problems with Randolph?"

"Only what I told you last time. Why?"

"There's someone asking questions. Digging into the Buchanan thing on Nassau. He killed some of Ryan's men when they took him for questioning. Right at this point we know nothing about his background. I've just spoken to Beringer and asked him to run a check on the man. It occurred to me that Randolph might have put him on our case. Got him to do some rooting for information he can use against us."

"Damn. I wouldn't put it past Randolph. It's something that old bastard would do. Hire someone to check out his suspicions. Let me go and talk to him. If the old coot won't play ball, you can have your people take him out. How does that sound?"

"Sounds exactly what I'd say if our roles were reversed."

"Randolph always goes to his club midmorning. I'll catch him there."

"Do it, Eric. Let's brush off these annoying flies so we can concentrate on the important things."

SENATOR ERIC STAHL confronted Senator Vernon Randolph in the quiet of his private club. Stahl was a member himself, and this wasn't the first time the pair had faced off. Stahl was aware of how serious a threat Randolph was. Stahl had made the decision to remove him, regardless of the senior politician's decision. There was something about Randolph that unsettled him. In essence Randolph was too much of an honest man. He didn't make it obvious; he didn't preach, nor did he try to press his views on others. Yet his standing in the Washington environment was unmatched.

Seated across from Randolph, Stahl felt the older man's blue eyes fixed on him. Randolph's gaze was unflinching.

"Eric, we have had this conversation before. Too many times. I am not interested in your proposal."

"From someone who admits to being a patriot I find your reaction disappointing."

"Why? Because I refuse to advocate your policies? Destabilizing the elected government of the country? Agitation. Almost an invitation to an armed uprising."

"Go out and ask anyone on the streets, Vernon. Ask them what they feel about the way the government has sold this country down the river. Weakened it. Taken away our right to freedom and the true spirit of the American way."

"That kind of rhetoric only appeals to the lowest intellect, Eric. Is that how you expect to gather your supporters? Where are you going to find them? In the gutters, the downtown bars and lap-dancing parlors?"

"Might work, too." Stahl grinned, trying to lighten the moment. "Vernon, we shouldn't be arguing like this. At a time like this we should be joining forces, not playing word games."

Randolph allowed himself a gentle smile.

"Eric, I mean every word I say. Please don't get confused. I despise your intentions, your policies, the people you associate with. It hasn't escaped my notice that you're in bed with Orin Stengard. He's your military clone. A warmonger who would bomb any country that dared to defy him. The man is a throwback to the 1950s. A different time and a different army. He should have been retired years ago. Thank God the man doesn't have his finger on the button."

"Be careful what you say about my friends, Vernon. I might have to send Orin to see you one dark night."

Senator Vernon Randolph ignored the implicit

threat. He leaned back in the deep armchair and studied Stahl.

"Eric, you're either very stupid or extremely arrogant. I'd have to choose the latter. Not that it makes all that much difference. What you're considering is ridiculous in the extreme. And do you honestly believe I'm going to sit back and pretend I don't know what you intend to do?"

Stahl smiled. "Vernon, I realize you're a man of high principle. I've always admired that part of your character. But I have to say in this instance it might not be the wisest choice. It could turn out to be unhealthy to say the least."

"Don't try to frighten me, Eric. I've been in politics too long to worry over words. And at my age threats tend to add a little spice to a life that's run for a long time."

"Playing the hero doesn't suit you, Vernon. Believe me, you wouldn't like what I could do to you."

"I intend to go ahead with the investigation I've been considering. You have something to hide. You're searching for Doug Buchanan. and you have an unhealthy interest in the Zero project. I'm going to drag it all out of the shadows and into the spotlight. The moment I have solid proof I'll take it to the President. You have my word on that."

"All right, Vernon. However you want it," Stahl said and turned to leave.

"Eric," Randolph said, "do your worst, and to hell with your damned games."

"A neat analogy," Stahl replied. "Just remember that games all have one thing in common. A winner and a loser. And you know well enough, Vernon, I hate to lose."

"THE EQUATION CAN'T be that difficult to grasp," Stahl said. "If Doug Buchanan is out there looking for some kind of sanctuary, there's only one man he'll look for."

He paused, savoring the moment, *his* triumph over every man in the room. He was still surprised at the revelation that had come to him on his return from confronting Senator Randolph.

"Senator, don't play fucking games," Cal Ryan said. "And pardon my language."

"No, you're right, Mr. Ryan. Excuse my indulgence. The man we need to locate is Saul Kaplan. Find Kaplan, and Buchanan won't be far away."

"What's the connection?" Ryan asked.

"Kaplan brought Buchanan into the Zero project, chose him as the man who would inherit Zero as his savior."

"You mean Buchanan is the guy who gets to sit in the control seat?"

"Exactly. He was chosen because he has all the military skills, is a man with a strong moral sense of right and wrong and he has terminal cancer."

"We playing games again? They were going to put a dying man in charge of Zero?"

"Two reasons, Mr. Ryan. Buchanan was aware that on his own he would have been dead in a couple of years, but once he became part of Zero, his biological functions, including his immune system, would be taken over by the machine. It would replace his natural bodily awareness and integrate it into the biocouch. Zero's capabilities are far in advance of anything in existence. You can appreciate why I want it under our control, Mr. Ryan. Our control alone."

"I'm starting to, Senator."

"With Zero in our hands, there won't be a nation that would dare to even think about threatening the U.S. We would be in total control of the nation and have the ability to make our enemies toe the line. If they refuse, Zero could be used to make them see sense."

"The ultimate authority."

Stahl smiled. "Zero tolerance, Mr. Ryan. Zero tolerance."

"Can we be certain Buchanan will head for Kaplan?"

"I believe he will. Buchanan has no one else to turn to. The Zero project was hit by an unknown force. Destroyed. No one is certain by whom. We suspect foreign interference. Regimes who see the threat Zero would pose to them. Which is why we need the project up and running. To counter such threats. If we bring Zero fully online, anyone contemplating a strike against the U.S. is going to know they would be under Zero's scrutiny. To answer your question, Buchanan is a man out in the cold. Who can he trust? He'll understand his position and he'll know he's a wanted man. Saul Kaplan was his mentor, the one man he knows he'll always be able to turn to. If Buchanan calls, Kaplan will help him."

"Where do we find Kaplan?"

"Right now we don't know where he is. Kaplan vanished from his university post weeks ago. Just took off. It could be he's heard from Buchanan in the past few days and the pair have arranged some meeting. We have to follow it up."

Stahl slid a folder across the desk. Picking it up, Ryan flicked through the data sheets.

"Everything there is on file about Saul Kaplan. Use it and find him. We need them both alive. Kaplan has knowledge about Zero we can use."

Ryan nodded. He gestured to his team and they followed him from the room, leaving Stahl alone. He remained seated for a while, then stood and crossed the room. He lingered at the window, watching Ryan and his people as they climbed into their vehicles. Stahl stayed there until the cars had driven out of sight. He made his way to the desk in a corner of the room, picked up his phone, punching in a number sequence.

"Are you available, Orin? Good. Where? That's fine. An hour?"

STAHL ARRIVED ten minutes early, which gave his security team time to check out the area around the meeting place. It paid to be careful. A man in Stahl's position needed to be cautious. He knew he had enemies. There was no point in making it too easy for them.

His team came back to report the area was clear. They climbed back in their car, and Stahl made his way down to the canal. Even though his car was some distance away, he knew his security men would have him in their sight.

The water was flat, not a ripple breaking the surface. Birds sang in the distance, calling to their mates. Stahl took a breath, allowing himself a moment of calm.

There was no doubt, he told himself, America was a beautiful country. It had everything a man could ever want or need. It was worth defending from those who looked at it through envious eyes. Terrorists, religious fanatics, countries who saw America as their adversary. The do-gooders and the liberals, even in America itself, who wanted to weaken it from within. The government legislators. The Communist sympathizers. The list was long. The threats came from abroad and from within America's own borders. Between them they would turn America into a soft target, with no military to speak of and the defense system pared down to the bone to appease the overwhelming lobby of pacifists and downright cowards. It was sometimes hard for Stahl to believe that America had been built by far-seeing, hardy pioneers, men and women who had crossed the primitive continent, creating the strongest, richest nation in the world. They had done it from scratch, using their bare hands and their burning desire to be free. In the end they had done just that. It had taken decades, spilled blood and the bones of the dead who littered a hundred dusty trails, but they had achieved a miracle.

And now, if it was left to the spineless administration, America would be weakened further, prey to any rogue nation that decided she was ripe for the plucking. There was talk of cutting back on defense, weakening the country's armed forces, taking the nation's protection out of the hands of the military. And there were too few politicians with the backbone to stand up in defense of those cutbacks. The Zero Option was ready and waiting, the ultimate weapon. In Stahl's eyes, even if the current administration brought it online, it would step back from utilizing the weapon's potential. Stahl would *not* hesitate to make the world fully aware of Zero and what it could do. His first act, once he was installed in the White House, would be a practical demonstration of Zero's capabilities. There was nothing like a hard strike to show the world America meant business. And a hard strike was what Stahl intended. Then the world could look on and see that the *new* American government meant what it said.

Stahl's hands were shaking as he plucked a cigarette from his silver case and lit it. He inhaled deeply, of smoke, letting the effect calm him. Just thinking about the enormity of his scheme unsettled him. Once he embarked on it there would be no turning aside. It would have to be seen through to the end. There was no doubt that there would be a global outcry. Condemnation. Accusing fingers aimed at America.

But what could they do?

With Zero online and able to target anyone, what could they do?

Damn them all!

America needed a hard man at the helm. Someone not afraid to take on the bitchers and the whiners and the appeasers, a man who could tell the enemies of the U.S. to go to hell, because the country had the best, the finest, the most deadly weapon under its control. Once Stahl had Zero in his camp, he could bargain his way into the White House and show the American people he wasn't fooling. And when he had the administration firmly manned by *his* people and the military under the command of Orin Stengard, then it would be the turn of the global community to see that America had turned the corner and was really back as the strongest nation on Earth.

Stahl flicked ash from his cigarette and watched it fall into the water at his feet. He felt a little better after his internal rant. Sometimes his bitter feelings got the better of him, and it proved therapeutic when he gave vent to them.

He heard footsteps close by. Stahl turned and saw Orin Stengard walking toward him. He was in civilian clothing. Sharply creased slacks and an expensive leather jacket over a pale cream shirt.

"Eric," Stengard said by way of greeting. "You made this meeting sound urgent."

"I wouldn't have asked to see you if it hadn't been."

"So?"

"I was correct. Randolph has been making more of his threatening noises. I offered him the chance to join us, but he turned the offer down point-blank."

"Is it bluster, or does he actually know something?"

"I think he's starting to became suspicious. You know what he's like. He's worked out you and I are close. He also knows about Buchanan being alive."

"How the hell did he find out about that?"

"Not from me. Look, Orin, that old bastard has been around for a long time. He has contacts all over, a finger in every department of the administration and the military. He's a one-man CIA. He's done favors for so many people you couldn't read the list on a long weekend. That man has survived so many changes of government it's worth a fucking medal."

"All right. So what does he want? A payoff? In on the deal? What?"

"I'll tell you what his intentions are, Orin, and believe me I know what I'm saying. Randolph wants to take us down. The man is a dinosaur. He has principles and morals. He doesn't have enough at the moment, but the minute he does he'll take his findings to the President and spill beans all over the fucking Oval Office carpet."

Stengard ran a hand through his thick, dark hair. He looked down at his highly polished leather shoes, cleared his throat, then looked out along the peaceful canal.

"We get rid of him, then. No ifs or buts. Senator Randolph has reached the end of an exceptional life in politics. It comes to us all, Eric. None of us is immortal. You have any problems with Randolph's imminent demise?"

"Do I look like a man with a problem?"

"To be honest, Eric, yes, you do. You need to learn how to relax. Tension never won any battles. Go with the flow. See the problem, work it out and send in the troops."

This time Stahl had to laugh.

"I have to hand it to you, Orin. Here we are getting ready to make a hostile takeover for the government of the United States. We have teams of covert mercenaries on the loose. A fully armed orbiting weapons platform over our heads just waiting to be switched on. And all you can say is 'Relax.' How the hell did you get where you are in the military?"

"By following my instincts. Letting the other poor idiots run around and get sweaty. Watching them work their butts off so they were old men before forty. I waited and listened, and took the chances they were too scared to tackle. They fell behind while I moved up the promotion ladder. And before you say it, yes, it *was* as easy as that. The military and politics are not so unalike. We plot and connive. Cultivate our allies and get rid of our enemies. Build up a store of favors we can call in. Make sure you always have your back to the wall and an eye out for the main chance." Stengard turned so he had Stahl full face. "After that little speech I think we both should watch the other. After all, Eric, aren't we after the same thing? Total power? High positions and control of the most awesome piece of hardware ever conceived? Tell me, Eric, do you still trust me?"

"If I told you, it would place me at a disadvantage."

"Spoken like a true politician."

"Can I leave you to deal with Randolph?"

Stengard nodded. He turned to make his way back to his car, Stahl at his side. He had his door open before he spoke again.

"Have you ever heard of a man called Belasko? Mike Belasko?"

Stahl shook his head.

"Name doesn't mean a thing. Should it?"

"No. Forget I asked. You'll not hear it again."

As HE WAS DRIVEN back to his own office, Stahl wondered briefly who Mike Belasko was. The name occupied him for a few minutes as he tried to make a connection. When he failed he dismissed it sat back in the comfortable leather seat, watching the Washington landscape flash by.

If things went as planned and they gained control of Zero everything he saw outside the car, as the old saying went, would be his. It was a pleasing thought.

CHAPTER THREE

Stony Man Farm, Virginia

Bolan was on his third coffee when Hal Brognola arrived. He took one look at the soldier and reached for the pot himself, pouring himself a mug before dropping into the chair behind his desk. Brognola looked like a man who hadn't slept for a long time. He took a long swallow of coffee, leaned back in his seat and stared at his old friend while he formed the words he wanted to speak.

"What the hell is going on, Striker?"

"I was hoping you could tell me. I'd planned to spend some R&R with Jack on Nassau. I touched down and found out it had gone to hell—Jack in hospital, Jess Buchanan kidnapped. I picked up some information on the perps and headed back for the mainland only to get hijacked at the airport and ended up having to fight my way out of a bad situation. That's it. I dropped off the security tape I located at Jess Buchanan's airstrip. Aaron is running it through the computer now to see if we can get some names for the faces. End of story. Now it's your turn."

"You up for another ride?" Brognola asked.

"Sure. Why not? I'm not even going to ask where."

"One of your admirable qualities, Striker. Flexibility."

Bolan scowled at his longtime friend and ally. "Don't push it."

Brognola allowed himself a brief smile. He drained his coffee mug and stood.

"We'll check with Aaron before we head out."

AARON KURTZMAN was alone in the Computer Room. He spun his wheelchair away from his workstation as Brognola stepped into the room, with Bolan shadowing him. One look at the Executioner's expression and Kurtzman knew it was no time for levity. He had been updated on what had happened from the moment Bolan had arrived in Nassau.

"I ran your security tape through the military database. You and Jack were right with the military connection. I came up with two positives. Your blond guy is one Calvin Ryan. Ex-Army. Retired a couple of years back from his last unit. Worked his way up through the ranks. Quite a record. The guy is a professional, a hard hitter. Desert Storm. Grenada. Headed a team of infiltrators for his commanding officer. You'll like this. Colonel Orin Stengard."

"Steel and Thunder Stengard?" Brognola said.

"The one and only. Makes all the other hard-liners look like pacifists."

"The guy is always in the news with his views on why America needs to pull up the drawbridge and turn the country into an armed camp. Given his way, he'd have kids in school being taught weapons drill and issued with M-16s."

"Any suggestions on what Ryan has done since he left the military?" Bolan asked.

Kurtzman shook his head. "Nothing on file."

"You said two IDs."

"Only got a clear image on one other man. Paul Meeker."

"One of Ryan's former military unit?"

"How did you know that?"

Bolan shrugged. "Just a guess."

"Every time you start guessing, I get a cold finger down my spine," Brognola said. "You have any other insights?"

"One observation," Bolan said. "Orin Stengard has been known to associate himself alongside Senator Eric Stahl. Another might-is-right believer, and a man who has more than a passing connection with the armaments industry."

"Connection is a nice way of putting it," Brognola said. "The Stahl family has been in armaments since the 1930s. It's where he gets his money. The man is worth billions."

"Is this the Eric Stahl who fronts the Third Party?" Kurtzman asked.

"Stahl *is* the Third Party. The guy wants to be President. He was elected on his manifesto in his home state because he has one hell of a following in the Fortress America camp. We might not like his views, but a lot of people do. Stahl makes no concessions to political correctness, or tiptoeing around the issues. He says it as he sees it. The country is losing face and the ability to defend itself because we fudge the issues and let our enemies tell us how we should act. According to Stahl, we should think of the U.S. first and if it upsets the rest of the world, so what?" Brognola glanced across at Bolan. "Time we left."

"You guys on a date?" Kurtzman asked.

"Not the kind you're thinking about," Brognola said.

"See what you can come up with on the wallet and the car-rental details," Bolan said as he followed Brognola out the door. "Check those Glock pistols, as well. I'll catch you later."

"You know where to find me," Kurtzman said to the Executioner's back. He swung his wheelchair back to his desk and bent over his keyboard.

He had been working on the car-rental information Bolan had brought in. The credit-card detail ran him into a firewall on his first attempt. It went so far, then threw up a block. That was its first mistake. Kurtzman didn't like being denied access to information. So he had pulled back and brought up one of his own programs, using it to bypass the card company's firewall. He had just requested his program to worm its way into the card company's database when Bolan and Brognola had visited. Now they had gone, Kurtzman turned back to his computer's search and checked on the results. A smile creased his face as he read what the search had produced. He was into the card company's database. His program had overcome the firewall put up by the security system. All Kurtzman had to do now was trace the ownership of the card, and it would point the finger at whoever was financing the people who had attacked Jack Grimaldi and Jess Buchanan.

THE BLACKSUIT PILOT behind the controls of the helicopter nodded as Bolan and Brognola settled in their seats behind him.

"Any update on Jack, sir?" he asked.

"Nothing new. He's going to be out of action for a few weeks, but he'll be okay."

"Glad to hear it. Hope everything works out okay. He was really looking forward his break on Nassau. All he talked about the last few days before he left."

"He'd be pleased to know people are thinking about him," Bolan told him.

"Yeah, they sure are, sir. Hell of a guy."

Bolan sat back as the chopper rose into the air and gained altitude.

"Hell of a guy" didn't even scratch the surface when it came to describing Jack Grimaldi.

RAIN PELTED the helicopter as it touched down on the well-tended lawn behind the White House. The pilot shut off the power and the rotors began to slow, making a soft pulse of sound as they cut the air.

A pair of dark-suited Secret Service agents came out to meet Bolan and Brognola as they ran across the grass to the entrance that would admit them to the President's residence.

"The President is expecting you," one of the agents said. He was staring at the slight, telltale bulge under Bolan's jacket.

"You need to take it?" Bolan asked, preempting the agent's thoughts. He opened his jacket to expose the holstered Beretta 93-R.

A muscle in the agent's jaw twitched slightly. He cleared his throat.

"The President has sanctioned your right to keep your weapon, sir."

"I appreciate that."

The agent held Bolan's gaze for a heartbeat.

"If you'd feel more comfortable, I'll hand it over," Bolan said evenly.

"That won't be necessary, sir. Thanks for your cooperation." The agent turned his gaze on Brognola. "Same concession goes for you, as well, Mr. Brognola. Would you both come this way."

The agents led the men to a thickly carpeted hallway that deadened the sound of their passing. They paused at the door to the Oval Office. One of the agents tapped on the door, which was opened by one of the White House staff members who spoke briefly to the agent before withdrawing. He reappeared moments later, beckoning to Bolan and Brognola.

"The President is ready to see you."

Bolan let the big Fed step inside first, then followed close behind. The staff member retreated, closing the door behind him, leaving the men alone with the President of the United States.

The Man came from behind his desk, holding out a hand to greet Brognola. The President's jacket was draped over the back of his chair behind the desk and his sleeves were rolled partway up his arms.

"Hal," he said.

"Sir."

The President turned his attention to the Executioner. It was a rare happening for the President to actually meet the man he was in the habit of sending out to do dangerous work on behalf of the nation. Before he even had words with Bolan, the President realized this was someone he could trust. The soldier had a presence, a quiet confidence that reached out and confirmed his devotion to country and duty. It was a rare thing, especially in the current climate of mistrust and deceit, and despite being hailed as the most powerful man in the world, the President found he felt safe being in the same room as Mack Bolan.

"Glad you could make it, Striker," the President said, holding out his hand.

Bolan took it, feeling the firm grip of the President.

"Did Hal fill you in with the details?"

"No, sir," Brognola interrupted. "I wanted this to come directly to him when the three of us were together."

"There's fresh coffee over there. Help yourselves before we start." The President crossed to the tray resting on a small table and poured himself a mug. "Anyone?"

"Black for me," Bolan said.

"Nothing for me just now," Brognola said.

Bolan took the mug the President handed him. He waited until the Man had taken his place behind his desk, then settled himself in one of the comfortable chairs facing the desk. Brognola sat on his left.

"Cards on the table, gentlemen," the President said evenly. "We have a problem brewing and you, Striker, however you want to call it, seem to have become involved." The President allowed himself a quick smile. "Not the first time that has happened, either."

"No, sir."

"Hal has given me the details of your involvement from the start, up to the present, so we don't need to go through that again. I also understand that your people at Stony Man are working on material Striker brought back with him, Hal?"

"Yes, sir, and we do have some feedback already," Brognola said. "It's a little early to give us definite connections, though."

"Cards on the table?" Bolan interrupted, leaning forward in his seat. He caught Brognola's warning glance but chose to ignore it. "I'm picking up a feeling of urgency, so I'm going to play my hand.

"From evidence I picked up in Nassau and the people who were waiting for me at the airport, we came up with two names. The man in charge of the team who took Jess Buchanan and attacked Jack Grimaldi is an ex-military man named Calvin Ryan. The other man is Paul Meeker. Meeker was part of Ryan's special-ops team. Their commanding officer in the army was Colonel Orin Stengard, and Stengard is a known associate of—"

"Senator Eric Stahl," the President said. He glanced at Brognola. "Hal? What do you make of this?"

"Right now they're just names and tenuous connections, Mr. President."

"But in the context of what I'm about to explain to Striker, don't you feel those connections are too strong to ignore?"

"As we're off the record and this goes no further, my personal feelings are that Stengard and Stahl are involved right up their necks, Mr. President. On past records concerning their political and personal views, I have to admit to being downright biased against them."

The President nodded. "That wasn't too hard to say, was it, Hal?"

Brognola glanced across at Bolan. "Happy now?"

"Getting there."

The President placed his coffee mug on the desk. He looked directly at Bolan.

"One thing Senator Stahl and I agree on is the defense of the United States. Where we part company is on the application of any defense system. Eric Stahl is a 'shoot first, consider the implications after,' kind of a man. I have no problem with having the best defense system available so that we can, as a nation, be in the position of having full protection in times of crisis. I do not see a defense system as a means of threatening and bullying other nations. That isn't going to get us anywhere.

"However, we live in parlous times. We moved into a new era in the wake of September 11. No doubt about that. The world has changed. We need to change with it. Peace, however defined, has to be worked at. It's going to take a hell of a lot of talking, and in the meantime there are still going to be those states and groups, terrorists if you will, who refuse to take the quiet option. So, gentlemen, we need to be able to protect ourselves from the rogue states until such times come that allow us to step back from the firing line. We owe that to the people of the United States.

"Three years ago a project was conceived and initiated by the U.S. The project is called the Zero Option. In simple terms Zero is a self-sustaining, orbiting weapons platform. Its purpose is to act as a defensive deterrent. Because of its capability no potential enemy of the United States would be able to launch anything against us. Once Zero detects a launch, it responds by targeting it with its own built-in missile system. The incoming missile would be destroyed while it was still in flight. Zero is equipped with detection and tracking capabilities of the highest specification. The system has been tried and tested. The tracking system is locked into the Slingshot satellite ring we put up earlier."

"We had a run-in with the Chinese and the North Koreans over that," Brognola said.

"Some run-in," Bolan commented. "From the way you're talking about Zero, Mr. President, I'm guessing this orbiting platform is up and running."

"Construction and final interior equipping was completed six months ago. There was a great deal to do. You have to appreciate the sophistication of the interior systems. Once all that had been given the all-clear Zero came partially online. A secondary function of Zero is information gathering and transmitting to our Earth command station. Coupled with Slingshot, Zero can pinpoint any known location, listen and see what's going on. That part of the Zero platform is already operating. We have, in essence, the best observation station in existence."

"That isn't the whole story, sir?"

The President glanced in Bolan's direction. "No. Zero's primary function is still on hold. And it will be until the final piece of the puzzle is in place. That brings me to why you're here. But first I have to explain the way Zero will be controlled. A somewhat unique way."

"To do with Doug Buchanan?"

"Doug Buchanan will be Zero's guiding hand and

decision maker. The platform can perform its mechanical functions, yes, but every one of those operations requires a command decision initiated by human intelligence. An intelligence that can assess the parameters and reach a decision based on experience and the capacity to make judgments with considerations for the consequences. Something a machine doesn't always regard as necessary."

"So Buchanan will be in command of the platform?" The President looked across at Brognola.

"This is where your knowledge of Zero stopped before, Hal. Now seems to be the time to bring you up to speed, as well as Striker."

If Bolan was surprised that Brognola already had insight into Zero, he didn't show it.

"Doug Buchanan will become part of Zero, yes, but I mean a *part* in the sense that a process will assimilate him, via what is termed a biocouch. His physical body will fuse to the couch, the connections being made by neural implants designed to merge living matter with the implants already within the couch. In the simplest terms Buchanan will become Zero will become Buchanan. Don't ask me to go into too much detail because Saul Kaplan lost me after the first couple of pages."

Bolan considered what the President had told him. He was as aware of bio- and cybernetic engineering as most. He was *not* aware it had developed this far.

"Research into this field has been going on behind the scenes for years," the President said. "Saul Kaplan has been one of the most energetic participants in the advancement of this science. When he put his concept forward at the start of the Zero project we realized just how far he had gone. This man-machine bonding hadn't been part of the Zero equation until Kaplan showed interest. The man is brilliant, creative, and he had everything mapped out when he made his presentation to the oversight group."

"How did Buchanan become part of this project?" Brognola asked.

"You mean why would a man offer to put himself through such a trauma?"

"Yes, sir."

"Doug Buchanan is a serving officer in the U.S. Air Force. Impeccable record. He is also a man who loves his country and has dedicated himself to serving it any way he can. Not unlike the people in this room right now. We each do what we can in individual ways. In Doug Buchanan's case he had reached a point in his life where he needed to make a critical decision. He has an incurable cancer. It will kill him, and there isn't a damned thing anyone can do to stop it. That was true until Buchanan and Kaplan came together. Saul Kaplan offered Buchanan a way out. I have to admit it turned out to be the most dramatic way, but once Kaplan had explained it, Buchanan volunteered to join the Zero Option project."

"The merging of Buchanan to Zero means the bio-couch will replace many of Buchanan's bodily functions. Zero will both nourish and monitor his life patterns. It will, as I understand it, kill off the cancer cells and sustain his life for as long as he remains integrated. His life expectancy will be extended, and the pain he would have experienced from his cancer will be eliminated. There will be, of course, substantial changes in his level of physical ability."

"He won't be able to leave this biocouch?" Bolan said.

"Exactly. But as Buchanan himself said, by the advanced stages of his cancer he would be confined to a hospital bed anyway. At least with Zero he would still be able to contribute something."

The President paused. He sensed that both Bolan and Brognola were trying to come to terms with what he had just told them. He allowed them their time by getting up to refill his coffee mug.

"Doug Buchanan is an intelligent, forward-thinking man. He took a long time considering the options open to him. There was no pressure put on him. No one had any right to push him into something like this. I made that a stipulation when Kaplan first came to me with the concept. Buchanan's decision was related to his life as it would be if he decided not to join Zero. In the end he came to me and we discussed it at length. He saw the challenge in the project. Looked on it as a step forward in his own life and something important for the defense of the country."

"So what happened?"

"The project was established at a facility in the New Mexico desert. This had been closed down some years previously, and when Zero came along it was decided this facility would be an ideal place—isolated, with all the things Kaplan would need. The facility was re-opened and equipped under Kaplan's supervision. The Zero team was composed of only a small number of technicians, plus Air Force personnel and security. They worked day and night to have everything ready for when the Zero platform reached completion. They were almost there when a nighttime strike by enemies unknown destroyed the facility, the equipment and the personnel. By the time a rescue team arrived, the facility was totally destroyed. Everything. There were no survivors. The intensity of the explosions and the thermal devices used had reduced the place to ashes. Even the bodies were consumed to the point where it was impossible to make a count.

"I have to mention something at this point," the President added. "Saul Kaplan had removed himself from the project some time back. He lost faith in the whole thing, I believe now due to some conflict he had with the Air Force command. I didn't learn about this until too late. He simply walked one day. Apparently he refused to do what they wanted. I had some heated discussions with the people involved and made it clear I wasn't pleased with their behavior and attitude. But the damage was done, and we were too far along to abandon the project. I'm telling you this because I did speak to Kaplan some time later. He had taken a post as a lecturer in a Midwest university. Even though I apologized for the attitude of the Air Force, I was unable to persuade him to return." The President smiled. "In the end Kaplan hung up on me. I took that as his final no."

"Is this a way of saying Kaplan might be involved in the strike against the facility, sir?" Brognola asked.

The President shook his head. "This wasn't revenge by a disgruntled ex-worker. Saul Kaplan is too much of a decent man to even consider something like this. Don't forget that his protégé, Doug Buchanan, was at the facility. Kaplan wouldn't do anything to hurt that man."

"Are there any theories on the strike force?"

"Nothing yet. We believe it may be the work of some foreign organization that may have found out about the Zero project and was simply making an attempt to prevent it becoming a reality. There are nations who would feel unjustly threatened even by the thought of something like Zero watching over them. Think about it, gentlemen."

"How was Buchanan's survival picked up?" Bolan asked.

"A locator chip was inserted into his skull during the initial implant operation. Miniature transmitter no larger than a pinhead apparently. It gave out a constant signal to a listening device at the facility. There was also a duplicate device here in Washington at the Defense Department. A backup. After the strike the signal went down. It was assumed it was because Doug Buchanan had died. By chance the line was left open. Or perhaps someone was hoping against hope. The upshot was that Buchanan's signal started up again about eight days ago. No one knows how long it had been transmitting before it was spotted. There was a trace put out, but the signal stopped again before a fix could be established. It came on again two days later. Since then it has been intermittent and for the past couple of days nothing. It could have been damaged during the attack on the facility. But at least we know Doug is alive. The signature from the signal chip was his. No doubt."

"Going back to the strike," Bolan said. "We now know that Doug Buchanan survived. He's on the run somewhere. Someone wants him. The attack on Jack Grimaldi and Jess Buchanan suggests these people want Buchanan alive."

"Doug Buchanan also carries a code sequence inside his head," the President explained. "It was implanted along with the neural net. That code will bring Zero fully online. The weapon arrays will activate and Zero becomes a fully armed platform."

"If Senator Stahl and Colonel Stengard got their hands on Buchanan, they would be in an extremely powerful position."

"Which is why I want Doug Buchanan back in safe hands, Striker. Our hands. The other possibility to be aware of is this unknown organization that carried out the original strike getting to know Doug Buchanan is still alive. If they do find out, I anticipate further attempts to kill Doug."

"I understand the need to keep this between ourselves, sir," Bolan said, "but there must be a few people around you who are aware of current happenings.
Someone could be involved in leaking information. It
has to be said, sir."

The President nodded.

"Yes, I understand, of course. I have at least three people on my close staff who have knowledge about Doug
Buchanan's resurfacing. The information was passed
along before I could do anything to keep it under wraps.
And yes, Striker, I'm aware that any one of them could be
passing that information to, shall we say, interested parties. As I said at the commencement of this meeting, no
one knows why you and Hal are here. I told no one about
the reason for your visit. Be that as it may, I am not so naive
as to believe someone couldn't make an educated guess."

Bolan nodded.

"As long as we all understand that. Mr. President,
you need to find out *who* and get them out of earshot."

"I understand your concern. Any leak from here
could be placing you in the firing line."

"And anyone else involved, sir."

The way Bolan said it caused the President to hesitate. He locked eyes with the Executioner and read the
warning there.

"Me?"

"If the people we've been theorizing about are as
hostile as we believe, you could be in danger on a close-
up and personal level, sir."

"You mean a last resort if the Zero thing doesn't gel?" Brognola asked.

"Bottom line? Yes, I do."

"If we're going along that road," the President said, "we have to consider the team from the original Zero project. Many of them are still involved with Zero. Work is going on to resurrect the project, and now that Buchanan has shown up, it means we could still bring Zero online. If we can locate Buchanan and have him brought back into the project."

"I'll have that coffee now, Mr. President," Brognola said. "I need it."

The President turned to Bolan. "Find Douglas Buchanan before anyone else, and Saul Kaplan, too, if you can. He could be in danger as much as Buchanan. At this moment in time, Striker, you are the one man I can trust above everyone else." The President glanced across at Brognola. "With the exception of Hal, of course."

"Too late for flattery, Mr. President," Brognola said.

"I'm between a rock and a hard place, Striker. If, as we suspect, there's a leak, there might also be a connection to the military community. My problem is how do I give someone the job of plugging a leak when I don't know if he, or she, is the one responsible? I would like you to deal with this for me."

There was a long pause. Brognola looked at Bolan, unsure what the Executioner was thinking.

"All right, Mr. President," Bolan said, "I accept."

"You'll do this for me?"

"On my terms, sir."

The President didn't miss a beat. "Your terms. What ever you need."

"No interference," Bolan said. "I'll need clearance to the highest level in case I need to go places. No questions asked how I carry this through."

"Agreed. As usual, you liaise with Hal and he talks to no one but me."

Bolan leaned forward. "I have one more thing to ask, Mr. President."

"Go ahead."

"Jack Grimaldi is vulnerable where he is. I don't want him left in that Nassau hospital. I want him moved to a secure facility."

"I'll see to it immediately."

"Thank you, sir."

The President handed Bolan a thick file. "You'll find everything you need in there—data on the people involved with the Zero-Option project, background on Saul Kaplan's concept. It's amazing reading when you're new to it. We need Zero back under our control." The President took a deep breath. "Do what you need to resolve this matter. Sabotage of the Zero project is an act of aggression against the United States, and I'm making a stand. Take whoever is responsible down and make our people safe."

Bolan stood and took the President's hand.

"Godspeed," the President said softly.

"Thank you, Mr. President.

"Open line, Hal," the President told Brognola.

The big Fed nodded. "It'll be 24-7, sir."

BOLAN BARELY SAID a word during the flight back to Stony Man. He sat immersed in the data file the President had provided. It was only as the helicopter started its descent that he sat back, closing the file.

"You haven't read any of this?" he asked.

Brognola shook his head.

"You'd better. It'll keep you awake at night."

They met Barbara Price the moment they stepped inside the Annex. Her expression told them they were about to hear bad news.

"Jess Buchanan's body was found a few hours ago. She washed up on a Nassau beach."

"Damn!" Brognola said.

Bolan didn't say anything, but there was no misreading the expression in his eyes as he turned and headed for the Computer Room.

"The Nassau police sent us these photographs," Price said as they entered Kurtzman's domain.

Brognola studied the images Kurtzman had printed off from the download. They made for uncomfortable viewing.

Jess Buchanan's naked body showed graphic evidence of the things done to her before death. The vital, healthy young woman had been subjected to terrible physical abuse. The injuries would have painful in the extreme yet not life threatening. They had been inflicted for the sole purpose of making her talk. To give up any information she might have been holding.

"How could they?" Price asked.

Bolan touched her arm. She looked at him, searching for answers.

"It's why we're here," he said. "Somebody has to settle the account for Jess Buchanan. For all the Jess Buchanans. If we don't, who will?"

"But…"

"Don't ask why. It never makes any sense. It has to do with someone deciding they're above the law. Beyond justice and outside the normal boundaries of civilized existence."

Bolan took a final look at the terrible images. He thought of Jess Buchanan alive and enjoying her life. That was over now, ended in a nightmare of horror and pain. He gently placed the photographs facedown on Kurtzman's desk.

"How did she die?"

Kurtzman checked his printout.

"Single shot to the back of her head."

"Was it a .45 ACP?" Bolan asked.

"Yeah."

Bolan recalled the Glock pistols he had taken from Cal Ryan's men.

Glock 21s, chambered for .45 ACP bullets.

"Aaron, find out where those pistols came from," Bolan said.

He left the Computer Room and went to his quarters,

where he had a shower and put on fresh clothing. He packed a couple of duffel bags. One with extra clothing and personal items. The second bag he filled with weapons: a 9 mm Uzi, with a threaded muzzle to take the bulky suppressor he added, his .44 Magnum Desert Eagle, complete with belt and holster. There was also an M-4 carbine. The compact version of the M-16, chambered for 5.56 mm, was a handy weapon for close-quarters firefights. There were extra magazines for each weapon. Bolan also included his blacksuit, combat harness and boots. In side pockets of the duffel were additional items he might need, including a couple of keen-edged knives, a garrote and a selection of grenades. A medium-sized backpack went into the duffel.

Bolan was going out to face enemies who had already shown their hand. Cold-blooded murder was nothing to them. Then there was the strike against the Zero facility. Bolan had to keep reminding himself that he could possibly be dealing with two totally independent groups—one that seemed intent on getting its hands on Doug Buchanan and the secrets of the Zero project for its own agenda, while the other appeared to have Zero's total destruction as its goal. The way things were shaping up, Bolan had foreign and domestic enemies out there. From his perspective they were all the same and would be dealt with on his terms.

AARON KURTZMAN already had a printout of the findings he had extracted from the credit card database.

"Makes interesting reading," he said, sliding the sheet across his desk.

Bolan picked it up and scanned the information as Kurtzman explained the facts behind the printed data.

"Skinned down to the bone, it tells us that the credit card used to hire the rental on Nassau and the cards from the wallets of the guys you tangled with in Washington were issued to a company based in Albany. Accord Sights. I ran a background check. The company retails telescopic sights for hunting rifles. It isn't a large concern, and employs only twenty people. They work through mail order in gun magazines. The office in Albany just accepts orders, processes them and passes the details to a distribution point in Pittsburgh."

"Got to be more to it than that," Bolan said.

Kurtzman scrubbed a big hand across his face, his bright eyes giving him away.

"The scope company is a wholly financed subsidiary of Stahl Armaments Corporation. I had to untangle a mess of corporate firewalls and go through the list of SAC holdings, but you can't hide forever. Somewhere along the line there has to be a connection. Might be halfway around the world, or in this case just a few hundred miles. Sooner or later the real owner has to show."

"So Senator Stahl is involved. That gives me a starting point. Looks like a trip to Albany is on the cards."

"Here's your cell phone," Kurtzman said. "This will get you through from anywhere. Tied in to our satellite feed. Direct dialing through to Stony Man. Got text messaging. You can link to a computer and contact me. I'll send any fresh data I find."

"Thanks."

"Take care now."

"ALL THE CREDENTIALS you'll need for Mike Belasko. Driver's license, passport, credit card. ID that says you're from the Justice Department. Contact number on the card will get through direct to us so we can confirm your ID."

On Price's desk were the wallets Bolan had confiscated during his clashes with the opposition. The cash from each wallet was on her desk. He scooped up the money and put it in his own wallet, along with the notes that had been supplied by Stony Man. Bolan had long ago abandoned any qualms about using the enemies' finances against them.

"Didn't I hear somewhere that in the old days you had a war chest? Where you kept all the cash you liberated from the Mafia?"

Bolan smiled. "Long time ago. I still have a slush fund."

"I'm intrigued."

"One day I'll reveal all."

Price smiled. "I can't wait."

"I'd better check in with Hal before I move out."

"I think you'd better. I'll have your car ready when you get back."

BROGNOLA LISTENED to Bolan's detailing of the information Kurtzman had come up with.

"Keep in touch."

"Oh, you'll be hearing from me."

"Yeah. That's what I'm worried about. I get the feeling I'll need to double the contingent of cleanup teams."

There was a brief pause.

"Striker, are you okay with this?"

"I'm okay. Jack's involvement won't go away. Or Jess's death. But it won't compromise the mission."

"That's all I need to hear, big guy."

Bolan turned to leave.

"Take care."

Bolan allowed a thin smile to edge his mouth.

"Hal, that's what I do. I take care of things."

Brognola shook his head. "Go on," he said. "Get out of here."

CHAPTER FOUR

Hong Kong

General Tung Shan remained silent until the waiter had finished laying out the meal and left the room. He helped himself to some of the food, poured a cup of black coffee—something he looked upon as a luxury—and settled back on the leather couch.

"So, what do you have to tell me?" he asked.

There were two other men in the hotel suite. They sat facing the General, seemingly reluctant to speak.

"Well, someone say something."

The man on Tung's immediate left cleared his throat. His name was Shao Yeung. He was Tung's security adviser, a young man who was prematurely balding. He had a thin face with prominent cheekbones. To the casual observer he looked ill, almost skeletal, but his outer appearance meant nothing. Shao had an incisive, quick mind. His observations were always acute, well defined. He wasn't a man given to making light conversation. If he hadn't been a vital part of Tung's team, the general would never have associated with the man.

"Yes?"

Shao poured himself a cup of coffee then directed his attention to the general.

"I didn't want to say anything until I had all the facts, General. Now that I am completely satisfied my information is genuine, I can report."

"And?"

"One of my contacts inside the United States has confirmed that there was a survivor from the Zero facility. Since the strike our team has been monitoring American activity. The first suggestion that a survivor exists came a week ago. Since then I have requested daily updates. We now have confirmation. As you may be aware key members of the Zero group, namely those who were to be part of the final group, had tracer chips implanted during the early stages of their induction into the program. They knew nothing about this. The implants were a safeguard so that the controllers of the project could maintain a watch over these individuals at all times. Following the strike against Zero, it was assumed that everyone had died. It appears we were wrong to make that assumption. One of the tracer chips activated a week ago. So it appears one of the team is still alive. Unfortunately the chip appears to be damaged. The signal has become erratic since the original showing."

Shao paused, watching the general closely. Knowing Tung as he did, it was possible the man might explode into one of his rages. If that happened, they could all be in danger. General Tung's loss of control was legendary. If matters failed to go the way he expected, Tung became a wild man, striking out at anyone within reach. People or objects. Neither was safe when Tung went on the rampage. No one dared stand up to him during one of these episodes. When someone had tried to resist, Tung had beaten the man almost to death. The incident only added to Tung's stature. He was a feared, respected commander, well-thought-of by his superiors. He got things done. He never failed, and his methods were approved of by the shadowy people in the background, because fear and intimidation were part of their armory. They used terror tactics on their own people, as well as on their opponents, because it kept them in line. Made them realize that they could easily become victims if they failed to satisfy those who governed them.

Tung remained silent as he drank his coffee, leaning his powerful bulk back in the soft leather of the couch.

"I believe the furnishings in this hotel come from Italy," he said finally. "It is commendable that their craftsmanship in leather is so constant. The quality never varies. Unlike their government. Why is it that a country such as Italy, famed for the genius of its artisans, is unable to maintain a stable government? Very strange, don't you think, Yeung?"

"Something to bear in mind, General," Shao agreed.

Tung fixed his gaze on the younger man. He smiled suddenly.

"I'm not going to disembowel you," the general said. "I can hardly blame *you* for the failings of the strike team in America when it was our friend Chosan who holds responsibility for that."

The man named by Tung was seated farthest from the general. He was a dark, stocky man, dressed in a well-cut gray suit and a white shirt, with a maroon tie fastened in a perfect knot. He wore black leather shoes polished to a high sheen. His black hair was cut close to his skull. He sat with his hands resting casually on his thighs, and even though he picked up the harsh tone of Tung's voice, he held his relaxed position, sure of his ability to defend himself.

Chosan Xiang didn't consider threats worthy of a response. He also knew that Tung was aware of his attitude. They sparred verbally whenever they met, each deriving enjoyment from scoring off the other. Chosan was no fool, nor was he an amateur. He had served General Tung for a number of years, always successfully, and asked little in return. The revelation that his planned attack of the Zero facility had not yielded a one hundred percent success rate was an irritant. Chosan had lived too long and fought too many battles to allow a single mistake to become more than it was. He understood the importance of what they had done. He also knew that Tung had a great deal riding on the elimination of the Zero project, so he remained silent, waiting to hear what the general planned to do.

"If there is a survivor, the Americans will have become aware of him. If this man has an implanted chip, then he must be one of the select members of the project. That makes him doubly important to everyone involved." Tung bent forward to refill his coffee cup. "Yeung, I want our people on this immediately. Have your U.S. contact provide us with everything he can on the background. We need to know what the Americans are doing. If there is a survivor with the knowledge to resurrect this project, the Americans will surely do everything they can to bring him in alive. That means they will be able to start the Zero project again. We cannot allow this to happen. We must locate and destroy him. Find out who they are putting in the field. This Zero project *must* be terminated. Allowing the Americans to bring this weapon online would place us all under threat. There is no way we would be able to create anything capable of matching Zero in the near future. We have no option but to destroy it so that the Americans themselves cannot use it. Yeung, this is your priority. Chosan will provide whatever field operatives you require. Use him. He has the contacts you will need in America."

Shao nodded. He was aware of the responsibility being placed on his shoulders. He glanced from the general to Chosan. The man returned his gaze and held it, his expression almost amiable, because he knew, as did Yeung, what would come next.

"Chosan, alert your people," Tung said. "And, please,

no mistakes this time. Make sure that when Yeung needs assistance, your people are in place."

Chosan Xiang stood and inclined his head in the general's direction.

"If I may be excused, General, I will start immediately. Shao Yeung, I will meet with you shortly and discuss what is to be done."

Shao nodded. He watched Chosan leave the room. His body language wasn't missed by Tung. He waited until Chosan had closed the door before he turned his attention back to Shao.

"What is it, Yeung? Do you not trust him, or are you afraid of him?"

Shao drank some of his coffee as he collected his thoughts. When he glanced up he saw that Tung had a thin smile on his face.

"Is it so obvious?"

"I see that there is something you consider worth being cautious about," Tung said.

"I am disturbed in his presence," Shao admitted. "I respect his profession and I know he is extremely capable, but it unsettles me."

Tung nodded. "I understand your caution. You are a planner. An organizer. I admire your ability to look at a problem and solve it in your head. I need that input. Chosan, on the other hand, is a soldier, a weapon. Proficient. Deadly. In his way he is like you. Once he has his target he goes directly for it. No deviation. No qualms about how many will need to die in order to achieve his goal. That is where you are different. You deal in statistics. Chosan deals in violence. You are not a man of violence, Yeung. That I understand. In the presence of someone like Chosan, you sense *his* violence and it disturbs you."

"Exactly, General." Shao looked Tung in the eye. "Does that disappoint you, General?"

Tung laughed. He reached out with a large hand and patted the man on the shoulder.

"Of course not. There are soldiers and there are scholars, and one needs the other. Right now I need both. Now let's eat this damned food before it goes to waste. To be honest one of the reasons I like coming to Hong Kong is the food. It's far better than anything on the mainland. We'll finish this then get down to business."

XIANG CHOSAN closed the door to his room and crossed to stand at the window where he could look out across Victoria Harbour, the choppy water thronged by boats. Beyond was Kowloon, its lights gleaming through a thin mist of rain.

Chosan remained at the window for some time. He removed his jacket and draped it over a nearby chair. He rolled the sleeves of his white shirt to his elbows, exposing powerful forearms. There was a puckered scar on his left arm, a reminder of the time he had been shot during a firefight in Taiwan while on an operation.

Finally turning from the window, Chosan crossed to the telephone and picked it up. He asked for an outside line, then dialed a number and waited until it was answered. The voice on the other end of the line was American.

"I need to meet you. I will be flying out in the morning from Hong Kong. The usual place." Chosan received an acknowledgment, then replaced the receiver.

Beside the telephone was a pack of cigarettes and a lighter. Chosan helped himself to a cigarette and lit it. Trailing smoke, he made his way back to the window and stood looking out across the harbor.

His thoughts were a soldier's thoughts. Chosan had a military mind-set and as soon as he was given an assignment he lived and breathed it, pushing aside any other considerations. Looking out across the harbor he saw little of the activity beyond the glass of the window. He was already marshaling all aspects of what lay ahead. He saw possible problems in the fact that he would have to utilize mercenaries for any assault on American soil. He would have preferred to use his own men, but that would be difficult to achieve. Not impossible, but it would have to be carefully arranged. A purely clandestine assault would minimize the risk. But this operation would be drawn out. A search-and-destroy mission, and his own men would stand out in such a situation. Americans were different. They could walk around openly, without being challenged. Their presence, even in remote areas, would go unnoticed. Which brought Chosan back to his original concern. That he was going to have to depend on men who were working for monetary gain, rather than doing it out of duty, as had been done for the original strike. It wouldn't have been Chosan's choice if there was any other way.

He stayed at the window, silently going through what he needed to do, lost to the passage of time. It was only a tap at the door that brought him out of his reverie. He crossed to the door and opened it. Shao Yeung stood there looking, as always, calm and utterly composed.

"May I come in?"

Chosan stood aside and gestured. He closed the door as Yeung walked into the room.

"I have arranged to meet my contact from the American mainland in two days," Chosan said. "Do I have your approval."

Shao turned to gaze at the man.

"Of course. I am as committed to this as you are. Where military tactics are concerned, I defer to you always. I hope you will afford me the same courtesy."

"That is where we differ. I am conversant with the tools of the soldier. You are skilled with words and politics. However, we have the same goal, so let us pursue that as amicably as possible."

Shao inclined his head in a silent response.

"Can I provide anything for your meeting with your contact?"

"Yes. The one thing that always brings a spark of interest to an American's eyes. Money. One thing you *can* depend on is American loyalty to the dollar."

"You would prefer to have your own men do this work?"

"Very perceptive, Shao Yeung. The answer is yes. I would be far happier if our own people were doing this, but the situation necessitates using a degree of outside help. For the initial phase at least we will have to depend on paid help. Never the ideal choice."

"If it was a simple matter of inserting our people, carrying out the strike to a satisfactory solution, would you feel more secure?"

"Of course. There is no question."

"Then why not use the Americans to locate the target and then insert *our* people to make sure there are no final mistakes this time?"

"I had thought about that," Chosan said. "It would increase logistical needs greatly. There would also be the timing element."

"But not an impossibility?"

"Anything is possible."

"Then formulate two plans of operation. If it becomes feasible, we will use our people for the final strike. Ask for whatever you need, and I will see that you get it. Money is no object. Our partners in this exercise have contributed a great deal of finance. The outcome is as important to them as it is to us."

Chosan smiled. "Yes, I must not forget our *brothers* from the Pacific Rim Coalition."

"Do I detect a note of cynicism?"

"I've been around long enough to understand the

complexities of the politics and national desires of certain of our sister nations. Right now they are a coalition based on survival. They see this Zero project as a long-term threat to them all. If the Americans achieve their aim, we will all live under its threat. The U.S. would be able to pinpoint whomever it wanted and force them to act in a certain way. That frightens heads of state. Knowing the Americans they would be able to select the nations they wanted to be in control. Anyone who upset the U.S. would find themselves singled out, and would their enemies do anything to stop the Americans? I think not. The Pacific Rim wants to be master of its own destiny, even if it includes committing hostile acts against a neighbor. But it wants to be able to do that with impunity. Not with the U.S. waving the Zero big stick at them. So while the threat from Zero exists, all these Pacific Rim nations are going to work together. They also understand that we have the better chance of seeing this through to the end. Which is why they are contributing financial and material assistance, and leaving the dirty work to us."

"I thought I was the thinker and you the man of direct action," Shao said.

"There are few warriors who are not also thinkers."

He considered Chosan's last remark.

"Then I had better tread carefully when I am around you."

Chosan smiled. It was a friendly enough gesture, but

Shao had a feeling there was more behind it than Chosan was showing.

"Our people in Hawaii will be informed of your arrival. Funds will be available for your use while you are there." Shao paused. "This contact you have. Do you trust him?"

"As I said, this American will keep his loyalty as long as I maintain his financial incentives. However, I sense your apprehension."

"He is an American above everything else. Is there not a possibility he may decide money does not wipe away loyalty to his country? One of the overriding things about Americans is their patriotism."

Chosan's growing appreciation of Shao's perception increased.

"When you use people who are doing it for money, there is always the chance of betrayal. It is a double-edged sword. Even using our own people based in the U.S.A. brings its own risks. An agent living and working in America might not be used for years. During that time it can have a negative effect and the agent becomes comfortable with the enemy society. The day the call comes, the agent finds he does not want to give up his new existence." Chosan shrugged. "Nothing in life is certain, except the indisputable fact that we will all die one day."

"So, a philosopher and a soldier," Shao observed.

"Hardly that. Just someone who has seen all the faces of humanity." Chosan lit another cigarette. "I should go and get ready for my flight tomorrow."

"Yes. As soon as my intelligence team has the details

on this missing man, I will let you have it. We need to identify our target. There will be no chance for error this time around. We are lucky to get a second chance. I don't think it possible to get a third if we fail again. General Tung has instructed me to arrange a meeting with our allies. They need to be kept aware of what is happening."

Chosan grunted in sympathy. "Rather you than me. Give me combat any day. Far less stressful on the nerves than being a diplomat."

Shao had to agree. The meeting with the representatives of the Pacific Rim Coalition wasn't at the head of his list of fun things to do. His instructions from General Tung had been quite specific. Shao's task was to insure they were kept happy. Pacified. Any doubts removed. That had been made extremely clear when Tung had issued his order. Apart from being a hard-line warmonger, the general was a practical man. His intuition warned him that keeping the PRC members up to date with the proceedings was politic. And being a pragmatic man, Tung had no qualms when it came to using any and all practices to gain his end result.

Shao Yeung, at that moment, felt slightly envious of Chosan's flight to Hawaii. He would have preferred to have been on the plane himself.

Hawaii

XIANG CHOSAN'S PLANE landed twenty minutes ahead of schedule. He had slept for most of the flight, so he was feeling well refreshed. It was late afternoon. Chosan picked up his single piece of luggage and made his way to the customs desk, where he presented his passport.

He was traveling on a UK passport, which had been prepared for him back on the mainland. He had used the passport on a number of occasions, and the entry visas showed he had been to a number of countries over past few years. Some were genuine, others simply excellent forgeries. The Chinese were past masters at deception. The forgeries were prepared by a special department within the Chinese secret service.

"Mr. Ling, what is the purpose of your visit to Hawaii?"

Mr. Ling smiled. "A little business. A little pleasure. I trade in fine arts all around the Pacific. My company is based in the UK." Chosan presented a business card that confirmed his identity and an address in London. The company did exist. It had operated for a number of years and was used by the Chinese as a clearinghouse for information and intelligence operations for China in the UK and Europe.

"How long have you been in Hong Kong?"

"This time? Only a few days."

Chosan continued to display his gentle smile. Whatever thoughts circulated inside his head he maintained his outer calm.

The customs officer nodded.

"Would you place your bag on the counter and open it."

"Of course."

Chosan did as he was requested. A second customs officer appeared and began to examine the contents. Chosan stood silently by. Security at airports had been stepped up in the wake of September 11, and he had been forced to submit to searches on other occasions.

"The briefcase."

The search continued. It produced nothing because there was nothing to find. Chosan traveled clean. His possessions were exactly as any innocent traveler might carry.

After a long five minutes his bags were returned, as was his passport, and Chosan was welcomed to Hawaii and told to enjoy his stay. After he had tidied his belongings and closed his bags, Chosan passed through the customs area and went outside to locate a cab for the twenty-minute ride to Waikiki.

IN AN OFFICE behind the customs desk, a tall, broad-shouldered customs agent turned away from the computer screen he had been studying. He picked up a phone and punched in a number.

"This is Kanaka. Put me through to Hardesty." He waited until his party came on the line. "Stan? Hi. This is Tom Kanaka over at Honolulu International. You got time to come over? I think you'll be interested in something we have over here. We've just picked up on one of those forged passports the Bureau asked us to look out for. Yeah, those. The Chinese forgeries. Don't worry.

The guy is being tailed as we speak. Give us time and we'll know where he's staying and who he's going to meet."

Waikiki

CHOSAN MET his contact in the bar of his hotel. He had made time to shower and change before making his way back downstairs. As usual, the hotel was crowded with tourists from the mainland. There was constant traffic back and forth of loud shirts and shorts, the click and flash of cameras. Chosan had to push his way through to get to the bar, which was decorated like something out of a Hollywood musical.

He spotted Hank Winston seated in a bamboo booth, a tall frosted glass in front of him. Winston was in his late thirties, a hollow-cheeked man with thin brown hair. His left eye was partially closed, giving him a lop-sided appearance. To Chosan he looked decidedly shady. Winston's appearance wasn't helped by his choice of clothing, which always consisted of gray pants and check-patterned sport coats.

"Hi," Winston said, rising to meet Chosan and taking his hand.

Chosan nodded and sat down. A waitress appeared and Winston ordered a fresh drink for himself and Jack Daniel's whiskey for Chosan. The American drink was a weakness Chosan gave in to whenever he was out of his own country.

"So, what can I do for you this time?" Winston asked, getting directly down to business.

It was one of the reasons Chosan liked dealing with Winston. The man never wasted time unless it had to do with the work in hand. He always cut straight to the chase.

"You recall our little venture involving the Zero project?"

Winston took a long sip from his drink, then cleared his throat. "I remember. Came out pretty neat, huh?"

"If you don't count the one man who survived."

"You shittin' me?"

"No. We have it confirmed. One man escaped the strike on the facility, which means we need to find him and anything he might have that could be useful to the U.S. military, who will no doubt be hoping to rebuild the whole project."

"What can I say, Chosan? Looks like we fucked up. Okay, whatever it takes. Tell me what you want to do."

"Find this missing link. Kill him and anyone associated with him who gets in your way."

"We got any ID on this guy?"

"That is being looked into as we speak. When we receive the information I will have it sent directly to you."

"Fine." Winston paused, his cheeks reddening slightly as he summoned the words he was going to need next. "We going to talk money?"

Chosan let the man stew for a while longer. To cover his discomfort Winston picked up his glass and drank, trying to hide behind it.

"Did you believe I was going to make you finance this yourself?" Chosan asked finally.

"Look, I wasn't sure how you'd take paying again. Some people might expect me to bankroll a second strike myself."

"I do not work like that. Nor do you. Money is the means by which we initiate our agreements. I will have my local people deposit whatever figure we agree into your account. My only concern is the timing," Chosan said. "Locating this target is paramount. We are under pressure to resolve this matter quickly. There are others interested in this man. If they get to him before we do, the consequences for my principals will be difficult to say the least."

"I'll be returning to the mainland on a noon flight tomorrow," Winston said. "Send me everything you have on the target through my e-mail system. I can advise my people to be ready to receive it. And I'll have them assemble a team the minute they get it."

"Can you have additional people on standby?"

"If you need them. Are there other targets?"

"Possibly. I will advise as soon as I have that information."

"Are you returning home when we complete?"

"No. I am going to be picked up here and taken to one of our ships. You will still be able to reach me via the satellite cell phone."

"Business trip? Or pleasure?"

Chosan allowed himself a quiet smile. "It depends on how you interpret those words."

The expression of confusion in Winston's eyes stayed with Chosan the rest of the day.

He hadn't explained himself any further, due partly to the fact that any explanation would have caused Winston a great deal of unrest.

Chosan's sea voyage would take him, and the assault team that would be on the vessel, toward America. He was preparing for any eventuality. In case Winston's strike teams failed, Chosan would have his backup. He was reluctant to use them, only due to the fact that an armed assault on American soil would leave his people vulnerable to capture, or worse. Chosan had no illusions where the Americans were concerned. Falling into their hands would be the last thing he would wish for his team. They were, to a man, prepared to die if it meant their strike had a successful conclusion. And each of them was fully aware of the price they would have to pay if caught. But they willingly accepted the risks. Death by their own hand was infinitely preferable to the torture they would suffer in American prison.

That was the business part of Chosan's trip.

If he did have to send in his people because Winston had failed a second time, then it would have to be. For Winston it wouldn't be the choice of a third attempt. He was on borrowed time already. Chosan could afford to be lenient this time around until, and if, Winston completed the assignment and the target was terminated.

Then there would be no further action needed. Failure this time would eventually result in the Zero project going ahead and the Americans becoming the single most powerful military threat to the rest of the world. If Chosan had to send in his team, it would fall to them to complete the mission. If that did come about, Winston would be under sentence of death. This time failure was *not* an option. Winston would die, and Chosan would undertake the action himself.

That would be the pleasure part of his trip.

CHAPTER FIVE

Albany, New York

Bolan sat at the wheel of his car studying the building that housed the offices of the Accord company. It was late afternoon. There were heavy clouds coming in from the east, casting a pall over Albany. His drive up from Washington had given the Executioner ample time to think about what had occurred since he had arrived in Nassau and learned of the incident involving Jack Grimaldi and Jess Buchanan. Subsequent events had drawn Bolan deeper into what now looked to be a major conspiracy.

The President's revelations had been an eye opener as far as Bolan was concerned. He was aware that the government had to be involved in defense projects that had to be kept from the public at large, simply for security purposes. He had no problems with that. Self-preservation was vital. Without it America left herself wide open to those who, for whatever ideological or deep-rooted opposition, wanted the country to suffer. Those who advocated nonaggressive stances, a weakening of America's defensive position, lived in a naive world. You didn't appease the scavenger by holding out your hands and walking into his trap. There had to be a line of defensive strength behind the negotiators. Any sign of weakness gave the advantage to the opposition.

The ongoing peace talks, which were taking place nonstop in various locations throughout the world, didn't hold much credence with Bolan. The complications of political, personal, religious and financial constrictions, all these were thrown into the pot. They created stumbling blocks that would determine the outcome. His contact with regimes determined to ferment unrest, who were ready and willing to create mayhem and inflict harm, shadowed Bolan's views.

Despite all the good intentions of the peacemakers, there was no way universal peace and harmony were going to spread across the world within the foreseeable future. Bolan wasn't being a defeatist. It wasn't in his nature. But he did possess a clear and unbiased view of the way things were. Nothing was going to change overnight. One day it might happen. It was a slow, agonizing process. A permanent chipping away at hate and prejudice. A small victory here. An agreement on small matters there. Concessions. Careful wording of proposals so that both parties could walk away without having felt they had been compromised.

Fragments of success that even when agreed on still needed nurturing, with a full knowledge that the smallest thing could set everything back in an instant. And it only took one act of violence, perpetrated by some single individual with a personal grudge, a political stance, to destroy in moments the long months of negotiation.

Mack Bolan saw all these things as he trod his relentless path through the murky reality of his war. He saw the horror and the pain, did what was needed to combat the needless destruction, and despite the continuing emergence of evil he remained resolute. If there was any form of stepping back and wavering, the dark side would win. Bolan refused to accept the thought. The battle always had to be engaged. His philosophy was simple—never, ever retreat. Take the war to *them*. Keep them on the run, looking over their shoulders.

The attitude of Senator Eric Stahl, with his advocacy of outright belligerence, added an even riskier note to the proceedings. Bolan had no argument with anyone who wanted to keep America strong. Stahl took that a dangerous step further. He would have turned America into an armed camp, bristling with offensive attitudes. Not the powerful giant holding out the hand of diplomacy. Stahl's vision for America would have her posturing and threatening, laying down her requirements to the world. And if regimes refused to toe the line, Stahl wouldn't hesitate to use his military strength to contain that refusal. He would push and threaten, and have no qualms about using weapons at his disposal. Which, if he seemingly had his way, would include Zero.

The capability of the Zero Platform, as Bolan had digested from what the President had told him and had read in the detailed file, made him aware of the awesome power contained within it. As a defensive weapon it would have no equal. Continually circling the planet, scanning and recording events, Zero would be able to monitor events on a twenty-four-hour cycle. Its information gathering would provide the American defense and security communities with vast quantities of data, allowing them to anticipate and counter any threat against the U.S., and even friendly states liable to be placed under threat. Added to that was the platform's weaponry. A collection of the most sophisticated missiles and lasers created. Many of the weapons systems were so new there were no details available beyond the fact they were installed in Zero. It came down to Zero being the single ultimate weapon any nation could possess. The President wanted it secure under government control, unlike Eric Stahl and his self-aggrandizing scheme to use it to lever himself into the White House.

Bolan glanced at his watch and decided it was safe to move. It was close to six-thirty. According to the information Kurtzman had extracted from the database, the company closed for business at six each day. He fired up the engine and drove across to the building's basement car park, keeping his speed down. He took the entrance ramp and eased the car inside. He had made a walk-by earlier, checking out the entrance-exit to the parking area. There were no barriers or shutters in place. He did see TV cameras located at the entrance and exit. They didn't worry Bolan. He was going to be inside his vehicle, and the fact his license plate might be monitored didn't concern him. Any trace of the number would come up against a Stony Man site that would show a legal background for the car. Bolan cruised the parking lot and found an empty slot, close to and facing the exit.

Under his jacket the soldier wore his shoulder rig holding the Beretta 93-R. His other weapons were in the duffel stored in the trunk. He unleathered the pistol and checked it, making certain there was a 9 mm round in the breech. He flicked the selector to single shot before returning the weapon to the holster. His only other weapon was a combat knife, carried in a snug sheath clipped to his belt at the base of his spine.

Stepping out of the car, Bolan used the remote to lock the doors, then made his way across the basement lot. Reaching the door that led through to the elevators, he located an empty car, stepped inside and pushed the button for the fifth floor. When it slowed and stopped he got out, waited until the corridor was clear, then moved to the fire door and went through. He took the concrete steps that led to floor six, easing open the door on the landing to check if the corridor was clear. Stepping through, he turned left and walked along the corridor until he spotted the entrance to Accord. Bolan walked on by, reached the end of the corridor, then turned about and approached the door again.

It had a frosted-glass upper section that bore the company name and telephone number. Bolan tried the handle, which opened under gentle pressure. He pushed the door enough to let him through. His initial glance revealed that the reception area was clear. He closed the door, taking a moment to turn the button lock.

The reception area was small, but expensively furnished with a light oak desk trimmed with polished aluminum. Beyond the reception desk were double doors, leading, Bolan guessed, into the main office area. As he closed in on the doors, he picked up the murmur of voices from the other side. He identified at least three speakers. One appeared to be angry at something one of the others said. Bolan took time to listen and heard almost immediately something that drew his interest.

"...the hell is Ryan going to say? Jesus, haven't there been enough fuckups already? Bad enough having Stengard on our backs. Now we got Ryan eating the friggin' furniture."

"It's easy for the colonel. All he does is sit back and give the orders to Ryan. Shit doesn't come down on him if things go hairy. We get to do the crap jobs. Like this thing with Senator Randolph. Why him?"

"We get paid to do the dirty work. It's as simple as that."

"And Ryan doesn't get smoked when his team does."

"Sound queer to you? How Ryan walked out without a scratch and his team got themselves killed?"

"You want to ask him how he did it?"

"Why don't you ask the other guy who was there?"

Four men were in the office, and they all turned at the unfamiliar voice.

They saw Mack Bolan, standing just inside the double doors, his back to the wall and the Beretta in his hand pointing directly at them.

"Who the fuck are you?"

Bolan directed his cold stare at the speaker.

"Belasko."

"How in hell did you find—?"

"Never mind about that right now. You should be working on how you're going to stay alive."

One of the three stepped forward, his face tight with rage.

"Those guys you killed were friends of mine. Good friends. Who the hell you think you are walking in here, waving that friggin' gun about? Figure it makes you a tough guy? Maybe I'll just come and take it off you."

Bolan could see the wild excitement in the man's eyes. He was hyping himself up into a state of uncontrolled rage. His sense would desert him, and he would make a try for Bolan despite being under the threat of the Executioner's gun.

"Back off, pal," Bolan warned. "This isn't a game."

"I'll give you fuckin' games."

Bolan saw the man tense, his shoulders lifting as he prepared to launch himself in the soldier's direction.

The muzzle of the Beretta moved slightly. The

weapon fired once, punching a 9 mm slug into the fleshy part of the guy's left thigh. The impact spun him and dumped him on the floor. He hunched over. Clamping his hands over the bloody of his wound, moaning in agony.

"We getting the idea this is serious now?" Bolan asked.

No one spoke.

Bolan moved farther into the room, keeping the three men covered. He bent over the man he had shot and quickly frisked him, finding a Glock .45 in a hip holster.

"I seem to be building quite a collection of these. You people getting a bulk discount? Maybe through Stahl Armaments?"

One of the men threw a glance at his partners. It told Bolan he was hitting the target.

"The name mean something?"

"Go to hell."

"Why don't we try Buchanan? Or Saul Kaplan?"

There was a door at the far end of the office. As Bolan spoke the last name the door crashed open, smashing against the inside wall with enough force to dislodge pictures hung there.

Bolan was distracted for a fraction of a second. He caught a glimpse of a moving figure charging through the door, a heavy revolver in his right hand.

His three captives clawed for the pistols holstered under their jackets, hauling them into view and jacking the slides back to arm them.

Bolan heard the metallic sounds and reacted instinctively, taking a headlong dive toward the bulk of a nearby desk. He hit the top on his left shoulder and rolled across it, dropping behind the barrier the desk offered, then put his strength into a push that turned the desk on its side. The thick, solid wood shielded him as autoweapons cut loose, the desk shaking as the bullets ripped into the thick top. He flicked the Beretta back to 3-round bursts.

The soldier moved to the far end of the desk, then leaned around the corner, his Beretta tracking one of the trio as the man moved to intercept. The moment he laid eyes on his intended target, Bolan was ready. There was no hesitation. He leaned out, the Beretta held two-handed, and fired a triburst, then followed with a second. His target grunted, stunned by the impact of the 9 mm slugs as they cored into his upper body. The second burst hit over his heart, the slugs cleaving through flesh and muscle, bone and organs. The ravaged body reacted and the guy went down hard, the pistol jarred from his grip.

"Goddamned bastard!"

Bolan heard the heavy crack of a gun firing. He moved in time to see one of the ex-captives twist around, a bloody hole erupting between his shoulders from the force of a heavy bullet. He hit the carpeted floor on his face, bone snapping under the impact.

There was a burst of sound as the remaining man rushed forward, gun up and firing. His shots were wild, his aim upset by panic at the sudden two-pronged attack. Bolan put a triburst into him, knocking him back over a chair. The guy went down screaming, his upper chest riddled by the Executioner's slugs.

Bolan pushed to his feet and moved cautiously across the office to stand over the man he had shot in the leg, scanning the shadows for his unknown ally.

"You want to tell me where Buchanan and Kaplan are?" Bolan asked.

The wounded man only stared up at the impassive figure towering over him. He knew if he had expected some kind of compassion from this man, he was going to be disappointed. The blood pumping from his leg wound took over as the main attraction, and the guy drifted away from Bolan's question.

"He won't tell you but maybe I can."

Bolan turned, discerned a faint shadow, the Beretta already tracking in on the tall and dark figure stepping out of the corner of the room.

"Easy there. I'm on your side."

The 93-R stayed on track, the muzzle steady as Bolan studied the newcomer.

He saw a man almost his own height, broad shoulders on a taut, lean frame. Brown face and thick jet-black hair. The guy was dressed in black, too, save for a white cotton shirt. Leather jacket, black pants, Western boots. The jacket was open, showing a belt that supported a waist holster, worn on the left for a cross draw. The weapon the holster carried was in the newcomer's right hand—a wood-butted, .45-caliber Colt Peacemaker, single-action revolver. The weapon was held casually, nonthreatening, but there was no mistaking the implicit threat it might present if matters changed.

"Easy to say," Bolan said, "harder to prove."

"If I was with them, you'd be on the floor, too, about now."

"Still doesn't tell me who the hell you are."

"Name's Joshua Riba." The man held out a leather badge wallet. He flipped it open to show a badge that had him down as a private investigator, licensed by the state of New Mexico. "My Apache name is Charriba. Handed down through the family. My great uncle Charriba was a hell of a fighter, they tell me. Had the Army chasing him all over New Mexico."

"Still doesn't tell me I should trust you."

Riba smiled. "I thought this had all been settled back in 1800s. We trust the white man and he trusts the Apache. Unless you want to start the Indian Wars all over?"

"I got enough wars of my own," Bolan said.

"The way you deal with the opposition, I'm not surprised. Look, why don't we get the hell out of here before more of these jokers show up?"

Bolan put his Beretta away. "Give me a minute."

Bolan made a search of the office. The only thing that drew his interest was a laptop sitting on one of the desks. It was switched on, some text on screen. Bolan hit the save button, waited for the function to complete, then switched it off and picked up the machine.

"Let's get out of here," he said.

They made their way down to the basement parking area. Bolan's car was still where he had parked it. Riba jerked a thumb behind him.

"Mine's outside, parked in back of the building. Red Cherokee Laredo. Follow me. I passed a diner on the edge of town we can use to talk."

He saw Bolan checking the area, his keen eyes probing the dark shadows.

"You trust anyone?"

A ghost of a smile crossed Bolan's lips. "That's a question I need to think about," he said and turned toward his parked car.

TWENTY MINUTES LATER Bolan sat nursing a steaming mug of coffee, sitting across from Joshua Riba in the diner.

"Why Saul Kaplan?" Bolan asked.

"I'm doing a favor for someone. A guy I know wants to find Kaplan."

"Douglas Buchanan?"

Joshua stared him out. There wasn't a flicker of recognition in the man's dark eyes. If he did know Buchanan, he wasn't giving anything away.

"Okay, let's do it the hard way," Bolan suggested. "The way you reacted back at the Accord building has you on the same side as I am. If I'm wrong, you put on a damned good show. But I don't think I am wrong. Somewhere along the line you and I are chasing the same shadows. You want Kaplan. I want Buchanan.

The pair seem to go together. There are other parties who also want Kaplan and Buchanan, but their intentions are less than honorable. So either we go our own ways and keep walking into each other, or we make a truce and pool what we have." Bolan paused. "That make sense?"

Riba considered Bolan's speech. He leaned against the back of the booth, tapping the fingers of his left hand against the edge of the table. Just as suddenly he sat upright, giving a slight flick of his head.

"Seems reasonable. But don't play games with me, because I don't play games."

"Okay. I know Kaplan and Buchanan worked closely together on a government project. Somewhere along the way Kaplan decided he'd had enough and walked off the project. He did a vanishing act. Turned up in a small-town university teaching science until a few weeks ago. This time he just fell off the edge of the world. The project Buchanan was part of was hit by an unknown assault force. The site was destroyed, and it was assumed that all the personnel had died. That was until a chip in Buchanan's skull started to send out a signal. It showed that he was still alive. Since then Buchanan has become a wanted man. He's wanted because he's the only man who can bring the project back to life." Bolan took a swallow of coffee. "Feel free to jump in anytime."

Riba allowed a hint of a smile to play over his lips. "You're doing fine."

"So how did you get involved with Doug Buchanan?"

"The night the project was hit Buchanan walked away without being spotted. He was hurt from being blown out of a building. Concussed. Some burns and cracked ribs. He just wandered away from the project and had no idea where he was going, or how far he'd walked. In the end he walked onto one of the dirt roads my tribe uses and stepped in the path of a truck being driven by my uncle. The guy took a nasty whack. Uncle John put him in the truck and brought him to our place. Apache settlement. My people tended his wounds and watched over him. He was unconscious for three days and nights. When he woke, his memory was part gone from the knocks he'd taken. So our local shaman came down out of the mountains and worked his medicine. Spent a couple of weeks with Buchanan. By the end Buchanan had recovered pretty well. He told us all about himself. What he'd been doing in the desert. All about the project. They call it the Zero Option? It was like he wanted to talk it out of his system. Then he started to tell about his cancer, but the shaman had already seen that and told Buchanan first.

"Buchanan started to get jumpy. He said something about people looking for him. Said he needed to move on because if they came looking and found us they would hurt us. He couldn't understand why it made us all laugh. Hell, he hadn't even realized we were Apache. But he still wanted to warn people and said he had to contact his niece, a young woman who lived on Nassau. He used the trading post phone to call her. He had to leave a message because she wasn't around at the time. You think she got it?"

Bolan nodded. "Yeah. It's how I got into this. A friend of mine was with the woman, Jess, when people came looking for Buchanan. My friend got beaten up pretty bad for being there, and Jess was kidnapped. They found her body two days later. The people who took her gave her a hard time before they killed her and dumped her body at sea."

"Sorry to hear that. So you're looking for these people because it's personal?"

"It started that way. Now it's more than just personal. The project Doug Buchanan was involved with is classified government business and goes right to the top. The problem is, the situation has become complicated. I'm pretty certain that the strike against the project was engineered out of the country, and it could be those people will still be out to get their hands on Buchanan. The White House wants him back to kick start the project."

"So who were these guys we tangled with?"

"There's a third player in the game. He wants Buchanan and Zero for his own agenda. Senator Eric Stahl. It looks like Stahl is in partnership with a Colonel Orin Stengard. He has his own teams out looking for Buchanan. Some of them are ex-military and used to be part of Stengard's covert military team. They have a simple procedure. If you're not Buchanan or Kaplan, you don't figure."

"They the same crew who put your friend in hospital and killed the girl?"

Bolan nodded.

"Last week I was complaining about life getting dull," Riba admitted. "Nothing ever happened. All I was doing was chasing bail jumpers and looking for wandering husbands."

"What happened to Buchanan?"

Riba rocked his coffee mug. "Doug's memory kept lapsing. One minute he was fine, then his grip started going and he was back where we found him. He didn't know who he was. But he still had that one thing he kept a hold on. Kaplan. Whatever else he forgot, that name stayed with him. He took off one night. Just up and went. No one knew until morning."

"He go on foot?"

"Borrowed one of my trucks. I'd told him it was there if he wanted to get around."

"You put out any traces on it?"

"No need. Found the truck at a rail depot about sixty miles away. Looks like Doug jumped a freight. My guess is he's gone looking for Kaplan himself. Like I said, he talked about the man a lot. I'd say he has a lot of respect for Kaplan. Doug knows he's in trouble. I got the feeling he believes Kaplan can clear everything up for him."

"Kaplan was the driving force behind Zero. He came up with the whole project—the concept, design, and he oversaw the building of the whole thing and worked with the people involved. My information has Kaplan and Buchanan being close. He needs a lifeline, something he can grab on to and use to pull himself back to reality."

"So Doug goes looking for Kaplan. We're looking for them both. And so are these shooters." Riba leaned back, flexing his wide shoulders. "So where do we start?"

"Joshua, what brought you to Albany?"

"It's my job. Remember? No big mystery. When Doug told me about Kaplan, it was clear he was concerned the guy might be targeted by the people who were looking for Doug. He told me where Kaplan used to live. So after Doug vanished I took off for Kaplan's house. Maybe I figured I'd find Doug there. A long shot, but sometimes they get results."

"He wasn't there?"

Riba shook his head. "I hung around for a while. That night two of the guys we took down showed up at Kaplan's house. Whoever they were, they know how to play the game. They broke in and spent a half hour in the place, looking for Kaplan, or anything they could find. When they came out I waited until they took off and tailed them." Riba grinned. "Two days and they didn't have a clue I was following them. They brought me right here to Albany and the Accord office."

"How did you get in?"

"Ever hear of back stairs? That building was older than my grandfather's lodge. By the time I worked my way into the storeroom you were already in the office talking to them."

"Joshua, you said you might know where Kaplan is. Is that true, or was it just to stop me shooting you?"

"Doug mentioned a place Kaplan used to go to when he was a younger man. It's pretty isolated, from what he said. Somewhere up in the Wyoming high country. Kaplan has a lodge there. It was my next place to look after Kaplan's house before those guys showed up."

"That's where we need to go," Bolan said. "I'll have my people run a check on Kaplan's recent incoming and outgoing calls. He might have a call divert on his phone. Any calls he might have received could have been passed on to a phone at this lodge. Maybe we'll get lucky with a location."

"Sounds good to me. Especially the *we* part."

"If I try to deal you out, you'll go on your own. One problem. The opposition can trace calls, too."

Riba grinned tightly. "You know how to bring a man down."

"First I need to check out this Senator Randolph connection. I need to know if he's in on this deal, or someone Stahl wants out of the way. You can organize for our trip to Wyoming. We'll take your truck. It's better suited for where we're going."

CHAPTER SIX

Claire Valens watched her partner cross the parking lot of the fast-food outlet, shoulders hunched against the driving rain, foam cups in his hands. She leaned over and opened the passenger door, taking the cups from his hands.

"You sure it was my turn?" he asked, shrugging out of his weatherproof coat.

"Jackson, would I lie?" she asked sweetly.

"Damned right," Byrde grumbled. "And cut the Shirley Temple act."

Valens laughed out loud. The sound was full and natural, exhibiting her spirit of enthusiasm and openness. As well as being one of Nature's beauties, Claire Valens possessed a sharp brain, the wit to go with it and a dedication toward her profession that sometimes made even Byrde take a step back and catch his breath.

"Okay, sometimes I might tell you *little* lies," she acknowledged. "But only so you won't get mad."

"Tell me about it."

Byrde sat back, sipping his coffee, absently watching drops of rain slide down the windshield.

"Doug Buchanan," Valens said.

It wasn't a question. Simply an uttering of the name of the man they were looking for.

"Did you finish reading his file?" Valens asked. "I mean really read it and take it all in?"

"Most of it. Why?"

"Could you have done what he did?" Valens paused before quietly adding, "I don't think I could. They didn't give us the full details on Buchanan when we were working at the facility. All we knew was that he had an important part in the project. But this…this is deep."

Byrde glanced at her, studying her profile, looking beyond to the woman behind it.

"I mean, the guy has terminal cancer and he still signs up for a project that would scare the pants off me."

Byrde steered around the mental picture her last remark conjured up and returned to the subject.

"Wasn't it the fact he *had* cancer that made him the prime candidate? After cancer, what could be scarier?"

Valens turned to gaze at him, a determined expression on her face.

"I knew that would be the way you'd see it. Everything in life is plain black-and-white as far as you're concerned. Am I right?"

Byrde drained his coffee cup.

"How long have we been a team, Claire? Three years? You came up with that line before the end of the first week. And it gets an airing every time I give my opinion."

"Hmm. So I don't have to use it often, then," Valens said.

"Just what else did they teach you at Lawrence Livermore? Apart from humiliating put-downs."

"Actually it was my best subject."

"That doesn't surprise me. What does is why you gave up that cushy post at GSR for a security field job. Come on, Claire, you had it made. Or was it because you heard I'd be partnering you?"

Valens didn't reply. When Byrde glanced at her, she was staring out the car window at a slight figure emerging from the house across the street. The figure was swathed in a long black raincoat, with some kind of floppy hat on his head.

They had been watching the house for just over two hours.

"That him?"

"Fits the description. Tall man. On the lean side. And the clothes."

"Too easy," Byrde said.

"What?"

"It's too damned easy," Byrde repeated. "People have been looking all over for this guy Kaplan the past few days. Somebody already broke in and found nothing.

We sit outside his house for two hours and next minute he shows up like he's going out to buy a carton of milk."

He began to check out the area, glancing over his shoulder to peer through the rain-streaked rear window.

"I don't like it, Agent Valens. Something doesn't sit right."

"Okay, *Agent Byrde,* what do you want to do?"

"Like it or not, we have to follow him. He's our best link to Buchanan." Byrde sighed. Resigned to the situation. "Let's go."

He pushed his hand inside his coat and drew out his handgun, checking the clip and working the slide to put a 9 mm cartridge in the breech.

"Calm down," Valens said, "I'm going, I'm going."

She started the car and reversed out of the slot they had been parked in. She eased the car across the lot, through puddled rain and took the exit, swinging onto the street. The traffic was light so she had no problem getting into a lane. The figure on the opposite side of the street was moving slowly, steadily, seeming to be in no kind of hurry..

The figure they were *assuming* was Saul Kaplan.

The man behind the Zero project. Kaplan had come up with the concept, had been the sole creator and the driving force behind the whole thing. It had been his genius and his relentless energy that had pushed the project along at a startling speed, bringing Zero from a paper project to reality in an unbelievable time span.

Claire Valens had only seen Kaplan in the flesh once. It had been at the Zero facility in the New Mexican desert. She and Byrde, as the security team assigned to Zero, had been taken there for a briefing before they became established as the on-site agents. One of the facility's military aides had been escorting Valens to a meeting when the lean, intense figure had approached and passed them in the corridor. The young lieutenant had waited until he figured they were out of earshot.

"Consider yourself privileged, Agent Valens," he had said.

"Oh?"

"That was the man himself. Saul Kaplan. He's the reason we're all here."

"The Kaplan who came up with Zero?"

"The very same."

Valens looked over her shoulder for a second look, but Kaplan had already vanished.

"Looking upon greatness is considered an honor in some countries," she said.

"Don't quote me," the lieutenant stated, "but greatness can be a pain in the butt when it comes to security."

"Do tell."

The lieutenant had been among the fatalities in the wake of the attack on the Zero facility. Valens had been able to recall his earnest expression, the way he believed without question the validity of what the Zero project would be used for once it was up and running. He had died for those beliefs. Valens envied him his devotion to duty and country—not that she didn't possess those qualities. Her problem was even though she did, she still questioned them, was always digging into things, turning them over to see what stuck to the other side of good intentions.

"I don't figure this." Byrde was still complaining. "What the hell is he doing wandering around in the rain?"

"Some people find walking in the rain to be quite therapeutic."

"Yeah?"

"Gene Kelly even sang and danced in the rain."

Byrde glanced across at her. "What has that got to with anything?"

Valens only smiled in her quiet way.

"Hey," Byrde said, "what the hell is that car do—?"

A black sedan had emerged from a service road, cutting across the street and seemed to be heading directly for their car. It accelerated suddenly, swinging in a wide arc that brought it on a trajectory directly in line with the agents' vehicle.

"Jesus, guns," Byrde yelled.

Valens peered at the car bearing down on them and saw a man's head and shoulders leaning out one of the rear windows. She saw that Byrde had been right. The man was wielding a stubby SMG, and he opened fire without any kind of warning.

A line of slugs peppered the hood of the agents' car. Valens hauled the wheel around, pulling the vehicle away from the attackers. The SMG fired again. Slugs hit the windshield, spiderweb cracks flashing across the glass.

The rear of their car slid on the wet road, and there was a solid thump as it clipped the rear of the attack car.

"Christ, Valens," Byrde yelled.

He had his window down and he leaned out, his pistol held in both hands as he pumped a half magazine at the other car. A window shattered in the rear.

Valens stepped on the brake, bringing the car to a jerking stop. She pushed open her door and exited the car, dropping to a crouch as she hauled her handgun from its holster. As she crouch-walked to the front end, the sound of autofire filling her ears, she sensed movement. She turned and saw the figure they had assumed to be Kaplan, coming across the street, his coat thrown wide open so that he could bring the combat shotgun he was carrying into action, the muzzle tracking in on Byrde, who was stepping out of their car, his back to the man.

Valens didn't hesitate. She braced her elbows on the hood and caught the shotgunner in her sights. She triggered two quick rounds and saw them punch into the target's chest, spinning him back a step. He stumbled to his knees, the shotgun's muzzle sagging to the ground. Valens triggered a third shot, seeing the impact and the spurt of dark blood from the target's head before he went down.

Byrde half turned, seeing what had happened behind him. He caught Valens's eye and nodded.

"Still someone in that car," Valens yelled, catching a dark flicker of movement inside the attack vehicle.

They turned in unison, weapons tracking, and fired within a heartbeat of each other. The driver jerked back against the wheel, blood splashing the inside of the windshield.

"I need to reload," Valens said.

"I'm covering you."

Valens ejected the spent magazine and replaced it with another from her pocket. As the slide snapped back into place, she moved to stand back to back with her partner.

"Okay."

She covered Byrde as he made a swift reload.

They scanned the immediate area. The street was silent save for the rain that was still falling, bouncing off the ground and washing away the blood that had come from the brief exchange.

"What was that all about?" Byrde muttered.

"Try setup. We walked right into this with our eyes wide shut."

The tone of her voice told Byrde his partner was angry.

Byrde was still casting around, weapon up as he searched the area, peering in through the windows of parked cars. A scattering of spectators were watching, on the edge of taking off if the situation changed.

In the distance, they heard the shrill sound of a police siren.

"Better get ready," Valens suggested.

They took out their badge holders and held them up as a police cruiser swept around the corner and angled in toward them. The front passenger door opened and a uniformed cop jumped out, shotgun trained on them.

"Hold it!" he yelled. "Put the weapons on the ground and get down yourself!"

Valens placed her pistol on the ground and walked toward the cop, holding out her badge.

"I said on the ground," the cop yelled.

"If you think I'm getting down there," Valens said tautly, "you can shoot me right now." She tossed her badge holder on the hood of the cruiser. "Read what it says, Officer. I work for the federal government, and Washington doesn't like its people getting their suits wet and dirty. I'm already wet, but I'm not going to get dirty, as well. See the ID card next to the badge? Call the number and you can confirm what I said. I'll stand here while you do it, but you tell me to drop once again, and I'll show you a trick with that Mossberg they don't have in the manual."

The driver of the cruiser stepped out, picked up Valens's badge holder and scanned the shield and the card.

Byrde had placed his own weapon on the ground. He advanced on the cruiser driver, holding out his own ID.

"I'd do what she says, Officer. That trick with the shotgun. I've seen her do it, and it takes about three weeks before you can walk straight again."

"Four weeks," Valens said. "And they don't always get to walk straight again."

"Okay, okay, you two," the cruiser driver said. "Just what the hell is going on here?"

"Jackson, you explain. I need to call home," Valens

said. She took out her cell phone, making sure the cops saw what she was doing and tapped a speed-dial number. It connected to their department, and she asked for their section chief. "Valens, sir. We have a slight problem here. The meet turned out to be a setup. Looks like the idea was for Byrde and me to be permanently retired from the assignment and the rest of our lives. No, sir, we're okay. But we have three DOAs on our hands and the local cops have arrived and are understandably nervous. I'd be grateful if you could just ease the situation. Thanks, sir, I'll put one of the officers on."

Valens held out the cell phone to the cruiser driver. He took it and identified himself as Officer Qualen. Valens glanced across at Byrde and shrugged.

FIVE MINUTES LATER the street was cordoned off by police cruisers, and an ambulance had arrived. With their identities confirmed, Valens and Byrde had their guns back and their hands full as they checked out the three-man hit team.

The trio was Caucasian. None carried any ID of any kind, their pockets were empty and they wore cheap, off-the-rack clothing, with all the labels removed.

"Do me a favor, Officer Qualen," Valens asked.

"As long as you forget that thing with the shotgun," Qualen told her.

"Oh, you boys and your guns," Valens said coyly. "Check these guys for prints and dental records. They have to have something we can ID them by."

"You got it," Qualen said. He pushed to his feet and beckoned to the medics. "Okay, guys, you can take them away."

He turned to his partner. "Danny, get on to the precinct. Have them send a tech down to the morgue. Tell them we need prints and dental on these three."

"Hey, what about the car?" Danny asked. "Those aren't local plates. Looks like an out of state to me."

"Call the number in," Qualen said. "Get it checked on the vehicle database."

Qualen followed Valens and Byrde back to their own vehicle. He ran an expert eye across the visible damage.

"I'll get a tow truck to haul this away," he said. "No way you can drive. Impact shoved your rear end out of line, and those slugs through the hood most probably made a mess of your engine."

"Looks like we need a cab," Byrde said.

"I can run you where you need to go," Qualen said. He studied the rain-soaked pair, grinning. "Looks like you need a change of clothing and a shower."

"Back to our motel would be fine," Valens said.

"Yeah, that shower sounds better all the time," Byrde added. "Hey, Claire, who soaps who this time? My turn or yours?"

"Damned if I can remember."

Qualen eyed them suspiciously, shaking his head.

"You pair," he said.

"We're a very close team," Valens said.

"Actually we're kidding about the soap," Byrde stated.

"Yeah, sorry. It's really baby oil. Warmed up and put on by hand."

THE FIRST THING they did after Qualen had dropped them off at the motel was to arrange for a replacement vehicle. While Byrde arranged that, Valens contacted their office again, using her cell phone.

"That's correct, sir. The local police are going to get prints and see if we can get anything from those and dental records. These people have done everything they can to stay anonymous. The other possibility is the car. Can I say something, sir, off the record? I have a distinct feeling we were set up by someone with access to our data files. It was too neat. They knew where we were down to the last minute. It's not as if we advertised our itinerary in the local press, sir, if you get my meaning. Yes, sir. We will."

"You telling the boss how to run his office again?" Byrde asked as Valens came off the phone.

"What I'm trying to do is keep you and me alive. By the way, are you going to fetch some coffee, or what?"

"Hey, I'm all wet."

"So it won't matter if you get wet again."

"I need that shower and dry clothes."

"Forgot where your room is? Next door. Remember?"

"Claire, you're all heart."

As he reached the door, Valens called out, "Jackson, that was a good call out there. Glad you were backing me."

"Works for me, too." He turned to look at her closely. "Hey, you okay?"

Valens grimaced. "I will be. I think it's starting to kick in." She raised a hand. It was shaking slightly. "I haven't really had time to think about it until now. I never shot anyone before."

"I knew if we stuck together long enough I'd have something in common with you, Claire."

"Just get out of here, Jackson, and go get that damned coffee."

Byrde grinned at her as he closed the door.

CHAPTER·SEVEN

Washington, D.C.

Bolan stepped out of the shadows and met Brognola midway across the clearing. The big Fed was hunched over, shoulders raised against the continuing rain. He didn't look happy. A cigar was clamped between his lips, and he constantly worried it as he faced Bolan.

"What's wrong with Florida?" Brognola grumbled. "At least they got sunshine."

"Good to see you again, too."

Brognola reached for Bolan's outstretched hand. "So what gives?"

"Albany was hot. Those people who work for Stahl have busy trigger fingers. No talking to them."

Brognola sighed. "Any feedback?"

Bolan handed him the laptop he had picked up at the Accord office.

"Aaron can poke around in this. See what he can find."

"The trace he was running down? He kept at it until he found a way around the block. It took him to the computer it originated from. When he unlocked the operator's password sequence, he came up with a name. Lewis Beringer. He works at the Pentagon, Air Force, on the Zero project. I followed it through with a contact. The word is that Beringer's section is under investigation for possible information leaks."

"You got an address? Beringer could be a man who needs talking to. He might give us some leads."

Brognola handed over a folded paper.

"It's coming down like you said. Leaks. Could be this Beringer has been passing stuff to Stahl. The Man is going to be pissed off."

"Then he needs to clean house. Until he can confirm that's been done, Hal, we can't afford to update him."

"Christ, Mack, you want me to stonewall the President of the United States?"

"I don't give a damn how you do it, Hal. He gave me full control of this mission. Right now I'm making a command decision. No more information reaches the White House."

"Great. Bang goes my pension."

"I'll make it easy for you. Just tell him I'm not in contact. We talked about this, Hal. The Man gave me a clean card for this mission. No interference. I make the rules and the field decisions. Hal, this thing is running wild. Since Buchanan came back on the scene everyone involved has started to push up the pace. I don't have the time or the inclination to hold back. If Stahl gets Zero online, he has the best hand in the game and no one can call his bluff."

"This is getting out of hand. Trouble is, I think you're right. This came from the Man himself. When Zero was up and running they had a security detail on tap. A couple of agents were assigned to the project. When Kaplan decided to detach himself, these agents were put on standby to bring him in if he showed. They were out on assignment when the strike went down on the project. Since then they've been doing some fieldwork, trying to locate Kaplan. When Doug Buchanan's electronic signature showed up, they were ordered to add him to their list. According to feedback, these agents, Byrde and Valens, were running a stakeout at Kaplan's house. They were pulled away from the house by a fake Kaplan and into an ambush. Report said they shot their way clear. Took out the hit team."

"Ryan's people?"

Brognola shook his head.

"No. We don't think so. The hitters were clean. No ID. Nothing. The local cops ran down the details of the car they were using. Turned out to be stolen with fake plates."

"Anything on the hit team?"

"It gets better. Fingerprints and dental records came up with some history. Seems these guys were professionals. They were known to the Chicago PD. They did some talking to their street informants, and it looks like someone had been gathering a hit team. They had mob connections. Drug trade. International smuggling. Contract hits. If it paid good, these people were into it. Byrde and Valens are going to keep looking to see if they can find a link."

"Hal, I'm going to need some identification on this pair in case I run into them."

"I figured you'd ask." Brognola pulled a padded envelope from his coat pocket and handed it over.

Bolan opened it and slid out a couple of standard ID photographs.. Full face. On the back of each plastic-encased photo were details on the two agents. Bolan scanned them both, finding himself lingering a little longer over the one of Claire Valens.

A strikingly beautiful young woman, her short, thick, chestnut-colored hair emphasized the natural allure of sculpted cheekbones. Haunting green-flecked eyes stared back at him and her generous, full mouth held a slight hint of a mocking smile. Bolan found himself wondering if the rest of her matched up to the head-and-shoulders shot.

"They can both handle themselves according to the reports I've read."

"I'm sure," Bolan said.

Brognola handed Bolan a third photo. "Lewis Beringer. His address is on the back. He lives in Arlington."

Bolan added the new photograph to the others. He slid them all into a pocket. "Anything else you need?"

"Couple of things. An update on Jack."

"He's fine. The President had him moved to a government clinic in Washington. I'm calling in to see him when I get back."

"Give him my best. Tell him—"

"I know what to say. What was the other favor?"

Bolan smiled at the comment.

"There was another guy at Accord, a PI called Joshua Riba. He's an Apache, and he helped me out. Buchanan spent some time at the guy's place in New Mexico after he got hit by a truck. Buchanan lost his way for a while, then took off to look for Kaplan. We figure he's on his way to Kaplan's place in Wyoming."

"And so might the opposition?"

"Exactly. Hal, I need air transport to get me, Riba and his SUV to Wyoming. I need to do this Randolph thing and maybe track down Beringer. I'll tell Joshua to get on down to Andrews. Get clearance for him so he can be ready to go when I roll in."

"Jesus, Striker, when are you going to ask for something *really* hard."

Bolan stared out across the shadowed park, his gaze probing the shadows. There was a troubled expression in his eyes.

"Striker?"

"They never give up, Hal. They cheat and betray, work against their own people, and for what? Power. Wealth. Some selfish need to be top dog and to hell with the rest. While they tie everything in knots in their own backyard, the real enemies are taking advantage."

"Don't make the mistake thinking Stahl and Stengard aren't enemies."

"No mistake there. They stepped over the line way back. No way they walk away and hide in the shadows, Hal. The game isn't played that way."

"Next up?"

"Senator Vernon Randolph."

"Randolph? You think he's involved?"

"Involved but not part of it, Hal. The way guys back in Albany were talking about him, he didn't sound like he was on their friendly list. Sounds like someone is going to make a visit, and I don't think it's to sell him life insurance."

"I'll get onto this airlift flight for you and Riba. Give him my name and tell him there'll be clearance for him."

VERNON RANDOLPH PUSHED away from his desk and left his study, making for the kitchen. As he crossed the hall he paused to check, not for the first time, that the front door was locked. He admitted to being a little paranoid, and for good reason. His confrontation with Eric Stahl had unnerved him to a degree. Randolph was no coward; he had never run from a fight in his life. Even so, he knew Stahl and the man's reputation for being a ruthless, manipulative egomaniac. When he had first gotten to know Stahl, he had been impressed by the driving force behind the younger man. As time passed and Stahl started to show his hand, Randolph realized the man was disturbingly single-minded in his purpose and the way he seemed intent on pushing it through. Randolph began to pick up murmurs, discreet talk that suggested Stahl had a hidden agenda behind all his outward bluster. Having been around the political circuit for a long time, Randolph had an inexhaustible supply of informants within the Washington enclave, including both political and military contacts. He had the ear of police and lawyers, streetwise informants, and had a certain clout within the security agencies. Randolph also had a reputation for a reserved honesty that added to his status. He was a man to be trusted, again somewhat unusual in the political arena. It meant people would talk to Randolph when they would walk away from others. He had never betrayed a confidence. Never admitted the source of any information. It placed him in a unique position.

Sometimes it placed him in difficult situations. Occasionally dangerous. Randolph was a survivor, and never complacent. He wasn't a man who considered himself untouchable, because he had seen too many who thought they were invincible, go down and in some instances stay down. He had attended the burials of a number of his contemporaries who imagined they were free and clear.

At this point in his life Randolph could have seen the specter of Death beckoning with a bony finger. If he had been a pessimist, that could have been the case. But Vernon Randolph veered toward the opposite. Life was precious, but at the same time it had to be lived to the full. Sitting in a safe corner, protected and shielded from danger, wasn't something he could subscribe to. So despite his personal misgivings about Senator Eric Stahl and his threats, Randolph had no other choice. He would carry out his promise to Stahl and present his findings to as many people as he could—the President himself if the need arose—and the hell with Stahl.

What the wayward senator had failed to realize was his biggest misjudgment about a man's character. He had committed the fatal error as far as Vernon Randolph was concerned.

Stahl had *threatened* the elder senator. In Randolph's book, that was the highest insult. He had never, from his youth, allowed anyone to try to make him back down. It was the most foolish thing anyone could do. Stahl could bring on his bully boys to do their worst. Randolph would see the thing through to the end. If he died in the attempt, then so be it, but he would take Stahl down with him if possible.

Randolph had that thought on his mind as he reached the kitchen. It was in shadow, with only a low-powered tube light shining from beneath one of the wall cupboards. He crossed to the bubbling percolator, chose a mug from one of the hooks under the wall unit and poured himself coffee. He stood sipping the hot brew, turning to look out the kitchen window at the shadowed expanse of the garden and orchard at the back of the house. It always gave him pleasure to look upon the garden. Amelia, his late wife, had been passionate about gardening, and the smooth lawns and flowering shrubs were her legacy. Randolph had no interest in the tending of the garden. Since his wife had died four years earlier, he had employed someone to maintain the look. It had been the least he could do. It was a living memory of his beloved wife. All he had from a long and happy relationship. They had no children so Randolph was alone in the house. As long as he had the garden to enjoy, he was happy.

He stood in the shadowy kitchen, sipping his coffee, wanting to stay where he was, but also aware that he needed to complete his work in the study. It was important he got everything he had collected about Stahl, Orin Stengard and his suspicions concerning their scheme in order.

He turned, placing his mug on the countertop, and reached out to flick the switch that would turn on the bank of floodlights and illuminate the gardens.

"Leave it, Senator," a deep voice said from the darker corner of the kitchen.

Randolph felt his breath catch in his throat at the command. Oddly there was something in the voice that told him he wasn't in any kind of danger from this man—whoever he was.

"What do you want?"

"I suggest you pick up your coffee and go sit at the breakfast bar."

"Are you serious? I don't understand what's going on."

Even as he asked the questions, Randolph found he was doing as he'd been told. He perched himself on one of the high stools. He peered into the corner of the kitchen where the voice had come from. It took a few moments before he made out the hazy outline of a man standing there.

"Something tells me you haven't come from Eric Stahl or Colonel Stengard."

"I haven't, but there are men outside who have, and they didn't come all this way to cut the grass."

"Are you serious? We should call the police. Or are you an officer?"

"No, and I'm not CIA, FBI or from any other agency you might have heard about."

"Then who the he—?"

"Senator, just enjoy your coffee. Those men out there are probably watching you through night-vision goggles. If you keep talking, they might spot your lips moving and wonder who the hell you have in here. We don't want that to happen."

Randolph managed a soft grunt of annoyance.

"Oh, no, we wouldn't want that happening, would we? Why not?"

"If they suspect you have company, they're not going to make their hit. They want you on your own."

"Sounds suspiciously like I'm a sitting target here."

"Exactly. Just do what you would normally. Now, shut up, Senator."

Randolph held back any further comments. He raised his mug and drank more coffee. He had almost emptied the mug when he heard a soft whisper of sound, which came from behind him. Someone was inside the house, coming from the front.

But hadn't he locked the door? He reconsidered his attitude. If these were professionals, locked doors and windows wouldn't keep them out for long.

He cleared his throat and slid off the stool, crossing to the percolator for more coffee, doing his best to maintain a calm exterior. He poured more coffee, realizing he really needed it, but was surprised to see that his hand wasn't even shaking.

Out the corner of his eye he saw a shadow slide across the tiled floor. The faintest whisper of sound. Very close this time.

Despite himself Randolph turned to face whoever was behind him.

MACK BOLAN SAW the intruder close in on the senator. The guy was in dark clothing, as was Bolan, and he held a dull-colored autopistol in his right hand. A bulky suppressor was threaded to the barrel. The Executioner had already moved to intercept, crossing the kitchen on silent feet, his own right hand reaching out to clamp around the intruder's wrist and force the gun hand toward the floor. The gunman reacted sharply, trying to break Bolan's grip, but he hadn't allowed for the Cold Steel Tanto knife in Bolan's left hand. The razor-sharp blade swept up, across the intruder's body, then Bolan arced it up, laying the edge of the blade across the man's exposed throat. The soldier cut hard and deep, drawing from right to left. The severing blade made a soft rasping sound. The intruder shuddered as blood began to pulse from his throat, making a gentle lapping sound as it burst forth.

Bolan snatched the pistol from the dying man's hand, reaching to push Vernon Randolph out of the way as he spotted movement outside the glass kitchen door.

A second figure, dark clad, brandished a stubby SMG, desperately trying to distinguish the shadowy figures in the kitchen.

As the bloody form of the first intruder dropped to the floor, Bolan reached out with his left hand and flicked on the exterior floodlights. The sudden glare caught the second intruder off guard. He threw up a hand to shield his eyes from the harsh light, offering Bolan a clear target. The Executioner raised the suppressed pistol he'd taken from the first man, acquired his target and triggered the weapon fast and hard. The pistol chugged out its silenced rounds in rapid succession, blowing out the door glass and hitting the intruder in the chest and throat. Bolan followed him down, pulling the trigger until the slide locked back empty.

Glass tinkled to the ground from the door frame as the last shell casing rattled across the kitchen tiles. The dying man on the patio let out a long, expiring sigh, his raised left hand flopping to the ground almost in slow motion.

"Jesus Christ," Senator Vernon Randolph said softly.

He was on his knees, his left hand resting on the floor. He felt something moist and wet against his skin, and when he looked down there was a pool of blood spreading out from the man on the floor beside him. The senator snatched his hand from the floor and saw it was dripping red.

Bolan dropped the empty pistol and unleathered the 93-R. He turned to help Randolph off the floor. The senator leaned against the kitchen unit. His heart was hammering, and a sheen of sweat glistened on his face.

"We need to move," Bolan told him.

Randolph had bent over the sink, turning on the water to rinse the dead man's blood from his hand.

"Move? Where? Are there more of them?"

"Could be."

"Are we leaving the house? I need to collect my laptop."

"Let's do it, Senator."

Bolan pushed Randolph toward the door that led to the main house. As they stepped through, he heard the rattle of equipment from beyond the shattered kitchen door.

The stuttering crackle of autofire followed them, slugs chewing at the doorframe, showering Bolan and Randolph with splinters. The Executioner shouldered Randolph to the left, away from the door, taking the right side himself. He turned, facing the kitchen, and saw the gunner stepping through the empty frame of the kitchen door. In the dim light Bolan saw the dark bulk of the SMG the man was carrying. He let the gunner cross to where the first intruder lay. The gunner paused, staring down at the corpse.

The Beretta tracked in on the guy's chest. Bolan stroked the trigger, drilling a silenced triburst at his target. The slugs slammed the gunner backward. He lost his footing and crashed sideways against the edge of the floor unit, his finger jerking back against the trigger of the SMG. A line of bullets stitched across the wall, misting the air with plaster.

"Let's go, Senator," Bolan growled.

They crossed the hall and reached the study just as a heavy object crashed against the main door. Glass shattered. Bolan could see shadowy figures on the outside.

"Get what you need, Senator, and do it fast."

Gripping the Beretta two-handed, Bolan triggered a pair of tribursts through the shattered glass, then heard someone curse wildly. Ejecting the depleted magazine, Bolan reloaded, moving to the opposite side of the study door, giving himself a clearer view of the front entrance.

The muzzle of an SMG poked through the opening and cut loose, the gunner sweeping the weapon back and forth across the interior. Bolan dropped to a crouch as slugs pocked the wall. Bracing himself against the door frame, he leveled the Beretta and triggered a burst. The SMG was jerked aside, the barrel banging against the opening. Then it disappeared from view.

Holstering the Beretta, Bolan plucked a fragmentation grenade from his combat harness. He pulled the pin, then moved quickly, keeping to the wall as he closed on the door. Keeping to the side, crouching below the level of the glass panels, he released the lever, counting off the seconds, then lobbed the grenade through the broken panel. He heard it drop outside. A man yelled a warning. Not fast enough. The grenade detonated with a heavy blast. Screams mingled with the rippling explosion. The house door splintered, the remaining glass panels blowing in across the hall.

Bolan shoved himself to his feet, Beretta back in his hand. He yanked open the battered, sagging door and filled the frame. Two men were down on the steps, bodies tattered and bloody, smoke rising from scorched clothing. They had taken the brunt of the blast and wouldn't be rejoining the fight. A third man was pushing to his feet, struggling to stay upright. His right leg was a mess of shredded flesh and splintered, bloody bone. He held up his right arm, staring at the mangled remains of his hand. Three fingers were gone, blood pulsing from the ragged stumps. He looked up at Bolan's dark figure as the Executioner showed himself.

"You weren't suppos—" he said before Bolan put a triburst through his skull, dropping him to the ground, surprise still showing in his eyes.

Bolan put away the Beretta and scooped up one of the discarded weapons, an M-4 carbine. There was a double magazine in the weapon, each holding thirty rounds of 5.56 mm ammunition.

He turned and went back inside the house and came face-to-face with Vernon Randolph. The senator was staring beyond Bolan, to the dead men sprawled inelegantly on the steps of his house.

"Remind me never to upset you, son," he said.

"Time to move, Senator. We need breathing space."

"I may never breathe again," Randolph muttered as he followed Bolan out of the house.

They skirted the exterior, cutting across the front lawn and into the trees that grew thick and tall along the frontage. Bolan pulled his cell phone out and punched in 911. When his call was answered, he spoke briefly and urgently.

"Better get someone out here. There's been a lot of shooting coming from Senator Randolph's place."

He cut the call, dropping back behind Randolph so he could cover him in case there were more gunmen.

When they reached Bolan's car, he unlocked the doors and told the senator to get into the back seat. Behind the wheel Bolan fired up the engine and eased out of the trees, back onto the driveway, swinging the car around and taking it out through the open gateway.

"Might be safer if you stay down, Senator. At least until we're in the clear."

"Sounds a reasonable enough request."

Bolan cruised steadily along the road. It wasn't long before he picked up the sound of police sirens. They were converging from a number of directions. Then he saw the flashing lights.

"Senator, you're going to have a lot of visitors at your place in the next few minutes."

Randolph sat up, leaning against the backrest.

"I don't even know your name, son," he said.

"Mike Belasko."

"It seems I owe you my life. I wonder what it's going to cost me?"

"Why should it cost you anything, Senator?"

"When you've been in politics as long as I have, son, you realize everything has a price."

"How about a cup of coffee while we talk?"

"Me buying?"

"If you want."

"Told you it would cost me something."

THEY WERE PARKED in the darkest corner of a fast-food outlet. Bolan had removed his combat harness, armed himself with the Beretta and donned a leather jacket before he went to the drive-thru and ordered coffee.

"This is something I haven't done for a long time," Randolph said. "Then this evening has been something of a surprise all around."

"Who sent that hit team, Senator?" Bolan asked, testing the water.

"Eric Stahl. Or Orin Stengard. Maybe both."

"A hunch? A definite ID?"

"You want an honest answer?"

"Damned right I do."

"Then as far as I'm concerned, those men were part of the conspiracy Stahl and Stengard are involved in."

"To do with the Zero project? Doug Buchanan and Saul Kaplan?"

"Yes. Stahl wants to gain control of Zero for his own

purposes. The man wants to be President. If the job was open, he'd try for God. Stengard is his military ally. Between them they are attempting to orchestrate a coup that would topple the government and put Stahl in the Oval Office."

"I don't see that as being an easy thing to do."

"If Stahl gains control of Zero, he's well on his way to doing it. The platform has the capability of placing ultimate power into the hands of the man who controls it. Mr. Belasko, have you been informed of Zero's destructive systems?"

"I know what it can do, Senator. It's why I'm trying to prevent Stahl getting his hands on it."

"With Orin Stengard in his camp, Stahl has a lot of backup. Stengard is a popular commander. He can muster a lot of sympathetic support throughout the armed forces. And he has the ability to command a great deal of ordnance. Using the internal military communications system, he can issue orders never to be heard by anyone out of the net."

"Has he been doing that?"

Randolph smiled. "You can see where I'm leading, Mr. Belasko."

"Call me Mike."

"All right, Mike. The reason I'm in the position I'm in is because I've been monitoring Stahl and Orin Stengard for the past few months. I have a lot of friends in the political and military communities, people I know who are opposed to the things that pair have been up to. I've gathered snippets of information from a great number of sources. On their own nothing very incriminating, but when you piece them together, like a jigsaw, a pattern starts to emerge.

"Stengard has been moving equipment around the country. Small consignments, sent to low-key bases. It's put into storage for a while, then moved on again. No one noticed, or if they did they weren't going to question orders with Colonel Orin Stengard's signature on them. Same has been happening to units of men loyal to old Iron and Steel. The deeper I dug, the clearer the picture. Over the past few weeks Stengard has reassigned a number of high-ranking officers to key positions where they have access to command facilities." Randolph drank his coffee. "It's all been done very quietly, helped by the cooperation of a small but dedicated band of top officers from all three services who have been doing the same thing."

"How did Stahl find out?"

"What I've been doing? No secret there. Stahl has been courting me for months. Probably from the inception of his conspiracy. I've been around a damn long time, Mike. Outlasted a number of Presidents. Made some enemies, but I think more friends. Along the way I've cultivated contacts and gained the confidence of a lot of people in politics, the military and the media. Stahl knew I was a patriot. Something I've never concealed. I love my country, never been ashamed to admit it, and I want America to stay strong. In my time I've made critical speeches as much as I have congratulated the various administrations. Eric Stahl took my attitude to mean I would be in favor of his scheme. He started to associate with me, working his way around to inviting me into his circle. I went along at first because I was curious, and also because I was sure he had something nasty up his sleeve. I was right. It came out one evening when we'd been drinking for a considerable time. He let slip some of his thoughts. Maybe testing me out. If he was, then it backfired because I told him exactly how I felt. And what I felt about him."

"He didn't like that?"

"Hell, no. The following day I received a curt telephone call from him. In simple terms he told me the courtship was off, and he wouldn't be contacting me again. No threats then. Just a hint that it would be better if I forgot our previous conversations and moved on."

Bolan shifted in his seat and studied Randolph for a moment.

"And that was when you started to take a covert interest in Stahl's business?"

"Yes. Something got under my skin. I knew I had to find out what it was before I could settle. So I started to run checks on Stahl *and* Stengard. The colonel's name had cropped up a few times during some of our earlier conversations, so I started to take a look at what they'd been up to. Especially Stahl's interest in the Zero Option project. The more I dug, the clearer it became that Stahl's interest in Zero borders on the extreme. For instance I found out he had been making discreet inquiries into the whereabouts of Saul Kaplan. By this time Kaplan had left his university post and vanished. My contacts informed me that Stahl had his people out looking for Kaplan."

"This information? Is it in your laptop?"

Randolph nodded. "Stahl and I just had a showdown. He said he knew I'd been digging into his affairs. I'll give the man credit. He didn't wrap it up. I either backed off and stopped trying to cause him problems, or he would see to it I wouldn't pass on any of the so-called incriminating data because I might have an inconvenient accident."

"I'd say you got to him, Senator."

"With Kaplan and Doug Buchanan on the loose, Stahl has to make his move soon. If they slip away from him, he loses his lever. Zero is the key."

"There's another equation in the game, Senator. My information is the people behind the original strike at Zero know about Buchanan's resurfacing. Until his implant chip started to transmit, everyone imagined Zero had been shut down. They thought the entire team had been killed. With Buchanan on the scene again, they have to make another attempt to hit him."

"Who are they?"

"No firm identification yet. Thinking is they're from out of the country. People who don't want Zero running because it might work against their long-range plans."

Randolph sank against the seat back. "Do you have any thoughts where Doug Buchanan might be?"

"A long shot I'm working on. Saul Kaplan has a lodge somewhere up in the Wyoming high country. It's pretty remote. Once I get you to a safehouse, I'm heading up that way. If we can figure it out, so can Stahl."

"Do you think Doug Buchanan will try to get there?"

"Buchanan has no one else he can trust. Kaplan is his last refuge."

"If I was Doug Buchanan, I would probably be thinking along those lines."

"Senator, do you know a man named Lewis Beringer?"

"Department of Defense. Why?"

"There's a suspicion he might be Stahl's inside man, passing along information on the project. Even helping in tracking down people Stahl wants to get his hands on."

"Kaplan and Buchanan?"

Bolan nodded.

"Are you going to look him up?"

"It might be worth a detour."

Randolph smiled. "You sound like a busy man, Mike."

"Right now it's 24/7, and no time out for good behavior."

"Then you'd better off-load me and go to it, son."

Bolan started the car and drove out of the parking lot. He pulled out his cell phone to contact Hal Brognola and arrange a safe pickup for the senator and his information.

He made a second call to Joshua Riba.

"How we doing?"

"Tolerable. How about you?"

"Are you at Andrews?"

"Am I. Listen, I haven't met your buddy, but a guy who can pull strings the way he does could solve the Indian problem in an afternoon."

"They got everything ready for us?"

"Damned great plane on standby. I'm in there now. My truck kind of looks lost. You know how big these damned things are?"

"Joshua, I have someone else to look up. Soon as I do that, I'll give you a call and let you know I'm coming in."

"I won't be going anywhere. These Air Force guys make a rare cup of coffee."

CHAPTER EIGHT

Chosan Xiang had arranged his transfer from Hawaii to a waiting seagoing motor yacht before leaving Hong Kong. With the caution that he always employed when on any assignment, Chosan had set up a diversionary arrangement in case he was being observed. Without being aware that a U.S. Customs agent was tailing him, Chosan went through his diversion tactic, picking up a different car and driving to a quiet bay where a pleasure boat had picked him up. Chosan had changed into leisure clothing, joining the skipper. They had spent a couple of hours cruising the Pacific, along with the many other pleasure craft, moving farther from the coastline until they were able to head out to sea. The motor yacht picked them up two hours later, and Chosan went aboard while another Chinese of similar build and dressed identically took his place. The pleasure boat then set out on its return to Hawaii, leaving Chosan in the hands of his Chinese crew.

With nightfall the motor launch moved out across the Pacific on a northeasterly course. Speed was pushed to the maximum, and the yacht remained at this setting until daylight. Just after dawn the yacht made a rendezvous with a Chinese navy submarine, Song Class, and Chosan made his second transfer. The submarine submerged the moment Chosan was on board, slipping quietly below the surface. The yacht turned about and began a more leisurely return in the direction of Hawaii.

On board the submarine Chosan met Shao Yeung. The younger man had asked to be allowed to join Chosan. His request to General Tung had been received with admiration. Tung liked his people to become actively involved in their assignments. Shao had convinced the general he could be of more help to Chosan if he was at his side. Tung made the decision to allow Shao his moment of glory. It made sense to give Shao an opportunity to experience life in the real world as opposed to being cloistered within the walls of officialdom.

Chosan had been surprised but not dismayed at Shao's presence. He accepted it because there was little he could do, and he admitted that Shao possessed certain managerial skills that would prove useful.

The submarine moved at maximum speed, deeply submerged, and took them on the next leg of their journey. It ended when they made their rendezvous with a diesel-powered freighter named *Oahu Star*. This was a Chinese vessel that plied the Pacific between Hawaii and the United States, carrying cargo for various companies, some legitimate, some covers for companies owned by the People's Republic. This time around the freighter carried electronic goods manufactured in China for distribution in the U.S.

It also carried Chosan's Chinese strike team, his own group of trained and highly motivated soldiers. They would be inserted into the U.S. if Hank Winston's team of hired killers failed to complete their mission.

Shortly after Chosan boarded the freighter, and the submarine had departed for its return to Chinese waters, he received the message informing him of the failure of Winston's assassins.

SHAO YEUNG TURNED from the rail as he heard footsteps behind him. He saw Chosan Xiang approaching. Chosan wore casual clothing and carried a thick tumbler filled with Jack Daniel's.

"Are you still convinced this was a good idea?" Chosan asked, raising his glass to the younger man.

"Coming along to help? Yes. Your Americans have failed once again. It is not your fault, but the general is not going to be pleased. If we work together, perhaps we can still salvage this operation."

"I admire your loyalty, Shao Yeung, and also your rosy view of the world." Chosan took a deep drink. "Let us hope we both survive. If not, we may end up building roads together in one of the northern provinces."

"Since I arrived on board, we haven't had a chance to talk properly. Tell me what happened to Winston's team."

"We learned that a security team originally based at the Zero facility was still operating. It seems they were not on-site when the strike took place. When it was learned that this man Buchanan still lived, they were assigned to hunt for him and Saul Kaplan. I informed Winston about them. Only so that he could watch for them. Instead he decided his team could remove them. He failed to inform me of this. He sent in his hit team from Chicago, and they set a decoy trap for these agents. However, the outcome was not what Winston had planned. The agents, one of them a woman apparently, fought back and killed Winston's assassins."

"And Winston?"

"He refuses to answer my calls. I cannot get in touch with the fool. Perhaps he finally understood something I said in Hawaii. It was only meant as a slight threat to make him realize how serious this assignment was. He believes I will come looking for him. To kill him. It is the first thing he has got right."

"Does this place us in a difficult position regarding our business?"

"Not really. I have contacted our own people in Seattle. Short notice, yes, but I believe that by the time we dock, everything we need will be in place."

"This was not how you wanted it to happen. If you lead this mission, you place yourself at great personal risk."

"What kind of a commander would I be if I sent out my men while I remained in a safe place?"

"I understand your loyalty and I respect it, which is why I want to help."

"Then do this. Contact your money people. Make sure that when we arrive in Seattle there is an unlimited supply of funds available. Remember what I said before. If you have enough money in America, everything is possible. When we make shore we are going to need weapons, vehicles and a helicopter. We have to be prepared for whatever our information contacts find out for us, and to be able to act on it."

Shao nodded.

"I will arrange things. Xiang, I believe we can do this. Together we can do this."

Chosan turned to stare out over the rail, watching the movement of the ocean. He took another long, slow swallow of his drink.

"They say the spirits smile on the young and foolish," he said very softly. "If that is true, they must be falling down with laughter by now."

"Did you say something?"

Chosan shook his head. "Nothing, Shao Yeung. Nothing of importance."

BY DAWN they were within one hundred miles of the Washington State coastline. Chosan's handpicked team of infiltration soldiers, four in number, were belowdecks, going through their plan of attack once more. They had done the exercise many times while the freighter made its way toward the United States.

Shao Yeung had made a number of satellite phone calls to his contact based in San Francisco, and by the time his business had been concluded a money transfer had placed close on four hundred thousand U.S. dollars into an account on behalf of a trading company that had been established in Seattle for almost four years. This was the Chinese intelligence headquarters for the Northwest U.S. and Canada. The function of the team was to gather, evaluate and pass on data gathered by other cells throughout the States, which was then sent to Beijing. A fleeting thought had crossed Shao Yeung's mind as he spoke to the contact in Seattle.

He was reminded of Chosan's remarks about such people, placed in quiet, unobtrusive positions, thousands of miles from the ever watchful eyes of their masters. In the relative calm and security of America, these operatives lived normal lives, mixing with the American public, fostering relationships, carrying out daily business. True dedication to the homeland would be diluted by the comforts and the freedom of the society they lived in. Shao could understand how easily those people could slip into their new roles as time went by, with little of the relentless propaganda they would be subjected to back home. He wondered how he might fare in the same situation and felt a tinge of guilt at his own reaction to that question.

He pushed the errant thoughts out of his mind, completing his transmission and ending it as quickly as possible. He left the radio room and made his way up on deck, crossing to stand at the rail. He looked out across

the expanse of water that lay between the freighter and
the American continent. He was angry at his own
thoughts, disturbed by them to a degree, and imagined
General Tung's reaction if he became aware of Shao's
traitorous distraction. It wouldn't be a pleasant experience.

Perhaps coming on this voyage with Chosan Xiang
hadn't been such a wise move after all. At least in Beijing he would have been far removed from such
thoughts. He had wanted to experience how a field operation ran. Now he was involved, he realized there was
more to these affairs than he had been aware of.

CHOSAN WAS addressing his team. He had gone over the
procedures, and the problems they might encounter. When
he looked on the serious, intent faces of his men, he realized how dedicated they were. Not one of them had raised
any complaints when made aware of the consequences if
they ended up in American hands. They were fully committed to the cause, to the elimination of anyone involved
in the Zero project. Their own fate didn't come into the
picture. If it happened that they were killed or injured—
or at worst captured—then they would accept it. When
they volunteered for Chosan's group, the expectations
were explained to them in clear, concise terms. No man
was accepted until he took that on board and it was drilled
into them over and over when they were being trained.

"Our sources within the United States are seeking information even as I speak. The two men who are our

targets." Chosan indicated the photographs pinned to the board behind him. "Douglas Buchanan, a major in the United States Air Force. He is important to the Americans as a vital element in the Zero Option project. Without him the orbiting platform cannot function. The other man is Saul Kaplan. He created and helped to build Zero. For his own reasons it appears he deserted the project and went into hiding. As long as he is alive, the Americans can use him to keep Zero going. So these two are the ones we have to eliminate. As long as they remain alive, they are a threat."

One of the team raised a hand.

"You have a question?" Chosan said. "Ask it."

"Why is it not possible for the Zero platform to be destroyed by a missile, sir?"

"A good question. The information we gained from our agents in America informed us that although Zero is not fully operational, it does have its own defense shield. Anything that poses a threat will be assessed by the on-board systems, and Zero will retaliate automatically. There are banks of missiles designed for this sole purpose. Zero would monitor an incoming threat, send out a warning and if that warning is ignored, the missile banks would launch. The technicalities involved in this are highly complicated. What I have explained simplifies the defensive shield. In brief Zero cannot be destroyed so easily. If it comes fully online, that prohibitive strike capability would become even more of a threat. Any missile launched against the United States would be destroyed and a follow-up would be an instant strike on the original launch site."

A deep silence followed Chosan's explanation.

"So you can see why this orbiting platform must not be allowed to come online. We must do what we can to keep it dormant."

"If we kill Buchanan, surely there will be someone to take his place?"

Chosan turned as Shao Yeung's voice reached him. The younger man had entered the room quietly and had been listening.

"Not immediately. It takes time to go through the medical procedures to prepare another candidate. With the destruction of the Zero facility, we set the Americans back a great deal. They will not have had time to replace Buchanan. Now he has resurfaced, his final assimilation into the project will make things easier for the U.S. government."

Chosan turned to smile at Shao.

"You see, Shao Yeung, there is always an answer to any question."

Zero Project Security Office, Washington

"*The question is* where the hell did Chosan Xiang go?"

Jackson Byrde rattled the printout in his hand.

"Hey, partner, you asking, or threatening to attack me with that thing?"

Byrde lowered the paper.

"I mean, dammit, we get a puzzle worked out, then the main guy goes missing."

"Maybe we should fly to Chicago and ask Winston. He was the last one to have contact with Chosan."

Byrde flopped into his chair, tossing the printout on his desk. He faced Valens across the office. Her desk was on the other side, facing his. She was hunched over in her seat, nursing a foam cup of coffee, her brow furrowed as she studied her own copy of the data.

The tie-in between Winston and Chosan Xiang had been one of those lucky meldings of request and response.

Following the police checks in the aftermath of the shoot-out between Valens and Byrde and the hit team, details began to emerge.

The hit men were linked to Hank Winston and his organization in Chicago. Routine checks into Winston's movements prior to the attempted hit revealed he had made a trip to Hawaii. It had been a short visit. He had returned to the mainland the following day, having met only one person during his time on the island. That was discovered when the U.S. Customs agent assigned to keep an eye on Chosan Xiang after his counterfeit passport had been spotted, observed Chosan in discussion with a man who was later identified as Hank Winston. The agent managed to get photographs of both men together and these were circulated to law-enforcement agencies throughout the U.S. The photographs and the written report that accompanied them went into the security network, being circulated to all agencies. As originators of the request, Valens and Byrde received their own copies, which answered some questions.

One remaining mystery was the disappearance of Chosan Xiang. The morning after his meeting with Winston, the Chinese vanished from sight. He had emerged from his hotel room and rented a car. He drove to Kapi'olani Park, traveled through the tunnel to the interior of the crater, then took the long walk to the summit of Diamond Head. He spent some time enjoying the view of the Oahu coastline before making the return trip down to where his car was parked. He then drove to a secluded bay, where he was picked up by a motor boat, which disappeared for several hours before returning to the bay.

The problems for the agent watching him began when the rental car was returned. It was the first time the agent had a close view of the man he was following since Chosan had returned from his cruise. The man who had driven the rental back to the agency had the same build, appearance and clothing as Chosan Xiang, but that was as far as it went. The man who emerged from the rental office wasn't Chosan. Somewhere between Diamond Head and the rental agency, he had given the agent the slip.

By the time this was discovered, Chosan Xiang had vanished. Questioning the decoy gained nothing. The man had his own identification, which was all in order. The rental had been taken out using that ID, obviously by Chosan, who had to have returned it to the decoy out at sea. The decoy, dressed in identical clothing, returned to land and continued on back to the rental agency.

A call went out for Chosan's arrest and detention. It never happened. He had gone to ground, or had left the island. The search went on, but there was no lead to his whereabouts.

Hawaii's problems were a long way from Washington. As far as Valens and Byrde were concerned, a few dark corners were suddenly flooded with light.

They had a connection now, one that confirmed suspicions that the strike against the Zero facility had been engineered by an outside agency.

Possibly China. And now with Chosan Xiang being linked with Hank Winston, that possibility was becoming stronger. China—a likely candidate for wanting Zero to stay earthbound. Zero off-line would let China, and some of its Asian neighbors, breathe a little easier.

And now that Doug Buchanan had resurfaced, China would be catching its breath and sending out the order to complete the original intent of the first strike. To eradicate anyone connected to the Zero project.

Valens and Byrde, being the investigating team for Zero, would have been seen as potentially a nuisance. Their probing into the Zero strike could have brought them up against the team hunting for Buchanan and Kaplan, so it would have been deemed worthwhile removing them from the scene. Unfortunately for the hit team it hadn't worked out as they had planned.

Valens and Byrde were still alive, and due to information gathering they now had a line on who was behind the whole affair.

"You got it all clear now?" Byrde asked, risking a cup of hot coffee being hurled in his direction.

Surprisingly Valens didn't react. She only made a sound that might have been yes, then sat upright.

"Where do think Chosan might have gone?" she asked.

"Back to Hong Kong, where he came from?"

"Maybe. But why not just fly out? According to customs, he had a return ticket to Hong Kong. As far as we know, he hadn't realized his fake passport had been spotted. So why the switch game?"

"Because he decided to go somewhere else and all that changing identities was just a precaution. Something he would do anyway. If he was up to something illegal, he wouldn't want it broadcasted."

"I guess you're right."

"Of course I'm right, Claire. Remind me when I was ever wrong."

"The hard drive on my computer isn't large enough to list the answers to that question." Valens finished her coffee. "I'm whacked. You staying here? I'm heading home to bed. Tomorrow is another day."

"*Gone With the Wind,*" Byrde said.

Valens was reaching for her coat. "What?"

"Wasn't that from *Gone With the Wind?* Scarlett O'Hara said it, didn't she?"

Valens scowled at him. "Good night, Jackson."

The telephone rang. Byrde snatched it off the cradle.

"Byrde. Yeah? Give me that again." He scribbled on a pad. "Thanks."

Valens sighed and dropped her coat on the desk. "Go on."

"We have a location for Saul Kaplan's Wyoming hideaway."

"I knew you were going to say that."

CHAPTER NINE

"It's Mr. Beringer, Senator. He insists on seeing you. He says it's extremely urgent."

Eric Stahl placed his book on the small table beside his leather armchair and took a sip from the wineglass in his hand.

Was it too much to ask? Just a few stolen moments of escape from the business of the day?

"Show him in."

His butler withdrew and closed the door to the study. Stahl stood, stretched lazily and waited until there was a tap on the door.

"Come in."

Lewis Beringer was in his early thirties, lean and with a slight stoop that had developed from years hunched over computer keyboards. Beringer worked on Stahl's behalf within the Zero project as a computer programmer. In the past he had extracted a number of files and data that had given Stahl his background knowledge on the Zero project. He was a careful man, not given to showing much enthusiasm, even when he achieved something worthwhile. This day, however, he appeared excited. Only someone who knew him well would be able to recognize excitement in Lewis Beringer. Stahl was one of the few. The moment Beringer entered the study, Stahl realized the man was almost drooling. Stahl tried to imagine what would have the power to generate such a reaction in Beringer. For a moment he wondered if Beringer had suddenly discovered women and had lost his virginity. He dismissed the thought instantly. Beringer would go through life not even noticing the opposite sex. His passion, his obsession, was his computers. Nothing else mattered to the lonely individual who spent his free time doing exactly what he did during working hours.

"What can I do for you, Lewis? Make it brief because I have a great deal to do this evening."

Beringer cleared his throat. He moved farther into the study, awkwardly peering around the room, as if he expected to see someone in the corner with a recorder and camera.

"You're safe here, for God's sake. This is my home, Lewis. I don't believe it's bugged."

"Well, these days you can never be sure, Senator," Beringer said. "Only the other da—"

He cut himself off when he recognized the impatient expression on Stahl's face.

"Do you recall instructing me to maintain a round-the-clock check on all of Saul Kaplan's stored data relating to the Zero project, Senator?"

"Yes. Cut to the chase, Lewis."

"Two days ago I picked up a data stream buried in some of Kaplan's files. They were ones I'd managed to rescue after the attack on the Zero facility. There was a program that had been installed during the creation of the Zero concept. It was intended to back up and store files if a major purge of the system occurred. It came into operation automatically when the facility was hit and the computer banks started to disintegrate. The files were badly corrupted, and I didn't think I'd get much from them. But while I was digging, I came across this hidden file. It had been buried so deep in the data stream there didn't appear to be any damage to it."

A slow burn of interest grew. Stahl saw the bright gleam of arousal in Beringer's eyes. He knew that whatever Beringer had found was important. The man wouldn't have come to see him if all he'd found was Kaplan's laundry list.

"Take your time, Lewis, and tell me exactly what it is you found."

Beringer reached inside his coat and removed a folded sheet of computer printout.

"It's all here, Senator. Details of the Zero Option. Just to give you an idea what I have on disk. All of Kaplan's run codes and number sequences. With this you can unlock Zero and gain complete control. Once you have Buchanan in that biocouch, the whole thing will drop into your hands."

Stahl reached and took the printout. He unfolded the crumpled paper and scanned the columns of figures and text. It didn't mean a great deal to him, but he understood it had to be the genuine article because of Beringer's excitement.

"Why hasn't anyone else found this, Lewis?"

"Because none of them are as good as me. They don't have the skill to dig through something that has been damaged as much as these files were and extract them. And also because I hid the files once I located them. I transferred everything to my own system and created my own codes so no one could get into them. Then I wiped the whole database from the rescued files so there was nothing left to find."

"And then you worked on them until you had the information restored? Very ambitious, Lewis."

"Ambition isn't your private domain, Senator."

The sharp tone in Beringer's remark caused Stahl to glance at him. There was a sheen of sweat on Beringer's furrowed brow and a look of defiance in his eyes. There was something different about the man, Stahl decided.

"You have this data safe, Lewis?"

"Yes. It's in my computer, safe behind a protected firewall. If anyone tries to break into the database, the firewall will simply delete the files. I also have a copy on a CD."

"Not with you?"

This time Beringer actually smirked. "Do I look that simple, Senator?"

"Lewis, am I detecting a note of mistrust? I thought we were in this for altruistic motives."

"Idealism won't pay my bills, Senator. Without wanting to appear materialistic, I don't have your limitless wealth." Beringer waved his hand around the study. "This room on its own is probably worth more than everything I possess. I've proved my worth on more than one occasion helping to gather information and pass it to you. Which has been good for you, but all it's done for me is, well, actually it hasn't done a thing. Except place me at risk. Right now my department is one of a number being looked at closely. We've all heard there is an internal investigation into information leaks. I have a feeling my time at the department is running out, Senator."

"Lewis, I told you I'll protect you if anything happens. You have my word on that."

"Your word isn't going to protect me if I find myself locked up in a federal prison. What the fuck good is yelling 'Senator Stahl will protect me' when my ass is being groped by some two-hundred-pound guy named Bubba? Tell me that, Senator."

"Let's not get carried away, Lewis. Sit down and we'll talk this through. Would you like a drink?"

"You're not listening, Senator. And no, I don't want a drink. Nor do I want to dance with you, or hold your hand while we gaze at the fucking Potomac. I'm in over my head because I imagined I was doing the right thing.

Senator Eric Stahl—the man who wants to put the world to rights. Jesus, I must have had my head up my own ass to believe what you told me. I'm going to spend the rest of my life in jail if I don't get myself out of this mess." Beringer pointed a finger at the printout. "Get your experts to check this out. It's a small part of the data I decoded. They'll tell you it's genuine. You want the whole thing? Fine. You can have it. But it's going to cost you, Senator. Five hundred thousand dollars. I think that's reasonable. A million would be better, but I'm not a greedy man. And I want it in cash. Not trace-able new notes."

"Lewis, this is a foolish thing you're doing. We can compromise."

"Oh? You going to offer me a personal check?"

"I was thinking more on the lines of you changing your mind. Lewis, I need you. We're at a sensitive stage in the program. Losing you would make things difficult."

"I can't afford to be associated with you any longer, Senator. This is my only way out. As soon as you get the money together, give me a call. You have my number."

Beringer turned, almost stumbling as he left the room. The moment he was out of sight, Stahl picked up the phone and dialed. He heard the front door shut with a bang as Beringer left the house.

"Orin? This is Eric. We have another problem. You'd better get over here fast."

He put the phone down, shaking his head at this sud-den, unexpected turn of events. Of all people he might have expected to pull out, Lewis Beringer hadn't even been on the list.

STENGARD ARRIVED within the hour. He sat and listened as Stahl related what had happened.

"We'll deal with this, Eric. You have Beringer's address?"

"Yes."

"Get it for me."

Stahl crossed to his desk and opened a drawer. He took out a slim leather-bound address book and thumbed through the pages. When he found what he was looking for he handed the book to Stengard. The colonel read the information, looked back at Stahl and gave a curt nod. He reached for the cell phone he carried and punched in a speed-dial access number. When it was answered he spoke quickly.

"Ryan, write down this name, address and telephone number." He gave the details, then said, "You'll be able to bring up this man's file on our database. His photograph will be there. Two objectives. One, Beringer has information relating to Zero on his computer system. And he also has a CD that holds files he's rescued from the computer system at the Zero facility. The disk is extremely important. It holds access codes and information that can't be found elsewhere. We need all that. Objective two, Beringer has, by his own actions, become a security risk. He wants money for the information he has. More or less threatened the senator with exposure if he doesn't get what's his. Let's not disappoint Mr. Beringer. Get the information, then terminate the little bastard."

CAL RYAN REPLACED the receiver. He reread the information Stengard had given him. Swiveling his chair, he tapped into the computer database and brought up the file on Lewis Beringer. He went to the photo ID and printed off a couple of copies. Pushing away from the desk, he crossed the room and went through to the lounge.

"Hecht, take Bodie and a couple of the others and get over to this address. Orders from the colonel. You're looking for this guy. He'll have a computer setup that you'll have to bring back. And he'll have a CD. We'll need that, as well."

Hecht examined the photograph. "What about him?"

"He doesn't make it. Understand? That comes from the colonel."

Ryan gave them the full story about Beringer, as related to him by Stengard.

LEWIS BERINGER'S Arlington home was set back from the road. It was reached by a narrow, unpaved lane that wound through tall, slender trees. The front yard of the house was in shadow. Beringer's four-year-old Ford was parked in front of the house.

Hecht rolled the black SUV to a stop before he reached the last curve in the lane, and he switched off the engine. He and Bodie sat in the front of the SUV, watching the house. The other two members of the team sat in back.

There were lights showing in the majority of the windows of Beringer's house.

"He scared of the dark or what?" Bodie asked.

"If I'd tried to run a scam on Stahl, I'd sit with all the fuckin' lights on, too, and with a good supply of fresh underwear next to me," Hecht commented.

Bodie slipped his Glock 21 from his pocket, checked that it was loaded, then took a stainless-steel combat knife from a pocket and held it up.

"He'll give us what we want." He turned to the men in the back seat. "Keep your eyes open." He held up his compact transceiver. They were all carrying them. "If I call, come running."

BERINGER PACED the living room. His stomach churned, and he kept breaking out in a cold sweat. He was nervous. Extremely nervous. Since returning home, he had become increasingly anxious about the outcome of his meeting with Eric Stahl. He knew the man's capacity for extreme reactions to unwelcome situations. Beringer was still trying to accept what he'd said to Stahl. When he left the senator's house, he had almost been physically sick. Beringer wasn't a courageous person. Normally he was the kind who stayed in the background, maintained a low profile and kept his mouth shut. His association with Stahl had been exciting at first, presenting him with all kinds of challenges. He admitted

to being in awe of Stahl and his outgoing personality.
That had dramatically changed. With the current mood
of suspicion in his department, the glamour had started
to fade. Listening to office gossip, Beringer began to realize the seriousness of what he had been doing. His
alignment with Stahl wouldn't save him if he was found
out as the mole in the department.

He was a traitor to the U.S. Government. He had taken
highly classified information and passed it to Stahl, who
wasn't cleared to have such data. He had also used his
computer access to get him into other government databases, enabling him to extract information Stahl wanted.
Beringer's familiarity with the Zero project had been the
reason Stahl had paid him such attention. With the current
problems Beringer saw he was nothing more than another
of Stahl's tools. His rosy image of Stahl had faded. The
man was using him, Beringer, as he did others, simply for
his own benefit. The special relationship was nothing. It
was simply a way for Stahl to use people, making them
think and feel that they alone were important to Stahl and
his cause when in reality the man was sucking them dry.

"You were a damned fool, Lewis," he said out loud.
The words echoed off the walls of the room.

He crossed to the cabinet where he kept his liquor
and poured himself a large, straight vodka. Beringer
downed it in one long swallow, then felt the tears well
up in his eyes. He felt his throat constrict, and he began
to cough, fighting for air. The vodka burned its way to

his stomach. He steadied himself, then poured another large drink.

When Stahl paid up, it could be vodka for every meal. He would be able to…

Beringer thought about that for a moment.

What if Stahl tried to get the information without handing over the money? Would he do such a thing? The main question for Beringer was, how far would Eric Stahl go to obtain something as valuable as the information Beringer had in his possession?

There was no need to wonder about that for long. Beringer knew the answer. Stahl was obsessed with his political-military schemes, to the point, Beringer believed, where he would go to any lengths to achieve them.

He swallowed his second drink. A little unsteadily he crossed the room and went to the array of desks that held his state-of-the-art computer setup. It was something Beringer was extremely proud of. He had built it over a period of months, always on the lookout for next-generation peripheral. For the extra memory. He was going to have to leave it all behind when he moved on. He had accepted that at least. When Stahl gave him the money, he would need to abandon his home and travel, establishing himself in some new location. That wouldn't be difficult with half a million dollars. He would take all his stored data in his laptops, his zip drives, and wherever he finally settled he would be able to continue to use his computing skills.

Bending, he opened a drawer in his desk and located

the handgun he kept there. It was a 9 mm SIG-Sauer P-226. Beringer had bought the weapon a couple of years earlier, following local burglaries. He had only ever shot it at a firing range, taking a short course in gun handling. Normally he hardly ever thought much about the weapon, only taking it out to maintain it. Now he felt a definite security as he lifted the pistol. He took out the magazine and thumbed the top bullet to make sure the spring hadn't jammed. He slipped it back into the butt, snapping it into place. Then he worked the slide to cock the weapon, then made sure the safety was on. He placed the pistol on his desk and went to sit down.

That was when he heard movement in the passage beyond the door to his room. He reached for the pistol, easing off the safety, and crossed to the door to listen.

GETTING INSIDE the house had been easy. Beringer had no security alarms or motion sensors. It hadn't taken the pair long to establish that. Once they had got in through the kitchen door at the rear they moved quickly through the silent house, checking rooms as they went. They made little sound as they cleared each room.

It was as they moved toward the front of the house, approaching the door that would open onto the living room at the front, that Bodie spotted a moving shadow at the base of the door. He touched Hecht's arm, indicating the shadow. It identified someone standing on the other side of the door. Close. Probably listening because a sound had penetrated.

Hecht caught Bodie's eye, motioned for his partner to get the door open and braced himself to one side, his Glock gripped two-handed.

Bodie took a step back, turned his left shoulder at the door, then launched himself at the panel. The solid impact sprung the door off its catch and drove it inward.

THE DOOR SLAMMED into Beringer and sent him stumbling back across the room.

He caught a glimpse of two armed men coming through the door. One held a pistol in cupped hands, the muzzle swinging back and forth. The other had his weapon aimed at the floor as he recovered from shouldering the door open. Beringer decided he was the least dangerous of the two initially and swung his weapon toward the other man, pulling the trigger the moment he felt he had his target in his sights. The P-226 exploded with sound, the volume seeming enormously loud to Beringer. He felt the pistol jump in his hand, and he had to close his fingers tight against the butt to prevent it dropping.

The 9 mm slug caught Hecht in the right shoulder, shattering the bone as it passed through, taking a sizable amount of flesh with it. The impact drove him backward. He collided with Bodie, just as his partner pulled the trigger on his own pistol. The wayward slug plowed into the ceiling.

Bodie, pawing at the blood that had showered into his eyes, pushing his moaning partner aside. By the time he had cleared his vision, Beringer had vanished. Cursing wildly, Bodie charged into the room, searching for his target. He pulled out the transceiver he carried and thumbed the button.

"Beringer got away! He might be heading in your direction."

BERINGER HAD DUCKED through the far door at the other end of the room, almost slipping on the wood floor as he ran for the front of the house. As he ran, fear propelling him forward, he became aware that he had left his CD behind. At that moment in time it was the least important thing on his mind. If he died, nothing would matter anyway.

As he made for the front door, he passed the entrance to the living room the two gunmen had used. It was still open and he caught a glimpse of the man he had shot. He was on his knees, hunched over, a bloody mass of pulped flesh and white bone protruding from the exit wound in his shoulder.

Beringer grabbed for the front door handle, almost missed it, then snatched the door open. As he stepped onto the porch, a gun fired behind him and a chunk of wood blew away from the door frame, splinters ripping his cheek. Warm blood started to course down his face. The sharp pain made him move again. He missed the second porch step and went down on his hands and knees, the pistol bouncing from his hand. A moan of panic rose in his throat. He lurched upright, spotting the SIG-Sauer in the pool of light from the house behind him.

As his fingers touched the butt, he heard a sudden volley of shots.

BOLAN HAD PARKED down the lane a distance, making his way on foot toward Lewis Beringer's house, keeping to the trees for cover.

He spotted the parked black SUV. One man was standing beside it, while a second sat in the back seat, the door open. He was smoking.

Bolan unleathered the Beretta and took a moment to check out the scenario. Two men with the SUV. How many up front, or inside the house?

Then he heard the first shot coming from inside the house. The two men at the SUV snapped into action. The guy inside scrambled out, a handgun visible now. The man already standing reached inside his jacket and drew his own weapon.

Bolan heard a faint voice, which had a metallic twang to it. The guy who had been standing outside raised his left hand, revealing a small transceiver.

The final words of the message reached Bolan as he closed in on the rear of the SUV.

"…heading in your direction."

Moments later the front door of the house was flung open, a figure briefly framed there. A shot sounded. The figure lurched down the steps, fell, losing the gun he carried. He remained on his hands and knees for a moment, then turned and reached for the gun he had dropped.

"It's Beringer. Get the bastard."

The man who had picked up the call on his transceiver stepped away from the SUV, his own handgun coming into play. He swung the muzzle in the direction of the man on his knees.

Bolan triggered a burst that took away the back of the gunner's skull. The impact kicked him forward and he flopped on his knees, his gun going off and driving a bullet into the dirt a moment before he fell facedown in the dirt.

Someone appeared in the doorway of Beringer's house. He aimed his own weapon at Beringer and fired. The computer expert yelled in agony and dropped to the ground.

Bringing up the Beretta, Bolan triggered a 3-round burst that impacted against the clapboards to one side of the door. The shots drove the shooter back inside.

The second guy by the SUV ran around the bulk of the vehicle, his weapon tracking toward the Executioner. He was too slow locating his target and was still looking when Bolan dropped him with a burst that cored through his chest and into his heart. The guy spun, arms waving. He slammed into the side of the SUV, dropping to the ground a deadweight.

Bolan ran to the SUV and jumped behind the steering wheel. The key was in the ignition. He fired up the engine and slammed the stick into Drive. He released the brake and jammed his foot hard down on the gas pedal. The big vehicle surged forward. Bolan flicked on the headlights, the bright beams flooding the front of Beringer's house. The soldier drove with his right hand, his left fisting the Beretta through his open window as he swung the SUV in close.

A figure stepped through the front door, one hand up to shield his eyes, the other waving the handgun he carried. The glare of the headlights prevented him from identifying any potential targets.

Bolan had no such problem. He jammed on the brake and brought the SUV to a slithering stop, kicking open the door and dropping to a crouch beside the broad front tire. He pushed upright, leaning against the hood, and took quick aim. He stroked the trigger and put three 9 mm rounds in the man framed by the headlights. The shots punched the guy backward and he fell out of sight.

Bolan went to where Beringer lay. He recognized the man from the photo Brognola had given him. The light from the SUV showed the bleeding wound in Beringer's left hip. The man moaned when Bolan rolled him on his good side. Checking the wound, he saw that it was a through-and-through, a clean shot that had missed the bone.

"Beringer, on your feet. We need to move in case there are more. And before any cops show up."

He hauled the man to his feet, ignoring his protests.

"Wait. I have important data I need to take away. Eric Stahl wants to get his hands on it."

Despite his misgivings Bolan helped Beringer back inside. They stepped over the body by the front door.

"I wounded one in the shoulder," Beringer said.

Bolan had already seen Hecht. The man was still down, blood pooling on the floor around him.

"In there," Beringer said.

Limping and in agony, Beringer went to where he had left his laptop and the CD containing the information he had rescued. He pushed it into a black leather carryall.

Bolan escorted him out of the house and helped him into the front seat of the SUV. Reversing from the house, the soldier drove back down the lane to the main road. He pulled in behind his own car and quickly transferred his duffel bags to the SUV. He climbed back into the black vehicle and drove off, heading for 66. He picked up the interstate and followed it west until the intersection with 495. Once they were on this route, Bolan stayed with it. The curving swathe of the 495 took them through Annandale, bypassing Alexandria and over the Woodrow Wilson Memorial Bridge and then along the final stretch of the highway until they reached the off ramp for Andrews Air Force Base. During the intense drive, Lewis Beringer said nothing. He sprawled in ungainly silence, holding the field dressing Bolan had given him against the bloody wound in his hip, inwardly contemplating an uncertain future.

CHALLENGED at the air base gate, Bolan produced his Mike Belasko identification. After a telephone call from the gatehouse and confirmation, Bolan was allowed through. He had an armed escort across the base to the waiting C-130 J transport.

Joshua Riba was waiting to meet him. The man glanced at Bolan's passenger.

"Did you do that?"

"No. A crew from Eric Stahl. Beringer has something the senator needs. Bad enough he wanted him dead."

Bolan picked up the carryall, along with his duffel bags.

"Is that what Stahl wants?" Riba asked, indicating the carryall.

"Beringer risked going back in his house for it. If it has something to do with Zero, Kaplan should see it."

"What about Beringer?"

Bolan crossed to the escort team and spoke to the sergeant in charge. Standing back, Bolan watched the Air Force escort climb into the SUV and drive off across the base.

"They'll take care of him until my contact decides what to do with him."

Bolan turned and climbed on board the Hercules. He made his way to the flight deck, where he spoke to the Air Force pilot. Riba had settled himself by the time Bolan returned. The sound of the turboprop engines firing up reached them. Once the engines had reached working capacity, the huge aircraft rolled forward, turning as the pilot made for the assigned runway. Once it was lined up, the pilot increased the power. The C-130 J eased forward, picking up speed as it coursed down the runway, the noise increasing until it broke free and pushed its way skyward.

"There's no going back now," Riba said quietly.

"That's never been an option," Bolan said.

CHAPTER TEN

Wyoming

Midmorning and Warren Air Force Base lay behind them. Riba was driving as they barreled along Interstate 80, west across the sprawling expanse of southern Wyoming. The air outside the vehicle was cool while inside the sealed vehicle the temperature was comfortable. They passed a few vehicles, mainly massive semitrailers shunting goods back and forth across the state, and local traffic. Riba kept his speed at a steady fifty, aware of the vigilance of local and state police when it came to breaking the speed limit.

When they had arrived at Warren, they found that Brognola had called ahead and arranged for them to be supplied with clothing and equipment. The Air Force also had food supplies and water. A pair of large steel flasks contained hot coffee.

Riba had helped Bolan load the gear into the back of the Laredo.

"Now this is what I call real clout."

On the road Bolan unfolded one of the area maps the Air Force had supplied. He studied it until he had their route worked out.

"Stay on 80 for the next two-hundred-odd miles. When we see the sign for Rock Springs, we exit and take 191 north. Another 150 miles should bring us up into the Gros Ventre and Wind River Mountain area."

"Still doesn't pinpoint Kaplan's place exactly."

"I spoke to my contact when you were asleep during the flight. They got results from that telephone intercept. Calls to Kaplan's home phone were rerouted to his place up here. Only a couple, but they were enough. A satellite sweep gave us a location."

Bolan took a folded printout that had been sent to the Hercules on-board computer system. It showed a satellite digital recon photograph with the distinctive shape of a timber lodge, close to the bank of a placid lake. He held it up so Riba could see it.

"I used the coordinates that came with the photo to work out on the map where Kaplan's lodge is. With that and your tracking skills, we should find it."

"Hey, I'm a strictly twenty-first-century Apache. GPS. Radar. I believe in progress."

Bolan grunted as he reached for one of the coffee flasks.

"Great help you're going to be."

"I still take my coffee black."

"No creamer?"

"What do think I am, some kind of pussycat? Your contact have anything else?"

Bolan showed him a couple more photographs.

"Mug shot from Chicago PD. Hank Winston. His people tried to take out the security team previously attached to Zero, now looking for Kaplan and probably Buchanan. Winston had been seen earlier in Hawaii talking to this guy. My people finally identified him. Chosan Xiang, People's Republic of China. He's military and works for a General Tung Shan. Apparently Tung is no lover of the U.S. Chosan runs a special squad that specializes in covert work. And from intelligence reports, not all of it in China."

"Do we figure this General Tung might be behind the original attack on the Zero facility?"

"When you start adding up all the information and the tie-ins, there's too much you can accept as pure coincidence."

Riba looked at the photographs again. "Okay, so this Winston and his team of hitters got stopped. Has he sent in a backup squad?"

Bolan shook his head. "Chicago PD can't locate him. He seems to have vanished. A local snitch came up with the story he emptied his safe and took off. The snitch got that from some of Winston's own people."

"Wait up," Riba said. "This Winston screwed up the first hit on Zero. He didn't know it, but he left Buchanan alive. Buchanan returns from the dead, and Winston's Chinese paymaster comes back and says 'Finish the job.' Am I still on the trail?"

"Fine so far."

"For whatever reason Winston's boys screw up again. Only this time they don't walk away. Next we know, Winston has left the Windy City, which leaves the question, what are the Chinese going to do about Buchanan and Zero? If they went this far to take out the whole setup, are they going to quit now? I mean we're not talking a fortune-cookie franchise here. This Zero system would mean hard times for the Chinese and their Asian neighbors."

Bolan stared out the windshield, leaving a silence for Riba to fill.

"Tell me if I'm just reaching here, Mike, but can we even *assume* what's jumping around inside my head? Such as this Chosan Xiang guy making a personal try at taking out Buchanan and maybe Kaplan?"

"One thing I didn't mention," Bolan said. "Chosan disappeared after his meeting with Winston. He didn't take a flight out of Hawaii back to Hong Kong. Or anywhere. He engineered a vanishing act to distract anyone watching him."

"So where'd he go?"

BOLAN TOOK THE WHEEL after a couple of hours. The interstate ran ahead, a man-made ribbon cutting through the immense spread of the Wyoming landscape, wide sky above, an endless flow of land beneath. They merged in the far, hazy distance, always leading him on yet never seeming to get any closer.

He checked his watch. It was going to be dark by the time they located Kaplan's lodge.

Washington, D.C.

ERIC STAHL LEANED over and picked up the telephone.

"Ryan? Please give me some good news."

"How about the location of Kaplan's lodge in Wyoming? Is that making you smile, Senator?"

"I almost had a funny thought. I guess that will have to do for the moment. I hope, Ryan, that you're in transit for Wyoming as we speak."

"Been in the air for almost thirty minutes, Senator."

"Ryan, no more fuckups."

"It has to be our turn for things to go right."

"No, Ryan, it has nothing to do with good luck. It has to do with not letting the other man keep on kicking your ass. Make your own good luck."

"Whatever you say, Senator."

Wyoming airspace

"BIG COUNTRY down there, Jackson."

"I guess."

"I thought all you boys liked places like this. Cowboys and all. Big horses. Big mountains. Big guns."

Byrde turned to stare at his partner.

"What is this with you? Always bringing big guns into the conversation."

"Never had one when I was a kid."

Byrde shook his head. He stared out the aircraft window and watched the mountainous Wyoming landscape slip by. He noticed there was snow on some of the higher peaks.

"What time you got, Claire?"

"Five to midday."

"We should be landing soon."

"You think we'll find Doug Buchanan down there?"

"I hope so."

HE AWOKE LATE, his body wet with sweat from yet another dream.

Or was it nightmare?

During the night, he had twisted and turned, his sleep crowded with dark, unsettling images, alternately hot, then cold, gripped in the embrace of soundless visions he couldn't escape. It was impossible for him to tear himself out of the paralyzing terror holding him captive. He was forced to endure the parade of silent images, and his single wish was to be able to yell his defiance. To at least scream out in order to break the spell.

He was alone, again, in a dark limbo that might have been eternal night or the cold of empty space. Underfoot he felt solid ground. At least something firm to support him. His body felt alive, with moving, insidiously crawling objects beneath his skin. He knew they were the implants, placed there as part of his transformation. His hands and arms floated into his vision, and he saw the moving shapes beneath his skin. The flesh was raised, like thick veins close to the surface, darker than the surrounding tissue. He could feel the rippling expansion. He knew that the same thing was happening all over his body, distorting its natural formation.

He felt a tearing sensation in his right hand and arm, and when he looked down he saw the flesh splitting open. There was no blood, just the snakelike protuberance of the implant. It arced about, like a blind snake, the blunt tip casting back and forth, searching for something that wasn't there. Again and again the implant tendril curled and uncoiled, restless in its quest to locate some unknown contact. Now there were more implants, bursting from his body, each new one probing the air around him, finding nothing, and then they all turned on him, the smooth, blind heads hovering in front of his eyes.

Even then he was unable to make any sound, remaining mute and terrified as the many slender implants merged into one thicker shape that struck at him suddenly, exploding in his face and sucking him into a vortex of utter darkness that sucked him down, turning and twisting him as it went on and on. And in his silent terror he found the strength to yell out and break the grip of the formless horror that had snared him.

Doug Buchanan burst into the light, sitting up with a force that almost threw him from the bed. He sat there, panting, his whole body aching, nausea rising from his stomach. He remained in his sitting position, his head against his chest, sweat dripping from his face.

That was how Saul Kaplan found him when he barged into the bedroom, concern etched across his lean face. He saw the twisted bed covers, the sweat that coursed down Buchanan's naked upper body and flinched at the expression in Buchanan's eyes when the man raised his head.

"What have we done to you, Doug?"

Buchanan wiped at the sweat running into his eyes. He took a deep breath, releasing it slowly.

"Given me a few sleepless nights, Saul."

He swung his legs to the floor and stood, swaying slightly, reaching out to place a hand against the wall until the sensation passed.

"Can I get you anything?"

Buchanan glanced at his watch. "I would ask for breakfast, but it's closer to lunch. A cup of coffee would be nice."

Kaplan shook his head, turning to go.

"Hey, Saul, don't beat yourself up over this. I knew what I was doing when I signed up for Zero."

"I don't believe any of us knew what we were doing, Doug. We only thought we knew."

"I'll go take a shower. Then we can talk."

Saul Kaplan returned to the kitchen. From the wide window he could look out over the expanse of the lake that lay just beyond his lodge. Seeing the tranquil spread of water, overlooked by the timbered mountain slopes, had always given him peace and a release from any concerns he might have had. It was the reason he had always resisted any offers to sell. It was a refuge from

the demands of his intense lifestyle and something he
valued above any amount of money. It was the first
place he had thought of when he had relinquished his
post at the university for health reasons. In part that had
been true because he had been unable to distance himself completely from Zero. He had imagined, at first,
that leaving the project would work, but he had been
wrong. The memories had been too strong. His attach-
ment too personal. His nights started to be sleepless,
leaving him tired and unable to give his full attention
to his work. So he had left, packing his bags, and had
set out for Wyoming and the lodge. When he had first
arrived, spending time settling in, he had been able to
return to the peace he had always found. Standing looking out across the lake had always brought him con-
tentment.

This day that idyllic panorama did little to ease his
conscience. Seeing Doug Buchanan confused and tor-
mented by the visions of his condition left Kaplan with
strong feelings of guilt. He was the one person who had
convinced Buchanan he was doing the right thing, that
he was embarking on an historic journey. Something
never undertaken by any other human being. His persuasion had been the pivot that had swung Buchanan to
his final decision.

"Damn you, Saul, you had no right."

He crossed to the sink and turned on the tap, filling
the coffeepot. He moved to the stove and lit the jet to
heat the water. His movements were automatic as he

took mugs from the cupboard and brought out the jar of coffee. His mind was elsewhere, drawing him back to a few nights ago when Doug Buchanan had showed up at the lodge.

IT HAD BEEN COLD, a thin rain whispering off the high peaks. When Kaplan heard the banging on the door he knew who it was. Buchanan had telephoned a couple of times previously, talking, sometimes rambling as he told Kaplan he was on his way. Kaplan, feeling both relieved and guilty, had listened to his friend's near incoherent speech. He understood that Buchanan had to have been suffering some degree of discomfort. Since the attack on the Zero facility, Buchanan would have been denied his drug injections, the treatment designed to ease him through the implant transition. It was possible for Buchanan to survive without them, but the loss of the treatment would have left him open to the change in his body, without the calming effect of the drugs. In his present state of mind, that loss would have simply added to his overall suffering.

When Kaplan had opened the door to see Buchanan standing there, soaked and weary to the bone, he was shocked at the outward appearance of the man. Buchanan had lost weight. It showed in his gaunt face, the dark patches beneath his eyes. Kaplan hadn't forgotten the ravaging cancer that was working away inside the man. That would be having its effects, too. It was a combination of both that had taken its toll on the major. Yet despite it all, he had found his way here to this isolated spot, searching for something he had been unable to find anywhere else.

He took Buchanan inside and made the man take a long hot shower. While he was doing that, Kaplan found fresh clothing for him. They were both of a similar height. Normally Buchanan would have been heavier, but his weight loss meant he was able to get into Kaplan's loose clothing comfortably. When Buchanan sat at the table, Kaplan placed hot food and coffee in front of him. Buchanan took a long look at the fresh steak and potatoes and set to eating it without a word. Kaplan let him finish his meal before he spoke.

"Tell me what happened after the attack on the facility."

"You heard about that?"

"Even though I walked out on the project, I still have contacts. They told me what had happened out of professional courtesy."

"And asked you to come back to start over?"

"Of course."

"They don't quit easily."

"Nor do you, Doug. Not like me."

"You can quit that talk right now. I know what was happening. They took Zero away from you, changed the rules and left you out in the cold."

"But I walked away from you, Doug. That was inexcusable."

"I forgive you, my son. My benediction for the week."

Kaplan smiled. That was the old Doug Buchanan, briefly revived. Always ready with a joke no matter how bad the situation might be.

"The night the strike came I was caught up in one of the explosions. Luckily it was the concussion. It threw me out of a window. I was able to crawl out under the perimeter fence and get into the desert. I hid and watched the facility being razed to the ground. Everything burned and flattened. I walked. I think I was looking for a phone to call in and tell what had happened. Things got a little hazy about then. The drugs had worn off, and I was losing it. It looks like I ran into this dirt road and a truck came out of nowhere and hit me. I didn't know a thing until days later. The guy driving the truck was an Apache from a local settlement. They looked after me. I'd taken some hard knocks from the explosion and then the truck. My memory was coming and going. I must have been in a hell of a mess. I'd drift off, then it would all come back. Go again. But those people looked after me. I did call my niece and tried to warn her people might come looking for me. I left her a message saying to tell anyone she hadn't heard from me. Then I figured if I stayed where I was, those people who wiped out the facility might find me and hurt the Apaches. So I took one of their trucks and drove until I found a railway. I jumped a train and started out looking for you and this place. Time was I didn't think I'd make it. You know what I did? I broke into a store along some country road and took painkillers. Food and drink. Christ, Saul, me. A major in the U.S. Air Force. Stealing."

"Some story, Doug. I'm just glad you got here."

"With a bit of luck we might get some peace and quiet up here." Kaplan's guilty look made Buchanan stare at his friend. "What?"

"I don't suppose anyone told you after I left. About the tracer chip they planted in your skull during one of the implant operations?"

Buchanan shook his head, too weary to even get angry at this new revelation.

"You mean someone can locate me by watching for a signal?"

"Yes. But if the chip had been working properly, you would have been found quickly. It may be that it isn't functioning on a constant basis."

"Oh, great. So we should be okay, then?"

"Let this be a lesson, Doug. Choose your so-called friends carefully in the future. I haven't proved to be exactly a faithful one."

"You keep on talking like that and I might suddenly agree."

"You should let me get you a doctor, Doug. You need proper treatment."

"No doctors. They ask too many damned questions. No doctors, Saul. Promise?"

KAPLAN HEARD the water bubbling on the stove. He made coffee and took the mugs through to the living room as Buchanan appeared, dressed and looking a little more relaxed. He took the mug Kaplan offered.

"I've had better nights," he said.

He wandered across the room and stared out through the panoramic window.

"What are you thinking, Doug?"

"That this isn't going to last. If I'm being tracked, chip or not, someone is going to make the two-and-two connection and come looking for you. Maybe it's time I moved on."

"Where to, Doug? Who do you trust? Think about what happened back in New Mexico. Who was behind the strike at the facility? If they find out you're still alive, I doubt they'll be waiting with open arms and a bouquet of flowers."

"So what do I do? Just keep on running? How long for, Saul? Until this damned cancer gets me? Yeah, I know, you wanted to get me medical help and I refused. Let's see how things turn out."

Kaplan sighed, embarrassed because there was nothing he could say to ease his friend's discomfort, physically or mentally.

"Do you have any weapons?"

"Weapons?"

"Guns. Pistol. Shotgun. Rifle."

"Yes. Here."

Kaplan led Buchanan to a locked cabinet in the far corner of the room. He produced a key and unlocked the doors, opening them.

In the upright rack were a shotgun and a rifle. In a drawer below were boxes of cartridges for the weapons.

"When I was younger I fancied myself as an outdoor hunter. I only went out a few times. I wasn't very good. And I suddenly realized I didn't want to kill animals, no matter how much I told myself it was for food."

Buchanan took down the rifle. It was in good condition, clean and oiled. It was a Marlin Model .375, a center-fire, lever action. The weapon held a 5-round capacity. The shotgun, a Ruger 12-gauge over and under, was fitted with expertly checkered and finished stock and fore end in American walnut.

Kaplan watched as Buchanan loaded both weapons.

"Are we going to need them?"

"I hope not, Saul, but it doesn't do any harm to be ready."

For what? Kaplan found himself wondering.

Buchanan caught his expression.

"Hey, I'm not thinking of shooting myself. I want to see this through one way or another."

THEIR ARRIVAL at the port of Seattle had been uneventful.

Shao Yeung, Chosan Xiang and his four-man team were down on the crew roster. They all had genuine papers that identified them as such. Once the *Oahua Star* docked and the usual checks had been made, the crew went about its business of unloading the cargo, which was moved to a dock warehouse to await final pickup, except for a pair of seagoing containers shackled to the deck. The freighter was due to stay in Seattle's port for a couple of days while it waited for a cargo for the return journey to Hong Kong.

Shao received a cell phone message from his Seattle contact to say that everything he had asked for had been arranged. He gave Shao a contact location, which Shao passed to Chosan, and arrangements were put in motion for the assault team to leave the ship.

That evening a semi-tractor and trailer arrived to pick up the deck container. The driver had all the necessary paperwork for the pickup. The container had been checked and sealed by U.S. Customs when they had come aboard to inspect the main cargo.

What no one had taken into account was the square access panel in the base of the container. It was just large enough to allow a man to crawl through and gain entrance to the interior of the container at the rear. This panel had been engineered and constructed at the Shanghai shipyard special-projects division. The small square of steel had been cut and refitted so finely it was invisible to the naked eye, positioned as it was between the natural formation of the container base. The neat fit had been further disguised by a fresh coat of paint, which had been weathered and faded by chemicals and salt spray. Chosan had used this method of covert entry previously.

Before the container was craned up off the deck a delay was created by the freighter's hoist operator, leaving it dangling a few feet in the air. The Chinese crew swarmed around the container, yelling and arm waving in the traditional way they were expected to behave. In the dark and the fortunate squall of rain that had swept in across waterfront, Chosan and his team released the false panel and climbed inside the container. The panel was eased back into position and secured by internal catches. The hoist operator, playing his part, shouted torrents of abuse at the deck crew and finally managed to get the container off the deck, over the freighter's side and onto the trailer, where it was locked into position, the base completely hidden from any prying eyes. By this time the dock security guard had tired of listening to the haranguing Chinese crew and had retreated to his dry security hut at the dock gate. He could still see the milling crew securing the container but decided it was less interesting than a cup of hot coffee and the football game playing on his portable TV set.

The tractor hauling the container rolled its load up to the gate. The driver, a Chinese himself, but with an American accent, leaned out of his cab, handing over the final docket for the security man to check and sign.

"These damned foreigners," the driver said.

"Yeah."

"How's the game?"

The security man handed back the signed paperwork.

"My kids could put on a better show. They pay 'em all that money and they run round like headless chickens. Might do better in the last quarter."

"I like *The Simpsons*," the driver said. "It's funny. Or maybe it's because of their color."

The driver opened the gate, trying to figure out what the driver had meant by his last remark. It didn't dawn on him until some time later. It made him think the Chinese had a weird sense of humor.

SHAO YEUNG STOOD in the wheelhouse and watched the container being driven away. He felt concern for Chosan and the assault team. He knew they were professional and were highly skilled in this kind of covert action. Even so he had a sense of foreboding that refused to go away. His admiration for Chosan Xiang had increased. The man was a true warrior, a hero of the People's Republic. Whatever the outcome of this operation, Shao would make sure that Chosan's dedication wouldn't go unnoticed.

CHAPTER ELEVEN

Wyoming

Saul Kaplan could hear the slap of the wind against the lodge's solid timber walls. He glanced across to where Doug Buchanan slumped wearily in one of the low armchairs set near the open log fire. Buchanan hadn't moved for the past hour. They had been talking for most of the afternoon and into the night. Now even Buchanan was talked out. They had sat together, neither man able to continue the conversation.

Kaplan had stood, heading for the kitchen. He decided to make coffee. He had been making coffee for most of the day. It gave him an opportunity to clear his mind. Buchanan had questions. So many questions, and Kaplan was glad to be able to at least try to answer them. He still felt guilty about deserting Buchanan, leaving him alone at the Zero facility. Secretly Kaplan felt ashamed of his actions. He realized there was nothing he could do to alter what he had done, but with Buchanan's presence at the lodge he could try to repair some of the damage. One of the difficulties was that Buchanan was still suffering from a degree of memory loss. His knowledge of Zero and the events before and after the assault on the facility would slip away, leaving him frustrated and unsure of himself. Then he would turn to Kaplan, his eyes searching the other man's face as he sought answers.

Now he had slipped into an exhausted stupor, content to sit and stare into the flames of the fire.

In the kitchen Kaplan stood at the sink, filling the coffeepot and looking out the window. It was dark, with barely any moonlight. Rain slanted down out of the gloom, and clouds were pushing across the pale gleam of the lake, rippling the surface. Just beyond the lodge, edging the clearing around the building, dark stands of trees swayed in the wind. Branches swung, shadows flickering. Kaplan was about to turn away when he paused and leaned closer to the glass.

He felt sure he had seen a figure moving out there. He looked again. More than one. He wasn't seeing things.

There were men out there.

And they were emerging from the trees and moving across the clearing in the direction of the lodge.

RYAN AND HIS MEN were equipped with radio communicators and headsets, which meant they were able to coordinate their approach to the lodge in the dark. They had flown in from Casper, Wyoming, using a Bell UH-1N Iroquois helicopter, from one of Orin Stengard's secure bases. The Bell, painted matte black, had carried Ryan, seven of his ex-military men and four local hitters who knew the area. They had been on the ground for almost two hours, working their way up the rain-slick slopes of the Wind River range. They were all armed with M-16 A-2 rifles and Glock 21 pistols. The Iroquois was below them waiting for exfiltration once the operation was complete.

Cal Ryan, sheltering against the thick trunk of a tree, sleeved rain from his eyes. The wind sloughing down off the high peaks was driving the rain directly at them.

"Boswell, how close now?" he said into his microphone.

The reply came back in seconds.

"Another half mile we'll be able to see in through that lodge window."

"Listen, once we have the place in sight, stay put. I don't want any lone plays. We wait until we're all in position before we go. That understood? Goes for all of you."

There were murmurs of assent from the rest of the team.

"Let's move out."

IN THE DARKNESS surrounding the lodge Chosan Xiang and his team crouched on the sodden ground, hidden beneath the overhanging branches of thick shrubs.

They were all clad in black combat suits, faces and hands darkened to avoid being spotted. The Chinese team carried 9 mm Uzi SMGs, fitted with 40-round magazines supplied by their American contacts, and had sheathed knives strapped to their belts. Each man had four extra magazines for the Uzi he carried, in combat webbing worn over their blacksuits.

They had arrived in the area in the late afternoon, locating themselves and then staying concealed until full dark allowed them to complete the journey that would bring them to the lodge.

The container trailer had left Seattle, picking up Interstate 90, and had stayed with it all the way through Washington State, the narrow wedge of northern Idaho, cutting through the Coeur d'Alene mountain range and across into Montana. Pushing steadily on, the rig had rolled through the Bitterroot Range, bypassing Missoula, following the western curve of Interstate 90 down toward Butte and eventually the crossing of the Yellowstone River, with the trace of the old Lewis and Clark trail running parallel with the interstate. Chosan and his team disembarked from the container after it parked off the main highway, late in the evening. After the twenty-four-hour journey, with rest stops for the driver and the opportunity for Chosan and his team to emerge from the container for relief and refreshments, the team, to a man, wasn't disappointed to see the rig drive on.

The Seattle contact had contracted for a helicopter to pick up Chosan and his team. The timing was exact.

Chosan heard the aircraft approaching within thirty minutes of their being dropped off by the trailer rig. The helicopter, a Bell Model 43, piloted by a Chinese, took off again the moment Chosan and his men were on board.

The pilot, a young man from Hubei Province, born in Wuhan on the banks of the Yangtze River, had lived in America for four years. He earned his living as a commercial helicopter pilot. Chosan spoke to him briefly, and the young man explained that he had been told exactly what he was required to do. He showed Chosan the flight chart and the course he would take. The young pilot was enthusiastic about his involvement in something so important for his native China.

Chosan and his four men spent most of the first hour of the flight checking and loading their weapons. They only sat back when that was completed. Chosan was able to relax during the long flight. The cramped conditions in the false section at the rear of the container hadn't helped to make the road trip very pleasant. He sat with his face turned to the canopy of the helicopter, staring out into the night. Of all the missions he had carried out for General Tung, this would be the most difficult. He knew, accepted and didn't allow to dampen his spirit, that the chances of a return home were thin.

If that was the need, then so be it, he decided. If he and his team succeeded and Buchanan and Kaplan died, then whatever happened to them didn't matter. Sacrifice was something Chosan and his men embraced. Five lives against the millions back in China. There was no question which had the greater importance.

The helicopter touched down in fading light. Rain was falling, cold against Chosan's exposed face when he climbed down out of the warm cabin. As his team gathered around him, Chosan signaled for them to follow him. They pushed across the treacherous slopes, making for the densely timbered terrain ahead.

The helicopter shut down, becoming still and silent. It would wait until they returned. Chosan had a personal communicator so he could alert the pilot.

They had a six-mile hike before they reached the lodge. Chosan had a plastic-covered map of the area, with the location of Kaplan's lodge marked on it. He and his team studied the map for long minutes, each man absorbing and retaining the directions given on the chart.

"The deaths of these two Americans is of prime importance. It is why we are here, why we have come to this place. To kill Buchanan and Kaplan. Nothing else matters. Not even our survival. They have to be removed. I know we have talked this over many times. Now we are here, within striking distance of the lodge belonging to Kaplan, all the discussion becomes reality. If we find both of them here, then we hit and hit hard. If there is only one, we do the same. If our assumptions are wrong and the place is deserted, then we withdraw and regroup. Something tells me we are not going to find that."

His team nodded in agreement. Under Chosan's directions they moved out, pushing deeper into the mountainous terrain.

Enemy territory.

"I STILL CAN'T believe it," Jackson Byrde grumbled. "That engine is only six weeks old. And it breaks down the minute we hit rough ground."

Valens didn't answer. She was in no mood for her partner's muttering. It was over an hour since they had abandoned their SUV. They were tramping through the undulating terrain, through brush and trees, over ground that was soaked underfoot from the continuing rain. It was wet and cold, the wind striking down through the canopy of branches.

They were at least equipped for the territory. They both wore heavy waterproof coats over their clothes, which consisted of combat-style pants and shirts and they had heavy-soled boots on their feet. Long peaked caps were pulled down over their heads. Each carried a personal communicator so they would be able to stay in contact if separated. Both agents were armed with their Beretta Model 92 pistols. Byrde was carrying a powerful flashlight.

"When they do this in the movies the search party has a dozen agents, choppers and searchlights," Byrde went on.

"Jesus Christ, Jackson, just shut the hell up."

Byrde grinned in the darkness. Right now Valens

was in fighting mode. If they came across anyone now, they would be in deep trouble.

He was about to make a facetious reply when he threw up a hand to stop Valens.

"What?" she whispered above the rattle of the rain on the foliage.

Byrde waited until she was alongside, then indicated the Bell 430 helicopter standing in a clearing beyond the fringe of trees concealing them. Despite the cross hatch of shadows, they could see a single occupant sitting inside the cabin.

"Something you see every day out here I guess," Valens said.

"Sure. Right next to the flying-pig circus. Here, grab hold of this."

Byrde thrust the flash into Valens's hand and opened his coat to ease out his pistol.

"I'll work my way around to the other side. When I'm ready, I'll give you a call."

Valens nodded and saw her partner vanish into the gloom. She worked her way along the tree line until she was level with the helicopter cabin, then settled down to wait. Byrde called in less than five minutes, his whispered words bringing a smile to Valens's lips. She transferred the flash to her left hand and pulled out her own weapon.

"Set," she said into her comm unit.

"Go!" Byrde replied.

Valens stepped out of the trees and ran across to the

helicopter. As she reached the rain-streaked cabin window, she caught a glimpse of Byrde on the other side.

Valens raised the flash and tapped on the Plexiglas canopy. Byrde did the same on his side of the cabin.

The young Chinese pilot reacted sharply, leaning forward to flick switches, panic driving his actions.

Valens reached out to grab the handle and open the cabin door. She leaned in and showed him the Beretta.

"Not advisable, sir. Would you please raise your hands and sit back, away from the controls."

Byrde had opened the door on his side.

"Do it. You understand what she said."

The Chinese pilot did what he was ordered. Whatever else he might have been, foolish wasn't it. He raised his hands and clasped them on top of his head.

Five minutes later the pilot was handcuffed to the frame of one of the rear seats. Valens stood watch over him while Byrde checked the map again.

"Looks like we're on track. Up that way."

"Let's go," Valens said.

MACK BOLAN and Joshua Riba were closing on the lodge when the Apache reached out to touch the Executioner's arm.

"Somebody coming up behind," he warned. "I make a couple of people."

Bolan and Riba were on foot, having left the Laredo back down the trail to avoid being heard.

They were both armed with weapons they brought

from the Hercules. Bolan had a 9 mm Uzi and wore the big Desert Eagle holstered on his hip, with the Beretta 93-R in a shoulder rig. In addition to his Colt .45 handgun, Riba had an M-4 carbine. He carried extra magazines in the pockets of a combat vest he had donned over the dark shirt he had changed into.

They had been nearing the lodge when Riba had picked up the sound of movement close by.

Bolan turned at the man's warning. He eased back into the undergrowth, the Uzi tracking the source of the sound.

Two figures, clad in heavy waterproof coats and peaked caps, stepped out of the shadows. The one in the lead had a flashlight.

The moment he saw them, Bolan felt a sense of ease wash over him. From their appearance and the way they were moving through the trees, he realized they were neither from Senator Stahl's camp nor from any other opposition force.

When a patch of light fell across the second of the two figures and revealed the female he had seen in the photograph Brognola had supplied, Bolan identified them as Byrde and Valens, the two Zero security agents.

"Hold it," he said and stepped up to one side and slightly behind the pair. "We're friendly."

Claire Valens responded sharply. "We'll be the judges of that."

She turned to face the Executioner, ignoring the Uzi aimed at her, and coolly looked him over.

"Wearing that getup doesn't suggest friendly to me."

"Appearances can be deceptive, Agent Valens."

"How the hell—?" Byrde said.

"My contact told me about you. He said you were on a similar assignment."

Valens stepped in closer, green eyes searching Bolan's:

"Your contact? Who the hell is your contact?"

Bolan admired her strength. Claire Valens, he decided, would be a young woman to stand up to.

"Let's just say we're all working to keep Doug Buchanan and Saul Kaplan alive, which isn't going to happen if we stand around here all night talking."

"It might make us easy targets," Riba suggested.

"I'm with him," Byrde stated.

"I don't want to make an issue," Bolan said. "You're looking for Buchanan because there's a threat to his life from out of country, headed by Chosan Xiang. Right? I'm looking for him because there's a threat from within the U.S."

"Threat? Because the government wants him back on the program?" Valens failed to conceal her disbelief.

"Specifically Senator Eric Stahl. The man wants Zero for his own purposes. And he has a partner. Colonel Orin Stengard."

"Proof?"

"I can give you that," Bolan said. "But not right now."

"Just who are you doing this for?"

"Friends who got caught up in it is part of the reason."

"What's the other?"

Riba raised a hand. "Equal job opportunities. Helping out Native Americans."

Bolan turned to go.

"Hey, you can't just leave...."

Bolan glanced at Valens. "Watch me."

He slipped away into the surrounding foliage, Riba close behind.

Valens glanced at her partner. Byrde shrugged.

"What the hell."

CAL RYAN'S SIGNAL went out to his team. He had received acknowledgment from them all, confirming they were in position.

"Let's go. And remember we need them both alive."

He meant Buchanan and Kaplan. An advance check by one of Ryan's team had confirmed that both men were inside the lodge. It had meant a great deal to Cal Ryan. Too much had been going wrong lately. He needed a successful outcome. If not for himself, at least for Colonel Stengard. The colonel was the one man Ryan didn't want to disappoint. He had too much respect for his former commander. Ryan had less respect for Stahl. The politician was—a politician. Too much for himself, with little real *respect* for those around him. Respect was something earned as far as Ryan was concerned, and Colonel Stengard had won his through the way he commanded his men, mainly in the thick of battle, where he showed why he was the kind of leader Stahl would never be if he lived to be an old man.

Ryan pushed away from cover and led the way across the clearing, moving in on the lodge.

THERE WAS a moment of confusion as Chosan's men realized they weren't alone in the lodge's vicinity. They had moved forward, heading directly for the lodge's front entrance, when one of them called out a warning, turning his Uzi toward the other armed figures converging on the lodge.

Chosan spun, seeing the armed men breaking into the open. He yelled to his men to defend themselves. There was no time to wonder who these men were. The newcomers had seen Chosan's team and were taking their own evasive action.

THE CRACKLE of gunfire reached Doug Buchanan, yanking him out of his stupor. He sat upright, reaching out for the shotgun resting beside him as Kaplan came running through from the kitchen.

"Armed men outside, Doug. Coming out of the trees."

A window smashed as a stray bullet shattered the glass.

"Stay away from the windows," Buchanan cautioned.

Buchanan moved across the room and pressed against the wall beside the main window, peering out.

He saw dark figures milling around on the open ground, saw the stab of flame as guns fired, and quickly realized that there were two groups firing at each other.

But who?

And why?

ONE OF RYAN'S MEN went down with a groan, struck by autofire. The whine and snap of bullets were all around. Ryan had identified the small group, five of them, who had come into view, and who were now close to the lodge. They had the advantage of being close to the building, allowing them a degree of cover he and his team didn't have.

The exchange of fire had destroyed the stillness around the lodge. Men were yelling, weapons firing. Bullets drilled into the timber frame of the lodge as Ryan's men fired back at the other group. There was a great deal of weaponry firing as the opposing sides simply fired for effect, each side attempting to gain the advantage while securing safe cover.

The darkness and the driving rain did little to help. It hampered visibility, and the wet ground did nothing to accommodate swift movement. One of Chosan's men went down on his knees as his feet went from beneath him. He struggled to regain his balance, and in that moment of indecision he was cut down by a sustained burst from one of Ryan's men. The shot man fell back across the ground, his chest glistening red.

CHOSAN SAW his man go down. He signaled for his team to fall back and gain the cover of the lodge. They obeyed and crouched in the deeper shadow at the base of the wall, returning fire as they did. One of Ryan's men went down, clutching at a shattered leg.

Turning, Chosan saw a short flight of wooden steps leading to a door. He moved forward, going up the steps, raised a booted foot and drove it against the door. He felt something snap and repeated the kick. The door burst open, swinging in with a crash.

"Inside. Quickly," Chosan yelled.

Two of his men went in, Uzis tracking ahead. Chosan followed. The remaining Chinese stayed outside, trading shots with the opposition, giving Chosan and his men time to do what they needed inside the lodge.

BOLAN HEARD the crackle of autofire.

"We too late?" Riba asked.

"Time we found out," Bolan growled and plunged ahead, heading down the slope that brought them to the lodge from the opposite side to the lake.

He made out dark figures in the clearing on the lake side of the lodge.

The gunfire increased; voices were raised in anger.

The end wall of the lodge contained a window. As Bolan cut across the ground toward it, he made out light in the room beyond. He slammed against the wall to one side of the window and then slid along so he could peer in through the glass.

He was looking in on the large living room: log fire, armchairs, and a tall figure wielding a shotgun peering out of the larger window that faced the lake.

A second man came into the room. Lean, with graying hair. He was yelling to the first man, pointing back the way he had come.

The first man turned from the window and Bolan saw his face.

It was Doug Buchanan.

Both men turned as something attracted their attention, Buchanan raising the shotgun.

Bolan moved back from the window, raised his arms to cover his face and ran at the window. He crashed against the frame, taking the whole of the window with him as he went through, glass flying in all directions as Bolan hit the floor on his feet, dropping to a crouch, the Uzi coming on line.

Beyond Buchanan and Kaplan moving figures came into view. Men carrying weapons.

"Major Buchanan, hit the floor," Bolan yelled.

To his credit Buchanan responded fast, reaching out to grab Kaplan and pulling him down, too.

Two of Chosan's men burst from the kitchen, Uzis seeking targets.

Bolan, already on-line, pushed his own Uzi forward, finger stroking the trigger. He cut down the nearest man with a withering burst to his lower body, the 9 mm slugs puncturing organs and punching out a bloody mass as they severed the target's spine. The Chinese toppled facedown on the floor, screaming.

The follow-up man triggered his Uzi in a pure reflex action to his companion's demise. The spray of 9 mm rounds went over Kaplan's head and struck the far wall of the living room.

Bolan was bringing around his Uzi when the savage boom of Buchanan's shotgun rocked the room. The charge, up close and personal, took away the target's right arm and a large chunk of his shoulder, blowing bloody spray into Chosan's face as he brought up short behind his injured man. The stricken Chinese fell to his knees, staring at the great raw wound where his arm had been. Blood was pulsed from the severed flesh.

Chosan Xiang wiped blood from his eyes, raising his Uzi as he braced himself for the shot that would, if nothing else, kill the man he had come all this way to find. In that brief moment he felt he would at least achieve that part of his mission.

It never happened.

In the scant moments before he pulled the trigger Chosan sensed a presence close by. He swiveled his eyes and caught a glimpse of a tall, black-haired man with a huge revolver in his hand.

"No way, you son of a bitch," Joshua Riba said and fired.

The .45 bullet took Chosan in the side of the skull. The Chinese felt as if he had been slapped hard. His head rocked and everything went silent, then it felt as if a great pressure was building up inside his skull. In the last second before death Chosan felt as if his head were about to explode. Then the bullet emerged on the opposite side, taking a large chunk of bone with it and a portion of his brain that spattered against the wall.

Riba had entered the lodge through one of the rear windows, Valens and Byrde behind him. They fanned out across the room.

"I don't think that's it," Byrde said. "There are more out front."

"I'll lay odds they're Senator Stahl's hired guns," Bolan said.

"What the hell is going on, Joshua?" Buchanan demanded, recognizing one friendly face among the group.

"We figure the Chinese were the same people who organized the hit on the New Mexican facility."

"So what has Stahl got to do with this?"

"He wants you alive, Doug," Bolan said, "so he can gain control of Zero and use it as a lever to get him into the White House. The man has a power complex, and he'll do whatever it takes."

"It's true, Doug," Riba said. "I've learned enough the past couple of days to agree with this man. Stahl is in bed with Colonel Orin Stengard. They're planning a takeover. But it all depends on them getting their hands on Zero. You're the only man who can get them access."

"You remember me, Major Buchanan?" Valens asked as she stepped forward. "Byrde and I were the security team at Zero. We've been looking for you, as well. To get you back to safety and away from anyone who wants to harm you."

Bolan had eased away from the group, checking out the front window. He could see the dark shapes in the clearing outside. They had formed a skirmish line, covering the lodge, and though he was unable to see any others, he knew that the place would be surrounded.

The Executioner calculated the odds of them all walking out alive if they put up any kind of resistance. The armed force out there was strong, and they had the advantage. Rushing out with all guns blazing might appear the heroic thing to do, but Mack Bolan hadn't survived for as long as he had by being foolish. He moved back, turning to look at the five people occupying the lodge. After all that had happened, he didn't want to see any of them get hurt.

Riba glanced around and saw Bolan watching the group. He sensed Bolan's mood, quickly got the feeling that if they put up any kind of resistance the men outside wouldn't hesitate to cut them all down if the need arose. The only ones who were safe at the present moment were Doug Buchanan and Saul Kaplan.

"No running for cover?" he asked softly.

Valens heard the question and was quick enough to pick up Bolan's shake of his head. She felt a comment rising to her lips but held it back, because she could tell by the look in his eyes that he hated the thought of surrender, yet at the same time there was nothing else they could do at this moment in time—if they wanted to stay alive.

Bolan could see the armed team moving toward the

lodge, weapons up and ready. He glanced back over his
shoulder, seeing Doug Buchanan and Saul Kaplan
standing together. The brief firefight had taken its toll.
Buchanan's effort had left him disoriented, staring
around the room as if he had no idea where he was. The
shotgun he had put to such good use had slipped from
his fingers and lay at his feet. Kaplan looked like an old
man, his face deathly white from shock. He had most
probably never been witness to sudden, violent death
before. If there was further action of any kind, Kaplan
would be more of a victim than anyone else.

Riba, Byrde and the feisty Claire Valens would fight
to the last—of that Bolan had no doubt. But the outcome would be the same. The opposition carried superior firepower, and they had the numbers, too. If Bolan
had been on his own, he might have fought back, concerned that he was only putting his own life on the line.
He looked again at the slowly advancing assault team
and made a swift decision.

He slipped the cell phone from his pocket and moved
to one side of the window as the number rang out. The
seconds it took before being answered felt an eternity.

"Striker?"

"Hal. Just listen. I'm at Kaplan's lodge. Buchanan
and Kaplan are here. Alive. So are Byrde and Valens and
the P.I. helping me out. Right now we don't have much
chance of shooting our way out. I'm going to take the
chance of surrendering to the assault team outside.
There are too many of them. If they take us… Listen.

Ask Aaron if he can check and see if the trace in Buchanan's skull is back online. If it is, you might be able to locate him when he's moved. It's the only way you might get to him before Stahl goes to work."

"Okay, now *you* listen," Brognola said. "The Bear might have something you can use as a bargaining chip. Beringer's laptop gave up some interesting information regarding Senator Stahl's dealings with Stengard. Seems Beringer had been keeping a file of his own as a lifeline. A section referred to Stahl's own files. Our pal Beringer had unlocked these files, using the senator's own password. He had some program that was able to break into Stahl's system and decode the password. Beringer says Stahl has no idea his files have been accessed. The senator isn't that smart when it comes to computers."

Bolan heard shouted commands outside the lodge. Someone yelling for them to put down their weapons and offer no resistance.

"Hal. No more time."

"The password is 'Freedom.'"

The lodge's main door crashed open, flung back against the wall. Armed men in black combat gear moved into the lodge. More appeared from the direction of the kitchen.

Bolan lowered the hand holding the cell phone before any of the assault team spotted it.

"Put the guns down," Bolan said to his companions. "Now isn't the time."

He dropped the cell phone to the floor, kicking it out of sight under a floor unit, then raised both his hands away from his body. He caught sight of Valens glaring at him, her eyes full of fury. He could take her rage. It was less harmful than getting shot.

The assault team filled the room. Bolan counted close to a dozen of them. They moved quickly to disarm Riba and the two Zero security agents. Two closed in on Bolan and took his weapons, frisking him quickly.

A familiar figure moved to the front of the group, taking off his black cap to expose short-cropped blond hair.

Cal Ryan.

He looked pleased with himself, smiling as he crossed to stand in front of Doug Buchanan and Saul Kaplan.

"It must be my fuckin' birthday. Two presents, boys. The performing monkey and the organ grinder together. Look after this pair. They're our meal ticket for this trip."

He pulled a cell phone from his pocket and punched a speed-dial number.

"Evening, Mr. Senator. Remember I asked if you were smiling a while ago? Well, you can do better than that. Try a damned good laugh."

Ryan listened to Stahl's reply.

"We got 'em both. Alive and kicking. Alive at least. We also have four additional guests. What do you want me to do with them?"

Ryan glanced around the room. His gaze finally settled on Bolan. His own smile widened.

"Tell the senator I have something for him," Bolan said, knowing he was playing a very wild card.

"What?" Ryan had to have been interrupted by Stahl. "Remember that bastard who capped my boys after the airport pickup? Belasko. Yeah, the one who shot my men. Seems he has something to say to you. Jesus. Whatever you say."

Ryan held out the cell phone to Bolan. The Executioner took it.

"Ryan tells me you have something to say," Stahl said.

"'Freedom,' Senator, just 'Freedom.' One of those words that means different things to different people. In your case it's the magic word that opens files."

The silence that followed gave Bolan more than hope. It presented him with a chance for them all to walk away from this alive, and that was worth a great deal.

"Put Ryan back on." Stahl's tone was flat. Cold.

Bolan handed the cell phone back to Cal Ryan.

"Ryan."

"Bring them all back."

"All of them?"

"Yes. We may need persuasion to convince Buchanan he should cooperate with us. If we have these others available, it might help to make him see sense. They might also be able to tell us how much others might know about our operation. Especially Belasko."

"Okay, Senator. We'll be moving out shortly."

"Remember, Ryan, we need them alive."

Ryan cut the call, then turned to stare at Bolan.

"He wants you all delivered alive." Ryan shrugged. "Beats the hell out of me, but he's the man, so he gets what he wants. He says alive, so it's alive you'll be. But he didn't say anything about getting bruised in transit."

Bolan realized what he meant too late. The M-16 in Ryan's hands swung up and around, clubbing him across the side of the head. The hard blow sent Bolan reeling. Before he could defend himself, Ryan was on him, casting aside the rifle to use his big fists. Brutal blows to his face and body sent the Executioner back against the wall. Still dazed from the rifle blow he struggled to fight back. He didn't succeed. Ryan hit hard and with little mercy. His attack was savage. By the time he was done, Ryan was out of breath and his knuckles were raw. Bolan, slumped back against the wall, had refused to go down. His face was bloody, his body aflame with pain. He felt rough hands grab his arms, hauling him upright. He shook his head to clear the fog of pain from his head and the blood from his eyes. He focused on Ryan's sweating face, stubbornly staring the other man down. Ryan raised a large fist, flexing his bleeding knuckles, lips curling back from his teeth.

"This isn't finished yet, Belasko."

Bolan didn't answer, but his expression remained defiant, and Ryan got the message.

Damned right it isn't over.

CONCEALED IN deep brush just beyond the lodge, Tang Mau had watched the larger force of armed men advance on the building and file inside.

He was the sole survivor of Chosan's team. Being ordered to stay outside the lodge when the others entered had saved his life. He had heard and seen the killing of his comrades. Realizing there were too many inside the lodge, he had dropped to the wet ground, crawling quickly away from the lodge. He had barely managed to slide into the deeper cover when the armed men had closed in on the lodge and entered the building.

Tang moved farther away, distancing himself from the lodge. The mission was over. Their task hadn't been fulfilled. His only problem now was getting away from the area, back to the helicopter where he would be able to make contact with Shao Yeung and inform him what had happened. There was nothing else he could do. He was alone in a strange country, with few who could help him. If he could return to Seattle and the freighter, he might have a chance. That didn't seem likely. So all he could do was to call Shao and ask for his help.

Over the next few hours Tang retraced the route back down the mountain, hoping to locate the helicopter if it was still there. The weather was still bad. Rain and wind. The darkness. Tang still carried his Uzi and he gripped the weapon tightly. At least he had that if he was confronted by anyone hostile.

He found the helicopter just before dawn. He had come in by a circuitous route, more by accident than by design. He could hardly believe his eyes when he broke through into the clearing and the helicopter was sitting there. Tang couldn't see the pilot at first, but as he neared the machine he made out the young Chinese in one of the passenger seats at the rear of the cabin. The pilot was sitting with his head back, and Tang realized he was asleep. He opened the rear door and saw straightaway that the pilot was handcuffed to the seat frame. Panic made him step back, bringing the Uzi into play as he looked around. He saw nothing, heard nothing.

Tang reached out to shake the pilot's shoulder. The man jerked awake, his eyes wide with alarm until he recognized Tang.

"What has happened?" Tang demanded.

"Two American agents found me. They handcuffed me, then went up into the mountains." The pilot checked out the area. "Where are the others? Chosan Xiang?"

"They are dead. It all went wrong. There were others there. An armed team of Americans. When Chosan and the others went inside, they were shot immediately. I only just managed to escape myself. We should leave quickly before anyone else comes."

"Can you fly this thing?" the pilot asked.

"I'm not a pilot."

"Then get me out of these handcuffs or we won't be going anywhere."

The pilot told Tang where to find the toolbox. From it Tang took bolt cutters and after some struggle he managed to cut the chain that held the cuffs. The pilot went to his flight seat and began the warm-up sequence.

Tang located the cell phone that had been left in the helicopter. He knew it had a number to connect him with Shao Yeung. He located the speed-dial list and found the number. It rang for some time before it was answered. Tang recognized the voice on the other end.

"Shao Yeung, this is Tang."

SHAO YEUNG FELT his spirits sink as Tang told him what had happened. Apart from the failure to kill Buchanan and Kaplan was the death of Chosan Xiang. It was a deep loss as far as Shao was concerned. An unnecessary loss and a sad one. Granted he and Chosan had only been involved for a short time. Even so Shao felt as if he had lost a good friend. Chosan had been a good man and soldier. The mission that had brought them all the way to America had been important. It had also been riddled with difficulties. The bitter thing was that Chosan had gotten so close to success.

Shao also thought about General Tung. He wasn't going to be pleased at all. Both attempts to eradicate Zero had come to nothing. Tung would be enraged. If anyone was standing too close when he received the news they would feel his anger. Shao would be on Tung's list, as well. As the only top-ranking survivor, he would carry the responsibility. The thought made Shao tremble. He was going to have to carefully consider his options.

"Tang, can you get back to Seattle?"

"I don't know."

"Will your pilot bring you?"

"I will ask."

"I will wait for you here if the ship leaves. I can arrange for us to stay somewhere. There is money available."

"All right. I will try and get back. Shao Yeung, thank you."

YEUNG PUT DOWN the cell phone. He wandered around the cabin, his mind busy with things he needed to do. Almost without conscious effort he picked up the envelope Chosan had handed to him before leaving.

"Open this and do exactly what it tells you only if I don't return," Chosan had told him.

Yeung opened the envelope and took out the single, thin sheet of paper. It was covered in Chinese characters, neatly brushed in the traditional style.

Yeung read the note. "If I am unable to carry this out, do it for me, my friend, Shao Yeung." A slow smile crossed his lips. It was typical of Chosan not to forget to pay a debt. He immediately picked up his cell phone and called the number Chosan had written down. When it was answered he identified himself by the name Chosan had instructed, relayed Chosan's message word for word, and promised to deposit the required amount of money to the noted account number. The man on the other end of the line thanked Shao for his call and broke the connection. There was nothing else to do. The man he had called was already in possession of an envelope that contained a photograph and certain details. As Chosan had requested, Shao destroyed the note.

He carried on with his own arrangements, which in the light of current events, confirmed to Shao that it would be wiser to stay in America rather than return to China. Until he had time to work out his own future Shao Yeung would adopt the identity on his ship's papers and find himself a new occupation. He had access to substantial money, and as Chosan himself had been at pains to point out, with money anything was possible in the United States. Shao Yeung decided it might be interesting to find out if that was really true.

CHAPTER TWELVE

SAC Corporate HQ, Maryland

Mack Bolan looked down on the vast spread of the manufacturing facility as the helicopter swung in for a landing. Immediately in front was the main administration building. Beyond the main building the manufacturing shops stood in isolation, surrounded by landscaped areas of trees and bushes, swathes of carefully tended lawns. The entire complex looked more like a hospital than a factory developing and producing an array of weapons ranging from .22 rifles, through heavy artillery, to the latest concepts in missile technology.

The helicopter overflew the main complex, dropping lower as it skirted the warehouse and freight yard at the rear of the site. Deeper into the site was a large, low structure. It had a stark, no-frills appearance and as the Bell Iroquois touched down on a large concrete pad fronting this building, Bolan saw the sign in front of it.

The sign stated SAC Research & Development—
Strictly Out of Bounds.

As the helicopter touched the pad, the jolt made Claire
Valens sit upright. She groaned as her stiff joints protested.
Restriction on her wrists made her look down. She was
bound by plastic cuffs, as were the rest of the captives.
She saw the red marks on her skin where the plastic loops
had chafed her and she muttered something under her
breath.

Bolan had seen this and failed to hold back a faint
grin. Even now Valens was putting up resistance.

He glanced around the cabin at the others.

Riba had his head back, his eyes almost closed, as if
he were dozing. Bolan knew otherwise. The man was
taking stock, watching and waiting.

Valens's partner, Byrde, had an angry expression on his
face. He hadn't liked the surrender, despite accepting it had
been the only sensible thing to do at the time. Bolan hoped
he wouldn't do anything without thinking it through.

Directly across from Bolan were Buchanan and Kaplan. They had said little during the flight. The soldier had
kept a close watch on Buchanan. The man looked to be
in a bad way. Weary, his face taking on a pale, unhealthy
pallor, Buchanan didn't look like a man capable of taking on something as complex as Zero. Next to him Saul
Kaplan was a man out of his depth. The events at the lodge
and the subsequent flight across country had driven him
into a shell of self-protection. He was a frightened man.

Bolan himself had absorbed the discomfort of the

flight without a word. His face and body ached from
Ryan's attack. It wasn't the first time Bolan had taken
a beating, and it wouldn't be the last. It hurt, but he bore
that, and at least it affirmed he was still alive. And life
was too precious to let go of. There were too many
things he had to do in this world. The next was going
to have to wait—for a long time if Mack Bolan had any
say in the matter.

The moment the helicopter made contact, one of
Ryan's men slid open the door and jumped out. More of
the armed team followed and they formed a line,
weapons at the ready, as Bolan and the others were
herded outside. When the remainder of Ryan's team had
exited the helicopter, they formed an escort around their
captives and pushed them toward the entrance to the
R&D building. Ryan was at the head of the line. He
paused at the doors and produced a swipe card he used
to activate and open the smoked-glass sliding doors. They
all stepped inside, the doors sliding shut behind them.

Ryan walked to the single elevator doors and used
his swipe card again.

Bolan made a mental note of that. He also watched
where Ryan pocketed the card.

The elevator was large enough to accommodate
them all. When Ryan punched the lower button on the
panel, the elevator dropped quickly. The trip was short,
so the car hadn't gone too deep. The doors slid open,
and they emerged onto one of the lower levels of the
R&D complex.

A single corridor stretched away from them. It appeared to go on for a considerable distance, fluorescent lights throwing harsh white light across the smooth walls and floor. Doors led off on both sides of the corridor at regular intervals. It was quiet. The air was fresh and cool, being pumped in through vents in the ceiling.

"You can go to your rooms later," Ryan said, grinning as if he had just made a humorous comment.

"I hope they run out soon," Valens said.

Ryan glanced at her. "Say what?"

"Your witty remarks. I don't know how long I can take them without throwing up."

Ryan was still grinning when he launched a looping backhand that cracked against the side of Valens's face. She stumbled, her eyes cold as she stared at Ryan.

"More where that came from," Ryan said.

"One of your specialties," Bolan said quietly. "Hitting defenseless women."

Ryan looked across at him. "A man needs a pastime."

"I've seen the evidence. After the woman was pulled out of the water."

"Hell, don't tell me that brought you into this?"

"It helped."

"Goddamned knight in shining armor," Ryan said. "Now I heard it all."

He moved on along the corridor. Reaching a pair of double doors, Ryan waited as they swung open, then stepped aside as his men took Bolan and the others into the room beyond.

It was fitted out as an office, with a large desk and high leather swivel chair. On the plain walls were large prints of SAC ordnance. Down one side was a computer layout, with a number of large-screen monitors and peripheral equipment.

Seated behind the desk was a man Bolan recognized from TV and newspaper images.

Colonel Orin Stengard.

He wore civilian clothing and had a large mug of coffee in one hand. As the room filled up, Stengard pushed the chair back from the desk and stood. On his feet he was an impressive figure: ramrod straight with good shoulders and a lean physique. He stepped around the desk and surveyed the captives like a man assessing prize cattle. Finally satisfied, he turned to Ryan, who was standing to attention.

"At ease, Cal. We're not on review."

Ryan relaxed. "As requested, Colonel. Major Douglas Buchanan, United States Air Force, and Dr. Saul Kaplan, Zero Option project."

"Proud to meet you, son," Stengard said, stepping up to Buchanan. "Hell of a thing you're doing for your country. Can't say I understand how it all works, but I'm sure the good doctor will explain."

"Maybe *I* should clarify something, Colonel Stengard," Buchanan said. "What I volunteered to do was for the elected government of this country. As far as I recollect, your name never came up as part of the project. Now, I can't speak for Saul Kaplan, but I'm pretty sure he'll tell you to go to hell, as well."

Stengard's booming laugh filled the room. "See, Cal, that's just what I'd expect from a man of Major Buchanan's stature. He's that close to getting himself shot for insubordination, and he still has the guts to stand firm. Resolve. Something we're short of in this country."

"And that's something you know all about is it, Stengard?" Bolan asked. "Resolve? Integrity? Do what has to be done and be damned who gets hurt in the process?"

Stengard turned sharply to face the tall man in black.

"Belasko, Colonel," Ryan said. "The one who gave us all the trouble."

"I've been hearing about you. Caused us a deal of inconvenience."

"My heart bleeds for you, Stengard."

"'Colonel' to you, Belasko," Ryan said, stepping in close.

Stengard put up a restraining hand. "Take it easy, Cal. Mr. Belasko is allowed his indiscretions. To answer your accusation, yes, I do have the resolve and the integrity to get done what needs to be done."

"At least we have that in common."

"And an optimist, as well. I admire that, Belasko. Then you'll understand what we're trying to do here. Get this country back on its feet. Build up its strength so none of those leeches out there can back us into a corner. It's time we made America great again. Time was the whole world listened when we talked. Now they smile in our faces, take our aid, then bomb us. Attack us within our own borders. Burn the American flag in their rat-infested streets and call *us* cowards and murderers. It's time we picked up the goddamned ball and showed them they can't treat the United States like so much dog shit on the soles of their shoes."

"And it's going to take you and Senator Stahl to do it?"

"Damned right it is, son. I'll tell you something else for free. We *will* do it."

"Not without Zero," Saul Kaplan said.

Stengard faced him, smiling, the cold, unblinking smile of the snake poised to strike.

"Which is why you and Major Buchanan are here. The keys that will turn Zero on and give us the means to send our enemies ducking for cover."

"Oh, please."

"Agent Valens. I've been hearing so much about you. Please, let's hear your contribution."

"I don't like swearing in mixed company," Valens said sharply.

"Colonel, she's got a smart mouth. You want me to—"

"Cal, let the lady speak. Remember this is still a democracy."

"As long as Zero stays switched off," Valens said. "The minute you and that lame-excuse senator get it back online we're all going to be in deep trouble."

"Are you suggesting we'll betray the American people?"

"Colonel, do I look that stupid? If I thought for a

minute you might get this circus off the ground, I'd
throw myself in front of the first train I could find."

"We have a disbeliever in our midst."

"Make that two," Joshua Riba said.

One of the assault team close to Riba turned and
drove the butt of his weapon into the man's ribs. Riba
bent double, coughing harshly.

"Enough of this crap," Stengard said. "Cal, get Buchanan and Kaplan down to the process room. It's time
we got moving on this. Have the others put in the observation room next door so they can see what's going on."

BOLAN WAS PUSHED into the observation room as the doors
slid open. It was a plain room. No furniture. The floor was
made of soft, sound-absorbing tiles. The others were
alongside him. As the door slid shut behind them, the far
wall lit up and revealed itself to be a floor-to-ceiling tough-
ened-glass sheet. It allowed them to see into the next room.

That one was double the size. One wall was fitted out
with an array of electronic panels and computer sta-
tions. Mobile pieces of equipment were lined up against
one end wall. The room gave the impression of an operating theater. It had a sterile look to it. Banks of lights
on flexible arms were suspended from the ceiling. The
effect was completed by what looked, at first sight, to
be an operating table.

Bolan moved closer to the glass screen that separated
the two rooms. He was looking closely at the operating
table. Only it wasn't an operating table. It was more like

a body-length adjustable recliner. There were arms at the sides, with short tubes protruding from the covering. There were more tubes coming up through the base padding, and where the head would rest was a shallow skull-shaped cap on a flexible arm.

"Jesus, it's the biocouch," Jackson Byrde said, his tone almost reverential.

Bolan recalled reading about it in the extensive reams of data the President had given him after his visit with Hal Brognola.

The biocouch, the point of transition where Doug Buchanan and the control center of the Zero platform would merge into a single, interdependent unit. The implants inside Buchanan's body would lock in and blend with those installed within the biocouch. This would create the environment and the catalyst that would form the human-machine biosynthesis coupling. The process would take a few hours as the couch began to feed Buchanan the synthetic fluids and neuro-wave transmissions. The evolvement of Doug Buchanan into Buchanan-Zero would culminate in his being able to take full control of the platform's functions via the electronic chips in his skull. They would only activate once the transition had completed successfully.

"How the hell did they—?"

"You are wondering how we got out hands on a biocouch?"

Stengard had followed them into the observation room, standing at the back as they observed Buchanan and Kaplan enter the room. A four-man team of technicians followed them in, and two armed guards stood against one of the walls.

"My contact in the Pentagon, who has unfortunately decided to opt out of our relationship, got the construction details as soon as the attack on the New Mexico site took place. We had to move fast before the shock of the strike wore off. As soon as that happened, there was a lockdown on everything to do with Zero, but we had what we needed."

"As far as you knew, Buchanan was dead," Byrde said.

"We had a few bad moments over that, I admit. Then common sense returned and told us the government would resurrect Zero. We could wait if we had to. But chance favored us and Doug Buchanan showed up again. Once the development team had the schematics it didn't take them long to construct a replica. We're very proud of it and the Room, as we call next door."

Bolan was observing the action through the glass. Both Kaplan and Buchanan were standing by the couch, obviously aware of what its presence indicated. Buchanan was slowly shaking his head.

The click of a sound system coming on reached the observation room. One of the white-coated techs turned to face Stengard.

"First problem, Colonel. Major Buchanan says he will not cooperate."

"I was afraid of that, Dr. Menard. Would you bring Major Buchanan to the glass, please."

The man named Menard went to Buchanan and took his arm, moving him across the room until he was standing at the glass.

Stengard faced him through the screen.

"Major Buchanan, what seems to be the problem?"

"You can't initiate Zero's activation without me, and I refuse to do what you want. This is not what Zero was created for and you damned well know, Colonel. The hell with you and your treason. I'll die first before helping you and that maniac Stahl."

"I don't think *your* dying will be necessary, Major. However, I see no alternative to showing you I mean business."

Stengard turned and crossed to where Ryan was standing. He stood close to the man for a moment, then returned to his former position, arms folded across his chest, close to where Jackson Byrde was positioned in front of the glass screen.

"Major Buchanan, this is no time for grand gestures. Believe me when I say I am not going to accept your refusal. You are not in command here. I am, and I say who lives and who dies."

Stengard unfolded his arms. In his right hand was one of the Glock 21 pistols. Stengard turned, raised the weapon and pressed the muzzle against the side of Jackson Byrde's head. He pulled the trigger three times in rapid succession, sending a trio of 9 mm slugs into Byrde's skull. The rounds cored in to demolish Byrde's brain, blowing out the other side in a spurt of red that spattered the window glass and splashed the side of Joshua Riba's jacket. Byrde slumped to his knees, then forward on his face, body jerking in final spasms.

"No!"

Valens launched herself across the room, despite her bound hands, and went for Stengard. She would have reached him if one of Stengard's men hadn't moved to confront her, his M-16 leveled at her chest.

"You can be next, Agent Valens," Stengard announced, the Glock leveled at her head. "You can join your partner."

"Ex-partner," Ryan said.

Stengard turned to the window and confronted Buchanan.

"Do we understand each other, Major? I have three more people here with me. I'm prepared to sacrifice each one of them until you see sense. Their lives are in your hands. If their deaths don't change your mind, I'm sure we can find further volunteers."

Doug Buchanan leaned against the window, his hands pressed against the cool surface as he stared down at Jackson Byrde's corpse and then across at Claire Valens. Tears were running down her pale, lovely face as she took in what had just happened so quickly and without any kind of warning.

"Major Buchanan, do not fuck with me. I am willing to sacrifice as many as it takes if you still need convincing. In the end it rests in your hands."

Buchanan turned from the glass and walked to the

biocouch. Dr. Menard and his assistants moved to strip off his clothing and replace it with a thin, body-hugging skin suit that had cutaways for the implant introduction. When the skin suit was in place, they helped position Buchanan on the biocouch.

"We're ready," Menard said over the intercom.

Stengard nodded. "Kaplan, time to go to work. As we were fortunate to locate you, we can use your expertise."

Saul Kaplan stood beside Buchanan, talking quietly to him as Menard and his team checked that Buchanan was fully settled before they activated the transition sequence.

A number of times Menard asked Kaplan questions. Finally Kaplan himself moved to the main computer station and keyed in codes that activated the process.

Bolan had remained in his earlier position, watching Buchanan. At first nothing seemed to be happening. The major appeared to be resting, his eyes closed, his breathing deep and regular. Then implant probes slid from the depths of the couch and at the same time the implants that had been inserted into Buchanan broke through the outer layers of skin and moved with precise motions toward the couch links. Despite his misgivings, Bolan found himself held by the pure fascination of this bonding of man and machine. He knew he was seeing something totally new. A startling and surprising advance in human technology. Doug Buchanan had proved he was a man willing to step beyond the normal bounds of mankind's need to explore his potential.

The window turned black, the sound from the Room shutting off.

"Ryan, get these people out of here now," Stengard said. "When Stahl arrives he wants to talk to Belasko. Make sure the other two are secured. I'm sure they have a lot to think about."

"Be a damned sight better if we got rid of them."

Stengard shook his head. "Not yet. They could still be of use if Buchanan or Kaplan find their consciences troubling them. Understand, Cal? Just lock them up for now."

"Yes, Colonel."

Ryan ordered a team to remove Valens and Riba, then he and another of his men turned to Bolan.

"Get someone to deal with that," Stengard said, indicating Byrde's body.

He turned his attention to Bolan. "A little persuasion and we prevail, Mr. Belasko."

"Enjoy it while you can," Bolan replied, his tone low and emotionless.

"Do I detect a threat there, son?"

"You understand what I'm saying."

Stengard straightened, his back ramrod stiff.

"I admire your guts, son. But don't try to fool me. I've been a soldier too long."

"And an insult to every American who ever wore his or her country's uniform."

Stengard's face darkened. He restrained himself with difficulty.

"You criticize *me?* Colonel Orin Stengard? Do you really understand what I've done for this country? How many times I've put myself on the line? And the men under me. We did everything they ever asked. And more. But the lily-whites in office want to weaken us. Strip us of everything America ever stood for. Jesus Christ, Belasko, we have to bend our knee to every pacifist, liberal, and PC loon whoever raised his sissy voice above a whisper. My God, man, have you taken at look at the country? All we do now is let the rest of the world sponge off us. At home people are gutless and can't even make it through the day without a counselor to hold their pasty hands. Spill a cup of coffee in your lap. Sue the coffee shop. Don't like the way someone talks to you at work? Sue the boss for work-related stress. What the hell is going on? America used to be a nation of independent, hard-working people who got on with life and gave the finger to anyone who tried to push them around. Not anymore. The government is screwing around with this country. It's time we took America back and showed the people the right way to do it."

"The Eric Stahl way? And your way? Use Zero to blackmail your way into power? Show the world America has its finger on the trigger? Do it our way or we'll put you out of business? How long before the curfews in U.S. cities? Go in and pick out the undesirables. Next thing it'll be the wrong color hair. Or eyes. I understand Stahl's politics, and frankly, Colonel Stengard, they're the worst thing that could happen to this country."

"Get this man out of my sight, Cal. Put him in a room and lock the door. Keep someone with him, because I don't trust him left on his own."

Ryan caught hold of Bolan's sleeve and dragged him across the room, his armed man close behind. The door slid shut, leaving Bolan in the deserted corridor with Ryan and his partner.

"Get moving," Ryan said.

Stepping behind Bolan, he raised a booted foot and placed it against Bolan's hip, shoving hard. The soldier stumbled. The armed man with him used the butt of his M-16 to strike their captive between his shoulders.

"Hey, Ryan, you think this asshole was ever in the military?"

"You never know. They'll take anybody these days."

Bolan was marched along the corridor to a short flight of steps. They emerged in another featureless passage, this one illuminated by soft strip lights.

"Hold it," Ryan said.

He shoved past Bolan to use a key card to open the sliding door. Out the corner of his eye Bolan saw Ryan hand the card to the armed guard.

"Inside, Belasko."

The room had a table and a number of metal-framed chairs. There was a water cooler and a coffee vending machine against one wall. It had the sterile appearance of a conference room.

"Stahl should be here in a while. Just keep him here."

Ryan turned and strode out of the room. The door slid shut, leaving Bolan alone with the armed guard.

"Go park your ass over there."

Bolan did as he was told. He sat on one of the chairs at the table, facing straight ahead. The guard took a chair at the far end of the table, his M-16 resting on his lap. After a few minutes the guard stirred restlessly. He reached up to push his cap to the back of his head, his eyes beginning to wander.

Bolan remained still.

The guard cleared his throat. Fiddled with the rifle. It was obvious he wasn't a regular serviceman. He might have been at one time, but now he would be on Stengard's mercenary list, a man who had lost his edge when it came to remaining impassive when left alone to guard a prisoner. He was more used to lazing around with his ex-service buddies, living on the pay he'd earned from his last contract.

No more than five or six minutes had elapsed when the guard pushed his chair back from the table and stood. He moved around the table and crossed to where the coffee machine stood. He looked it over, deciding he didn't have to pay for a drink, then peered at the instructions.

The guard was no more than three chairs away from where Bolan sat motionless, offering no resistance. He wedged the M-16 under his left arm and used his right to order his drink. The machine made soft sounds. The plastic cup dropped and the liquid flowed in. The machine clicked as the delivery was completed. Leaning over so he could clearly see the plastic cup, the guard made to take it out from the delivery recess. He made a sharp sound as the hot cup stung his fingers, then reached up to grasp it by the thicker lip at the top. It diverted his attention from Bolan for no more than a few seconds....

The guard was lifting the cup, turning his head to check his prisoner, when he heard a whisper of sound. He let go of the cup, maneuvering the M-16 into position. He got the impression of something dark, moving extremely quickly, and then Bolan was on him. The Executioner hit with the speed of a striking snake, dropping his bound wrists over the guard's head and yanking back hard against the man's throat. Bolan's right knee came up, ramming into the guard's lower spine with savage force. The guard gasped as Bolan's encircling wrists snapped tight against his throat, crushing the windpipe and closing with a viselike grip. Bolan increased the pressure of his knee to the spine. The guard began to choke, spitting bubbles of froth. The M-16 slipped from his grasp, the rubberized floor absorbing the sound. The guard reached up, fingers clawing at the arms around his neck. He began to thrash about, his movements uncoordinated. The color of his face darkened and his eyes stared wildly about. Bolan maintained his grip for the next long minute. The struggles slowed. The jerking eased, and the harsh breathing was reduced to a final, whispering sigh.

Bolan lowered the dead man to the floor. He located the sheathed knife strapped to the right thigh. He slipped it from the leather scabbard, reversed it in his clasped hands and slid the blade, cutting edge uppermost against the strip of the plastic cuffs. It took a minute of steady concentration, keeping the pressure of the blade against the loop, but the gentle sawing action eventually severed the plastic. Bolan rubbed at his wrists to aid the flow of blood to them.

He knelt beside the body and unclipped the combat harness the man wore. It held extra magazines for the M-16. Bolan slipped into the harness. He took the long-peaked black cap and put it on pulling it over his eyes. His disguise wasn't going to fool anyone for long. The fact he wore a blacksuit, of a slightly different design to Ryan's team, would help. He took the sheath for the knife and fastened it to his own leg, replacing and clipping the knife back in place. A search of the dead man's combat suit yielded the key card. Bolan picked up the M-16 and ejected the magazine, checking it. Then he snapped it back in place, cocking the rifle.

Bolan headed for the door. He raised the key card, pausing for a fraction of a second before he inserted it in the slot.

He had no idea what he might find when he stepped out of the room, but he was ready for anything.

Bolan was on a roll. He was armed and dangerous, in no mood for compromise. And if Colonel Orin Stengard believed America was going soft, it was because he hadn't witnessed Mack Bolan in killing mode.

The door slid open, presenting Bolan with an empty passage and a choice of which way to go. It wasn't a difficult one.

Bolan turned and headed back the way he had been brought in—to the upper level and a face-off with his adversaries.

CHAPTER THIRTEEN

Joshua Riba crossed the locked room and stood over Claire Valens. She was sitting on a low seat pushed back against the bare wall, her arms folded across her chest, staring vacantly at the wall on the other side of the room. He crouched in front of her, staring into her eyes.

"When an Apache dies, it isn't seen as a time to blind the eyes to what went before. We look back at the good times. Happier days when the person was alive. We remember the words he spoke, the laughter. While you keep those things in your heart, the person never dies. He is always with you. A man can live forever if his friends stay loyal to his being and his spirit. Jackson Byrde made you laugh. I see that. He was a strong partner, too."

Valens raised her eyes. "He was all that and more. I'm going to miss him."

"But you will not forget him?"

"I hope not. But in a year? Two? Will I still have the same strong feelings?"

"I believe in the Apache way. It says that a true friend will always have a place in their heart for one who has ascended to the spirit world. Times are you will have other things on your mind. But in the quiet times you *will* think of him. He has been part of your life. He will always be part of your life. As long as he has that, Jackson Byrde will never truly die."

Valens reached out to grasp one of his strong hands. "Thanks for that." She held him for a moment, then straightened. "Jackson would be chasing me to get off my butt and do something. It's time we did."

She pushed to her feet and began to pace the room, checking out every section, steadily and thoroughly.

"Pretty solid," Riba commented.

"But not built to be a prison cell," Valens pointed out.

"I guess not."

Riba followed her gaze as she looked up at the ceiling and the square air vent.

"What do you think?"

"Worth a look," Riba said.

They dragged one of the chairs directly under the vent. Riba stepped on the chair and reached up to push his fingers through the vent slots. Once he had a good hold, he tested the fixture. It had no screws, simply tabs that clipped into place. He pulled hard, and the vent came away in his hand. Riba stuck his head through the hole and peered along the box section that vanished into

the distance. It wasn't totally dark. There was faint il-
lumination coming from the strip lighting set in the
ceilings that intruded into the aluminum box sections.

"I can make it," Valens said as Joshua stepped down
off the chair.

The man patted his chest. "I can't. No way I'll haul
myself in there." He took her shoulders. "You sure you
want to do this?"

"Damned right I do."

"Okay." Riba grinned suddenly. "I'll stay here and
hold the fort."

"Let's do it."

Valens stepped onto the chair, reaching up to grasp
the inner edge of the vent. As soon as her feet lifted from
the chair, Riba stepped up, caught hold of her around
her waist and boosted her up. Valens pulled herself into
the vent. The size of the box section was large enough
to allow her to crawl on hands and knees.

"You okay?" Joshua asked.

"Fine."

"Take care."

Riba watched her move along the section until she
was swallowed in the shadows. He lowered his head and
shoulders, placed the vent back in place and locked it
in position. He put the chair back where it had come
from, then squatted with his back to the wall, facing the
door, and waited.

THE ROOM WAS nearly silent—the soft hum of electronic equipment was coupled with the gentle sound of

data sheets coming off the printer. The air was cool, a feather touch against the skin as it was pushed out of the air-conditioning units.

Saul Kaplan moved from checking readout data to stand over Doug Buchanan. The process had taken over fully now, and Buchanan's vital signs had told Kaplan he was reacting favorably. Although the initial signs were good, Kaplan found he was unable to gain any kind of comfort from them. The Zero concept had taken second place to his concern over Buchanan's experience since the attack on the New Mexican facility. Kaplan was unable to dismiss what he considered his failure to protect Buchanan. Walking out of the project had been a weakness. Now he admitted to himself that he should have stayed and fought the Air Force personnel trying to take away his control. He also realized he couldn't turn back time. What had happened was fact. Kaplan's only salvation rested on his being with Buchanan now, and making certain that the process went well.

Buchanan opened his eyes and stared up at Kaplan. The ongoing process combining fluid transfers and the activation of the implants and electronic generation of the neural network had drawn him into a state of balanced euphoria. He saw his surroundings through a soft haze of drowsiness. He felt better than he had for some while. His pain and discomfort had been drawn away. He felt rested, comfortable, concerns evaporated. He sensed Kaplan's presence and turned his head to gaze up at his friend.

"Saul, why the bad-day expression? You should be a happy man."

"Why? Because I got you into this mess."

Buchanan smiled. "They haven't beaten us yet."

"Doug, how are you feeling? Forget about me and my hang-ups. I need to get your feedback on the process."

"It's a good way to get rid of a headache. Saul, I feel great. No pain. No worries. What do the machines tell you?"

"They agree. The transition seems to be working. Your implants and those in the couch are working in harmony. Reciprocation is developing. The fluid transfer is almost complete. Your neural net will be online in the next couple of hours."

"Stengard is going to be waiting. The minute he knows we have a link with the platform, he's going to try and break into the control core."

"I may have a way around that. Doug, we have to remove the possibility of them overriding your link with Zero. *We* have to stay in command."

MACK BOLAN MADE his way along the passage. He reached the stairs, picking up footsteps in the corridor above him. Bolan pulled back as an armed figure began to descend. The Executioner caught a glimpse of a blacksuit, combat harness and peaked cap.

One of Ryan's assault team.

The man had his M-16 slung. The Executioner leaned his own rifle against the wall and drew the sheathed knife. He let the guy reach the bottom of the steps and turn into the passage before he moved up behind him, left hand snaking around the guy's body to clamp tightly over his mouth. The keen blade of the knife arced up and opened the exposed throat. Left to right, deep, severing everything in its path. The man reacted violently, hands reaching up to the gaping wound. All he found was cut flesh and a surging flood of warm blood that wet his hands and spilled down his blacksuit. He kicked and wriggled, his whole body going into a frantic dance of death. Bolan held him tight, fingers digging into the flesh of his face as he restrained the dying man. He didn't slacken his grip until the guy's struggles weakened and finally ceased. Bolan lowered him to the floor.

Sheathing his knife, Bolan bent over the dead man and relieved him of the extra magazines he carried for the M-16. Bolan slipped them into the zip pockets of his own blacksuit. He picked up his own rifle and went up the stairs quickly.

There was no easy way to do what he had to. Stengard and Ryan were commanding a ruthless regime here. Their intentions were obvious. Buchanan and Kaplan were the only ones safe from harm. At least until Stengard and inevitably, Stahl, had control of Zero. The moment they had that, no one would be safe. And that lack of security would extend from this isolated facility to become a global concern. Zero in the hands of Stahl and Stengard wasn't a matter to be treated lightly.

The main corridor stretched in both directions. Bolan could identify where Buchanan and Kaplan were being held. He didn't know where Riba and Valens had been taken. His main concern was Ryan and his team. He needed to trim them down to where they were no longer a tangible threat. If Buchanan hadn't been involved, Bolan could have aimed his strike at the building, too, creating a diversion that would have forced Ryan and his people into the open. That was out of the question. Bolan had no idea of Buchanan's dependency on the building's power source to maintain his biocouch. Taking out the power supply might kill him.

"*Hey,*" someone yelled behind Bolan.

He turned and saw one of Ryan's blacksuits coming down the corridor. The man was raising his M-16.

"You're not—"

Bolan triggered his M-16 and sent a 3-round burst into the man. The 5.56 mm slugs whipped the guy around and bounced him off the wall. He left a bloody smear on the plain wall as he slithered to the floor.

CRAWLING THROUGH the air system, Claire Valens heard the burst of gunfire. It was close. She wondered who had caused it. She had been moving for some distance now. Maybe it was time she got her feet back on the ground, she decided.

"WHAT WAS THAT?" Kaplan asked.

Menard shook his head.

"Doesn't concern us," he said. "We stay here."

"*I'm* not going anywhere," Buchanan pointed out.

Menard made his way back to the computer station, Kaplan close behind.

"Are these readings correct?"

Kaplan studied the figures. "Don't worry about the drop here and there. It's to be expected. It won't last long. When Doug's system starts to actually work with the couch's built-in electronic chip, his neural net will come in parallel. When that happens, we will know the melding has taken successfully."

Menard cleared his throat. "Dr. Kaplan, I know that apologizing doesn't absolve me of what I've done. I had little choice. Both Stengard and Stahl, they threatened me and my team. They said that if we didn't work on this project, we would die. Our families, as well. Stengard has a way of making you believe him. The way he killed that man today. If I hadn't been convinced before, that did it. How can you plead with someone like that?"

"You don't," Kaplan said. "As for apologizing... don't worry. Just stand in line behind me. Right now I have enough apologizing to do for all of us."

RIBA HEARD the door make a soft sound. It began to slide open and an armed blacksuit stepped through, into the room.

The Apache stepped away from the wall, the underside of his left hand slamming against the probing M-16 and knocking it up out of harm's way. He continued his move, swinging a powerful right fist into the face of the startled blacksuit. The sound of the blow was loud, the man's jawbone skewing sideways as it was driven out of its sockets. Riba followed up with a crippling blow to the stomach and, as the guy buckled over, Riba smashed his knee up into his face. Bone crunched and blood flew in a glistening spray as the guy went down on the floor. Riba snatched up the discarded M-16, using the butt to crack down on the guy's skull. He bent over briefly to snatch a couple of extra magazines from the harness, then ducked out the door and went looking for trouble. He'd heard gunfire short minutes earlier and knew it was Belasko kicking ass. He was sure the big guy could use some company.

THE CORRIDOR ENDED with a left turn. To Bolan's right were double swing doors, each with a small window. As he peered through, he saw a number of blacksuits already reaching for their weapons as they reacted to the triburst.

The layout of the large room beyond the doors showed the canteen area. Rows of tables and chairs, the kitchen at the far end, with a serving counter in front. There were lights on in the kitchen, but no staff. Bolan assumed Ryan's team would be looking after their own food preparation.

Eating was the last thing on any of their minds as they headed for the doors that would allow them to exit the canteen.

Bolan booted the doors open, the M-16 coming online as he picked his first target and blew the guy off his feet, spilling him back across one of the tables in a haze of red. The guy rolled over the edge and crashed to the floor as Bolan picked an oncoming pair and hit them hard and fast. Dark fragments of blacksuits filled the air as the 5.56 mm slugs hammered home and put the pair down in bloody heaps.

Bolan dropped to a crouch, swinging the M-16 at a figure coming in on his left. The enemy gunner fired first, his shots ripping chunks out of the absorbent floor covering. The Executioner twisted, turning his body to both avoid the line of slugs and to bring him in line with the shooter. Bolan's weapon crackled as he fired off a couple of tribursts, hitting the target at knee height. The guy yelled in pain, his legs giving way, and he crashed down on his face. Bolan hit him with another burst, seeing the prone figure jerk then fall still.

There were three more on the far side of the canteen, seeking cover rather than pushing forward with their attack. Bolan reached the cover of a support pillar and leaned around the corner. He spotted one of the trio working his way behind the serving counter, his own rifle sweeping back and forth as he looked for his vanished target. Bolan waited until the guy raised his head far enough above the level of the counter, then laid a burst into the guy's skull and saw him jerk back.

Combined fire from the two remaining enemy gunners pounded the pillar where Bolan had been hiding.

By this time he had moved on, down on his stomach, crawling under a row of long tables. He had pinpointed the pair, crouching behind a free-standing freezer unit. Bolan raised the rifle, taking steady aim before he hosed a cycle of 3-round bursts into the unit. The unit shuddered under the impact of the slugs. A couple of them went through the unit, distorting as they did, and hit flesh as they emerged. The damaged slugs tore bloody chunks out of the target's right shoulder, impacting against bone and splintering it. The hit guy backed away from the unit, his injury already starting to give him pain. He slumped against the wall, clutching his ruined shoulder, and made an easy target for the soldier's follow-up burst. The wounded man rolled across the wall, starting to bleed from the additional wounds in his lower chest.

Bolan ejected the spent magazine and snapped in a fresh 30-round clip. He cocked the M-16, picking up the sound of movement. He shouldered aside a table, pushing upright and saw the last man advancing across the canteen, his rifle sweeping back and forth as he tried to pinpoint his target.

They locked eyes in the same moment. Bolan had already acquired his shot. He triggered the rifle, dropping his man with a burst that chewed into the guy's chest and put him on the floor.

Bolan turned to leave the canteen. He left behind the stench of powder smoke and spilled blood, and knew it was far from over.

VALENS HAD PEERED through the air vent, checking out the area below. She was in some kind of storage section. There didn't appear to be anyone around. If there was, she would have to deal with them. She worked the vent cover out of the clips and pulled it up beside her, setting it aside. Now she was able to check out the area below with ease. It *was* deserted. She maneuvered herself around and slid from the vent feet first, hanging briefly by her hands before dropping to the floor.

The storage area held little of interest for her. Just boxes and cartons. Valens saw the exit and crossed to the door. It wasn't locked, and she was able to look out at the corridor. She eased the door open, checking both ways. The corridor was empty.

She picked up the crackle of gunfire.

Turning, she made her way along the corridor, seeking the source of the firing.

HEAVY GUNFIRE caught Riba's attention. He located the origin of the fire and turned to make his way there.

As he moved along the corridor, a door ahead opened and someone stepped out.

It was Colonel Orin Stengard. He had an autopistol in one hand. His head turned as he sensed Riba's closeness. The pistol swung around, and Stengard opened fire. The first 9 mm slug hit the wall above Riba's head. The next clipped his left hip. He hit the floor, rolling frantically, steadying himself and returning fire. The bursts from his M-16 ripped chunks out of the plaster wall and gouged holes in the door.

Stengard fired again, ducking back inside the room and dragging the door shut. As the door slammed, Riba cut loose with M-16, the stream of 5.56 mm slugs blowing holes in the door at waist height.

"Damn," he muttered.

Sitting up, he used his rifle to push himself to his feet. His hip was stinging from the bullet clip, blood soaking through his pants.

"Joshua."

It was Bolan. He moved along the corridor to join his comrade, spotting the blood-soaked pant leg.

"You hurt bad?"

"Just a graze. You?"

"Ryan's assault team is down a few men."

"Stengard went in there after we had our little set-to."

"That's one who isn't getting away," Bolan said.

He moved to the bullet-riddled door and tested the handle. The door opened easily. Bolan stepped to the side in case Stengard was inside, waiting for someone to show.

Nothing happened.

Riba braced himself against the wall on the other side of the door.

"Yank that door open and I'll lay down a few loads."

Bolan nodded. He grasped the handle, then pulled the door wide open. Riba triggered several bursts, arcing his muzzle right to left, until the M-16 magazine was empty. The moment he had stopped firing, Bolan went in fast, hitting the floor inside and rolling to the left. He held the M-16 ready for use as he scanned the confines of the room.

It was bare of furniture of any kind.

And there was no one else in the room. He climbed to his feet, double-checking the room.

It was empty.

Colonel Orin Stengard had disappeared.

CHAPTER FOURTEEN

Bolan spotted the exit door on the far side of the room. He sprinted across, flattening against the wall beside it.

"You want me to stay here?" Riba asked.

"Get to where they have Buchanan and Kaplan. Stay close."

"You got it."

As Riba disappeared, Bolan snatched the door handle and pushed it open. He peered out. An empty stretch of corridor lay before him. At the far end an open door showed daylight.

Bolan went down the corridor fast. As he neared the exit door he picked up the sound of raised voices.

VALENS HAD COME around the corner in time to see Orin Stengard pushing open the door that led outside. He had an autopistol in one hand and a transceiver in the other, and he was talking into it rapidly.

She paused at the open door, checking outside.

Wide lawns spread away from the building to a high security fence four hundred yards distant. On the far side of the fence thick woodland hid the facility from sight.

Stengard was standing no more than ten feet from the open door, still talking into the transceiver, the handgun at his side.

Valens picked up the sound of a helicopter coming in toward them. It swooped down from overhead, swinging around to approach the area fifty feet from where Stengard was standing.

It was a drab-colored Boeing CH-47 Chinook, a heavy transport chopper used extensively by the U.S. Army.

Valens wondered why Stengard was calling it in. Reinforcements? Or a means of taking Doug Buchanan and his biocouch away?

The reason was of secondary importance to her. Valens had only one thing on her mind.

The fact that the man standing in front of her had killed her partner. Shot him down in cold blood without a trace of regret, or concern, and for no other reason than to make a point.

Valens allowed she was letting her emotions dictate her actions. She didn't give a damn about that. Just as long as the cold bastard didn't get away with what he had done.

She launched herself from the door, crossing the lawn with long, powerful strides to quickly close in on Stengard.

The beat of the Chinook's twin rotors deadened any sound she might have made, so Stengard didn't know she was there until she slammed into him, the force of her attack knocking him to the ground. He hit face-down, the breath driven from his lungs, the transceiver flipping from his grip. He lay for seconds, stunned by the force that had put him down, and in that time Valens went for his gun hand. The heavy boots she was wearing made good weapons. She pounded down on his gun hand, breaking two fingers, then kicked the gun aside as it slipped from his grasp. As Stengard raised his head, blood streaming from his nose where he had hit the ground, Valens launched a kick that impacted against the side of his head. Stengard gasped at the pain, tasting blood in his mouth. He rolled with the blow and for the first time recognized his attacker. He had no time to register anything else because Valens kicked him again, the toe of her boot catching him on the left cheek, opening a ragged wound that streamed blood down his face. He arced over on his side, trying to ward off her continuing attack and failing. Valens's next kick took him in the stomach, and Stengard almost retched with the pain. The kick turned him on his back, and Stengard kicked out with his own feet and hands, desperately attempting to gain some distance from the enraged woman standing over him.

"Goddamn, you bitch, don't you know who I am?" he managed to blurt out, spitting blood.

"Why don't you tell me? I might be so stunned I'll surrender."

Stengard got his arms under him and pushed into a

half-sitting position. He was struggling for breath. His body hurt and he could feel blood all over his face.

"I could have you arrested and shot for what you've done."

Valens crouched and picked something up off the grass. As she rose, Stengard saw it was his own gun. She turned it so the muzzle was aimed at Stengard.

"I'm glad you brought the subject up, you gutless excuse for a man."

"What are you going to do?" Stengard sneered. "Kill me? A senior officer of the United States Army."

"Really? You could have fooled me."

The Chinook was hovering ten feet off the ground, sideways on. The side door, situated just behind the flight cabin, had been opened to reveal a figure manning an M-60 E-1 machine gun he carried cradled in his arms.

Valens, still in a high state of anger, hadn't even turned to look at the helicopter.

As she raised the pistol she had picked up, Stengard turned toward the Chinook and raised a hand, jerking it in Valens's direction.

BOLAN TOOK IN the whole scene as he came through the open door: Valens standing over Orin Stengard, the pistol in her hands aimed at him; the hovering Chinook with the door gunner arcing the barrel of his M-60 toward Valens.

Bolan raced across the grass, bringing up his M-16. He triggered a couple of bursts, the 5.56 mm slugs clanging against the side of the Chinook, close to the open door. The machine gunner jerked back, losing his aim before he could fire, giving Bolan the added seconds he needed to reach Valens.

He saw her startled expression as he came up to her, moving fast and reaching out with his left arm. Bolan hit her sideways on, the force of their coming together sending them both off balance.

The door gunner regained control and brought his weapon online again, triggering the M-60. A stream of 7.62 mm rounds arced in toward where Bolan and Valens had been standing when the gunner pulled his trigger, tearing up clumps of grass and earth. The thwack of bullets chewing their way into the ground filled Bolan's ears as he rolled Valens and himself clear. He pushed her aside and rose to one knee. Shouldering the M-16, he aimed and fired, sending bursts at the door gunner. His first burst clipped the gunner's shoulder. The next took him in the chest, kicking him back inside the chopper. The guy let out a startled scream. In his injured state he unwittingly kept his finger on the M-60's trigger, the muzzle spitting fire and spraying the Chinook's interior with a heavy burst.

What happened inside the Chinook would never be known. The burst could have hit the pilot, or caused some serious damage to control settings. Unknown cause still had a visible effect. The chopper surged nose up, then slipped sideways and started to tilt toward the ground.

Bolan had already hauled Valens up, turning her and

pushing her back toward the R&D building when the
Chinook started to yaw.

Behind them Orin Stengard was on his feet, taking
advantage of Valens being pulled away from him. He
saw Bolan grab the woman and head for the building.

Then he heard the faltering sound of the Chinook. He
felt the brush from the rotor wash and turned to see what
was wrong.

What he saw was the dark bulk of the huge machine
sliding in his direction, losing height with startling speed.
He saw the whirring blades of the aft engine, blurred
with their rotation, slashing down at the ground. The first
tip struck, cutting through the soft earth, the rotor bending, snapping, sending fragments through the air. He felt
something strike a hard blow to his left arm and when he
looked down his limb had been completely severed just
above the elbow. He saw the spurting blood and had time
for a short scream of pure terror in the instant before another blade ripped through him with total ease. His torso
was cut through from shoulder to waist, his life ending
in that shrieking moment of pain and noise and confusion.

THE CHINOOK LANDED hard, the sheer weight of the aircraft dragging it to earth with crushing impact. The main
structure buckled and twisted, seams splitting wide open.
Fuel lines were sheared and fluid began to gush from the
ragged ends. Electrical circuits shorted out, crackling
and sparking. Fire rose and spread quickly, curling its
way back to the punctured and leaking fuel tanks.

Bolan and Valens were feet away from the open door when the Chinook blew, sending a ragged swell of fire across the grassed area. The fire had a life of its own, expanding rapidly and throwing out heat that was intense enough to almost scorch their clothing. Debris began to rain around them. The billowing fire engulfed the metal carcass of the chopper. It burned the grass brown and shriveled leaves on the trees beyond the perimeter fence.

Valens slumped against the frame of the door, staring at the ravaged helicopter.

"Did we do that?"

"I don't think it was divine intervention," Bolan said. He took her arm and led her back inside the building.

RIBA HAD CLOSED the door to the Room. After he had done what he could to tend his wound, with Kaplan's help, he remained in the background, trying to make sense of what he was watching. The sight of Doug Buchanan stretched out on the biocouch had thrown him for a moment. The process had moved rapidly, and Buchanan had reached a stage where he was in a kind of limbo, neither fully himself nor completely integrated. Kaplan had explained this was a delicate stage in the process. In another hour or so Buchanan would take the short step from his normal existence into his new life. When that happened he would be part of the biocouch.

"Doug and the couch blend into a single organism, each dependent on the other. A kind of cybernetic organism. Man and machine working as a single unit."

"Like that guy on TV? *The Six Million Dollar Man?*"

Kaplan smiled. "A reasonable analogy, perhaps. Only Doug won't be running around bending steel doors and overturning cars. He will, if we take this to its logical conclusion, be on board the Zero platform, controlling its functions and providing his human intellect toward making important defensive decisions."

"That's where you got me, Doc. You're telling me Doug is going to be in orbit? Stuck in space with nothing but a deluxe computer to keep him company?"

Kaplan ran a hand through his hair. "There's a lot more to it than that, Joshua. If we get out of this in one piece and time allows, I'll explain. Right now my concern is Doug."

"Yeah. Sorry, Doc, just ignore me."

That was when they heard the distant, deep sound of the explosion as the Chinook blew.

BOLAN LED THE WAY back through the building. They encountered no resistance.

"Where the hell are they?" Valens asked, voicing Bolan's own thoughts.

"Maybe Ryan has made a discreet withdrawal," he said.

"Ryan doesn't have the brains to do anything discreet. That guy is seriously nuts. He'll be around somewhere regrouping. He hasn't quit on us yet."

"We're still one player short," Bolan said. "Senator Eric Stahl."

STAHL HAD his driver stop the car short of the R&D building when the Chinook exploded. He saw the flame and smoke rising into the air at the rear of the building.

"What the hell was that?"

Stahl's driver was one of Ryan's men, named Curtis. The man opened the car door and stepped outside, reaching for the cell phone in his pocket.

"Hey, Ryan, what's going on? I got the senator here with me out front of the main building. You want us to come in, or what?"

The conversation was brief. Curtis ended his call and returned to the limousine. He waited while Stahl lowered his window.

"The prisoners got free. They're inside somewhere. Cal suggests we back off until he gets things under control again."

Stahl felt angry and frustrated. And he felt like hitting out at someone. He glanced at Curtis, wondering if he could take out his rage on the man. He dismissed the idea instantly. Curtis was one of Ryan's team. Ex-military, and as such liable to tear off Stahl's head if he tried anything as reckless as violence. Like it or not, Stahl had to remain dependant on these people until he had Zero in his hands.

If ever.

It had all seemed so simple at the outset.

"What was the explosion?" he asked Curtis.

"The Chinook Colonel Stengard called in to uplift Buchanan and his baby couch."

"I believe you will find it's a deal more sophisticated than a baby couch."

"Whatever you say, Senator. Anyhow, it seems this Belasko guy took the chopper down."

Curtis returned to the car and swung the limousine around, driving toward the main complex and the road that led back to the highway.

Stahl settled back in his seat.

First Randolph walking away free and clear. Then that little bastard Beringer jumping ship. That had been a bad loss. The information Beringer had fished out of the damaged files from the Zero facility would have proved extremely useful. However, there had been compensation in the form of Saul Kaplan showing up when they had finally caught up with Buchanan.

Stahl wondered just exactly what Ryan had meant about the prisoners getting free.

How many did they shoot? Was Buchanan still in their hands? Was anything going to go right?

He thought of calling Ryan, but decided it wasn't a good idea. He took out his cell phone and speed-dialed Stengard. All he got was a dead signal. The damned phone wouldn't even connect.

Stahl was going to take Ryan's advice and make a retreat for the time being. His trip to SAC had been to speak with Belasko. The call he had received from Kaplan's lodge had startled him. How had Belasko gotten his computer password? There was more than enough in those files to implicate a dozen people, military and political. Stahl had spent time and money gaining the kind of information certain to insure cooperation from any one of the people in his own files. The data was for self-protection. If he needed to bail himself out, he could use the information to blackmail, coerce or damned well scare certain influential people. His data was his get-out-of-jail card. He intended to survive, one way or another, and if others had to go down to save *his* skin, then so be it.

CAL RYAN VIEWED the burning wreckage of the Chinook with more than a trace of regret. Its loss was going to make things difficult. Worse than the crippled helicopter was the body of Orin Stengard, or what was left of him after the helicopter's rotor had done its damage. Stengard had been burned by the explosion, as well.

Ryan stood over the body of his former commander, head bent in silent respect.

He was bitter over Stengard's death, but all he could do to make it right was to find Belasko and the woman. They had been seen with Stengard shortly before the Chinook had been brought down.

"Cal, they're back inside the building," one of his men said. "Belasko and the woman. And that Apache bastard is in the Room along with Buchanan and the Doc."

"Let's go," Ryan snapped. "We need the girl and Belasko alive for now. Leave the Room as it is. They can't go anywhere. Keep out of sight but watch the place."

THEY REACHED the corridor where the Room was situated. It looked clear. Bolan called a halt, and they surveyed the deserted corridor.

"Too damned quiet," Bolan commented.

"Where are Ryan's storm troopers? I'd expect them to be crawling all over the place."

Bolan felt uneasy. It *was* too quiet.

"We'll back off," he said, "until I can figure out what's going on."

"Okay."

Valens turned to check the way they had come, Bolan following suit.

Her warning yell came too late. The corridor exploded in a stark white flash that seared their eyes. A savage crack of sound pounded their ears, making them hurt under the pressure.

Bolan threw out a hand to make contact with Valens. He failed to connect. He stumbled blindly, hitting the wall.

Someone had thrown a stun grenade. He had used them himself in the past and knew that sight and vision would return—but not soon enough to prevent their being overpowered. Bolan felt hands grab him, wrench the M-16 from his grip and strip off his harness and the sheathed knife. All this in silence and with him unable to see his attackers.

He didn't even realize the blow was coming. Not until something hard struck him across the back of his skull and he pitched into a silent black void.

STAHL'S CELL PHONE rang.

"Yes?"

"Ryan. Senator, we have Belasko and the woman. You said you needed to talk with him."

"Have some of your men bring them to the old Stahl warehouses. East of the Washington rail yards. You know where I mean?"

"I know it, Senator."

"We may need to have a serious talk with Belasko. I'd prefer privacy. It could be too risky me being on-site at the moment. You understand my position, Ryan?"

"I understand, Senator. One other thing. Not good news. Colonel Stengard is dead. He was killed when the chopper was brought down."

Stahl considered the implications. Stengard had the military connections and the clout needed for the follow-up to getting Buchanan and Zero under their control. Stengard had been an important part of the project to embrace Zero and its ultimate power. Without him things would be a little harder to achieve. But as long as he had Buchanan and Kaplan in his hands, matters were far from over.

"Well, Mr. Ryan, it seems a field commission is in order. How do feel about taking over? Are you still in?"

"Do my best to match up to the colonel, Senator. It won't be easy. He was the best."

Stahl made sympathetic noises, allowing Ryan his moment of maudlin sentimentality.

"Take control of the situation in there. We can't afford to lose Buchanan at this point. Make sure he does nothing once he is capable of making contact with Zero. Let me know when that happens, and we'll make certain we end up with total control."

"Senator, we're sailing pretty close to the wind here. You still think we can bring this off?"

"I'm aware of all of Stengard's contacts. They still have the equipment and people in the right positions. If we can get control of Zero, then we have the strongest card of all, and this game is going to be ours. Ryan, no one ever achieved anything of significance without risk. What the hell, man, do you want to live forever?"

"Senator, I can see how you got to be where you are."

"Keep Buchanan alive until you limit the damage down there."

Stahl cut the call and leaned forward. "You hear that, Curtis?"

"Yes, sir. Shame about the colonel, but we're not in the business of baking cakes. People get hurt."

"Exactly. Curtis, head back to Washington. Rail yards near Union Station. I'll direct you when we get close."

"Doesn't sound like we're going to a party, Senator."

Stahl smiled. "Depends on your concept of what a party is, Curtis."

THE BLACK SUV swung in through sagging metal gates, bumping over potholes and through deep puddles. A rust-streaked sign proclaimed Stahl Warehousing. Within the high mesh fencing the blocks of large storage buildings were dark and run-down. The main company had ceased using them years ago. The area was littered with debris.

Behind the SUV came a second vehicle, a dark-colored sedan. Backup.

It was close to dusk. Shadows were creeping out from the corners and spreading across the site. It was raining again, and the gray sky was heavy with swollen clouds.

The SUV eased in through half-open doors, rolling inside the cavernous building. It came to a stop close to where offices had once been the operational hub of the Stahl distribution center.

The sedan stayed outside, armed hardmen climbing out to keep watch.

The rear doors of the SUV were opened. Bolan and Valens were hauled out. Although they were reasonably recovered from the effects of the stun grenade, Bolan remained silent, as if he were still under the influence. He had to be pushed around to make him do anything and failed to react when spoken to.

The hardmen who had accompanied them to the warehouse gathered in a loose group. There were four of them, three carrying M-16s and the fourth a combat shotgun. All wore holstered pistols.

The sound of an engine starting reached them. The sound rose as the limousine carrying Eric Stahl rolled down the warehouse and came to a stop alongside the SUV.

Curtis got out and walked to the rear door. He opened

it and Stahl emerged. He crossed to where Bolan and Valens stood.

"This is Belasko?"

"This is the guy," one of the hardmen said.

"He doesn't look all that special to me. How in hell did he get away causing so much damage?"

"Simple, Senator. He's good. Have to give him that. He's a nervy son of a bitch."

"And this must be Agent Valens." Stahl looked her up and down. "What a waste. Good-looking woman like this shouldn't be running around shooting off guns. Her place is in the bedroom giving special service."

"Senator, if that was true I'd expect to handle real men. So you wouldn't even be on my client list."

Stahl's face hardened. Behind him one of the hardmen choked back a snigger. The senator's eyes blazed with sudden anger. He lashed out with his bunched fist, catching Valens across the mouth and knocking her off her feet. Valens sprawled on the dirty feet, head down, blood dripping from her lips.

"No respect," Stahl said. "One of today's problems."

He swung around to face Bolan again. There was something in the man's blank stare that added to his rage.

"What's wrong with him?"

"Effects of the stun grenade. Takes longer to wear off some people."

"Jesus, that's all I need. I have to question this man." Stahl raised his hands in a gesture of futility. "I'm pay-

ing all this fucking money and what do I get? Shit by
the wagon load."

For a moment Stahl lost it. All his disappointments,
the setbacks, the losses. They boiled to the surface in a
flash of white-hot rage.

He lunged forward, swinging his fists at the man he
knew as Belasko.

They never landed.

Bolan erupted into action, knocking aside Stahl's
ill-judged attack. He caught hold of the senator's coat
and hauled the man up close, then swung him around
to collide with the nearest hardman. The startled man
tried to avoid the stumbling senator, but failed. Stahl
bowled into him, pushing him off balance, and gave
Bolan the chance to duck in under Stahl's flapping
arms. Bolan snatched the pistol from the hardman's
holster and jabbed the muzzle into its former owner's
side. Bolan triggered a trio of shots that cored into the
man's body and blew out the other side in a bloody
spray. As the injured man fell, Bolan turned and took
long strides toward the parked SUV. He dropped to the
floor and rolled under the vehicle, aware he only had
seconds before they came after him. He was almost out
the other side when the hand gripping the pistol snagged
against something under the chassis. The gun was torn
from his grip. Bolan heard it clatter across the concrete,
lost in the shadows. He came out on the far side of the
SUV, pushing to his feet and into the shadows near the
empty offices.

The belated crackle of M-16s followed him, slugs snapping and chewing at the office block, tearing out splinters of wood and shattering glass.

"Goddamn. Spread out."

"Find him."

"Bring in the guys from outside."

The final command came from a shrill-voiced Eric Stahl.

"Don't let him get away."

CHAPTER FIFTEEN

Bolan spotted a flicker of movement close by his left side, the subdued glimmer of light on the metal of a shotgun. At the same time he heard the scrape of a boot on the concrete as someone closed in from the front, the snap of a slide racking back, then forward to push a load into the breech.

Bolan reacted instantly. He moved out of his cover, his upper body twisting, bringing him around to face the shotgunner, his hands reaching to grasp the weapon. The shotgunner hadn't been expecting his target to confront *him*. His delay was all Bolan needed. The Executioner wrenched the shotgun from his hands, swiveling the deadly weapon and driving the hardwood butt into the gunner's face. Bone snapped and blood spurted. The man fell back, gasping, hands reaching up to cover his bleeding face. A rush of sound warned Bolan of a second attack. An M-16 loosed a burst that sent slugs reaching into the shadows way off target. Bolan sourced the position of the shooter. He was facing the target, the shotgun on track, finger against the trigger. Dropping to a crouch in the fraction of a second before the man fired again, Bolan triggered the shotgun, sending the powerful charge into the blacksuit's lower torso. The close range of the shot ripped the man's body open, splintering ribs and destroying his internal organs. The guy didn't have time to scream as he was kicked off his feet and thrown across the floor with dark blood misting the air around him. He landed hard, the back of his skull smacking against the concrete with an ugly sound.

"You fuck—"

The sound came from the ex-shotgunner. Bolan spun, still crouching, and saw the man fumbling for the handgun he carried. His left hand was still pressed to his bloody face.

Bolan jacked the slide and raised the shotgun. He fired into the bulk of the man's body, the charge ripping its way through flesh and muscle, carving a fatal path that put the shotgunner down in a tangle of flailing limbs and mushrooming gouts of blood.

He heard raised voices, the sound of running feet. Others were closing on his position. Bolan turned, pushing deeper into the shadows around the office block, shouldering aside piles of debris, broken packing cases, stacks of wood.

His exit from the building was an open gap where a wooden door had once hung. Now the opening led directly into the rain-drenched night. There was no easy, comfortable way of doing it. Bolan paused only briefly, working the slide to put another round in the shotgun's breech, then went through and outside. The crackle of autofire followed him, bullets chewing at the door frame, blowing a hail of splintered wood in Bolan's wake. He turned away from the door, ignoring the heavy downpour that soaked him in seconds. The rain was bouncing off the ground, silvery sheets driven by the wind that was gusting around the sprawl of empty industrial buildings.

Bolan moved on, shots following him, the snap and zip of passing bullets spurring him to find cover before luck gave up on him. He couldn't allow that to happen. There were too many scores to settled. Too much to be exposed.

Off to his right a dark figure ran out from behind cover, lifting a weapon. Flashes of fire and the crackle of shots forced Bolan to alter his course, and he took a headlong dive behind piled wooden packing crates. He rolled across the rain-drenched concrete, hearing the burst of fire chew and splinter the crates. Coming to his knees, the soldier swung around, picking up the slap of feet as his attacker closed in, maybe believing he had hit his target. Bolan picked up the man's sharp breathing as he bulled his way around the end of the crates, overconfidence allowing him to step into the open, his gaze searching the gloom behind the stack.

The shotgun was already up and leveled, and Bolan

stroked the trigger as the guy appeared. The shadows were briefly lit by the spout of fire from the muzzle. The reckless shooter took the charge full in the face. He went backward, his scream turning into a strangled gurgle as his pulped throat collapsed, blood filling his mouth. His body hit the concrete with a sodden thump, one heel drumming against the ground in a final spasm of resistance against the overwhelming pain.

Bolan crouched to pick up the M-16 the man had dropped. He slung it by the strap, then eased back into the gloom. Night had fallen quickly. The darkness didn't worry Bolan; it was his ally, providing cover as he prowled the site, seeking the enemy.

He had become the hunter now. In this savage world of betrayal and deceit, where men had turned against their own country to aid one man's selfish desires, there would be no mercy this night.

Mack Bolan had turned the game around. He had the advantage because he had seen the face of his enemies, and he was moving in for the kill.

He checked the shotgun. By his estimation he had two shots left. A nearly full magazine was in the M-16. It was enough for what he had to do here.

The noise of the rainfall covered his movements. Bolan skirted the immediate area and worked his way around to the front of the warehouse where he and Claire Valens had been brought. Crouching behind a stack of metal, he saw the parked sedan, one man waiting beside the car.

Bolan shouldered the M-16, taking his time as he made his target and put the guy down with a burst that cored in through the back of his skull. The impact threw him facedown on the concrete. The soldier moved immediately, staying low as he closed in on the building. He flattened against the door and peered inside.

He could see the parked SUV and Stahl's limo. A number of figures stood around the area, clothing wet from exposure to the rain. Bolan's pursuers had regrouped for a council. He could see Valens, slumped on the floor, her back against the limo. Senator Stahl and his bodyguard were there, too. Stahl was haranguing the troops, his arms waving around as if he were giving a speech.

Bolan went in through the door, staying in the deeper shadows as he moved to bring the group within range. Choosing his position, the soldier laid the shotgun on the ground, bringing the M-16 into position. He had flicked the selector to single shot.

He braced himself across the top of a steel drum, settling the assault rifle on his first target. There was no hesitation in Bolan's actions. Distance sniping was a skill he had acquired a long time ago, during his own military service, and that skill never went away.

His finger gently took up the trigger slack. The M-16's muzzle locked on to the target. He took his time, fixing the distance in his mind.

His finger squeezed the trigger. He heard the shot, felt the M-16 kick against his shoulder and immediately switched to the next target. Now that he had his range, Bolan continued his sniping, firing before his first target had hit the floor. A second man spun away from the group. The cartridge cases chinked against the concrete at Bolan's feet. He angled the muzzle around for his third shot, seeing the surviving three gunners splitting apart. He locked on and fired again, caught one directly between the shoulders, sending him in an ungracious dive. The man hit the floor facedown, the impact hard and uncompromising.

Stahl's bodyguard reached out and hauled the senator aside, pushing him behind the cover of the SUV. Bolan laid a number of shots at the vehicle, seeing a window implode and holes punched through the body panels.

Movement caught his eye. Bolan saw one of the remaining hardmen bending over Valens. The guy hooked his left arm under her and dragged her upright. His intention was clear—to use Valens as a shield. Bolan brought the M-16 on track, his muzzle focused on the man's head. Bolan knew he had a thin window before the guy had Valens fully in position, covering his body with hers and using her as a bargaining chip.

Bolan didn't dwell on the moment. He shut down his emotions, ignoring the pale mask of Valens's face as she put up a struggle. But he did see the bright smears of blood standing out against the flesh of her face.

He fired.

The M-16 cracked.

The 5.56 mm bullet took the man above his right eye, snapping his head back. He fell away from Valens, buckling at the knees, and went down hard, his rifle slipping from dead fingers.

Three to go.

Valens had dropped to her knees, but not out of weakness this time. Bolan saw her lean over and pick up the dropped M-16, haul it close to her body as she used the side of the limo to push to her feet.

Bolan allowed a thin smile to edge his mouth. He had to give her credit. Whatever else, Claire Valens was no quitter.

He spotted movement on the far side of the warehouse. A dark figure scuttling toward the door. The sole survivor.

Bolan went after him.

The hardman saw Bolan's determined figure and brought up his rifle, triggering wild shots as he kept moving. The soldier ignored the chipping concrete, pausing to shoulder his own weapon.

He fired twice, his shots taking the moving man through the side of his torso, shattering ribs and tearing organs. The man's full flight faltered. He slowed, struggling for breath. He began to cough, spitting blood. Then he sank to his knees and dropped to the floor.

Bolan turned away, heading back to where the two vehicles were parked. Somewhere in the shadows beyond were Stahl and his bodyguard.

And closer was Valens.

The crackle of an M-16 filled the warehouse; someone shouted.

Bolan picked up the pace and reached the SUV.

Valens had vanished.

Silence descended over the warehouse. The only
noise Bolan could hear was the rain pounding the roof.

The crackle of an M-16 alerted Bolan to Valens's
presence. He heard the bullets clang against steelwork.
There was a rush of movement, then a handgun returned
fire.

Bolan moved past the SUV, his M-16 across his
chest. He peered into the shadows at the distant end of
the warehouse, trying to make out shapes.

Something warned him of a presence.

The Executioner turned, bringing the rifle into target acquisition. A bulky shape lunged at him,
slammed bodily into him. Bolan fell back, hearing
someone grunt. A hard object cracked against the
side of his head, and he felt hot blood course down
the side of his face, soaking the collar of his blacksuit. He struck out with the M-16, felt the butt make
contact, heard the gasp of expelled breath. The brief
seconds of hesitation gave Bolan the chance to see his
adversary.

It was Stahl's bodyguard, Curtis.

Curtis lunged at Bolan again, bringing his handgun
in line for a shot.

Bolan dropped to the floor, sweeping his leg around
and knocking Curtis off his feet. The man grunted with

the impact as he hit the concrete. The Executioner rolled, then sat up, saw Curtis recovering and clubbed him across the side of the head with the M-16. The blow spun Curtis away. He lost his grip on the pistol, struggling to shake off the effects of the head blow.

They got to their feet together, Curtis bloody faced and uncoordinated, Bolan set now as he reversed the M-16 and put two shots into his target. The 5.56 mm slugs cored through Curtis's chest cavity and into his heart, punching him off his feet. This time the bodyguard didn't get up.

"Belasko, over here," Valens yelled.

Bolan followed the sound of her voice and found her with Stahl.

The senator looked disheveled, his expensive suit streaked with dirt and oil from the warehouse floor. A bloody smear marred the side of his face. His lips were split and bleeding. He was backed up against the side of the SUV, hands partway raised as Valens covered him with the M-16.

"Jesus, get this bitch off me," he demanded. "She's crazy enough to kill me."

"You want *my* help?" Bolan asked.

"I'm a United States senator. I have more influence than you realize. Harm me and—"

"Stahl, shut your mouth," Valens said. "Because of you, people are dead. My partner included. Murdered by that sick buddy of yours. The late Colonel Stengard. Right now your status is down to less than nothing."

"Senator, when the information in those files is made public your government takeover is going to disappear," Bolan said. "Once the President has the details, every one of your conspirator friends will feel the cold. You know what they do with traitors? Lock them away in a secure federal facility and lose the key."

Stahl thought about that for a moment, then he visibly relaxed.

"Belasko, it doesn't need to happen that way. We can work this out. Do you realize how wealthy I am? The Stahl Corporation is my legacy. I have more money than the Federal Reserve. I could make an accommodation. For you and the young woman. Think about it, Belasko. It has to be better than this. Risking your life for what? Some vague notion of justice and democracy? People get themselves killed, but nothing really changes. Money is power. It buys off the troubles of the world. Now, how does your job stack up to that?"

"Pretty good," Bolan said, his voice taking on an icy tone.

Stahl frowned. "I don't understand. What's so good about your life?"

"It allows me to deal with people like you, Senator," Bolan said, removing plastic riot cuffs from a pocket of his blacksuit.

"We'll just sit you down here, and I'll put in a call to a friend who'll arrange a pickup. I'm sure you'll have a lot to tell the Feds."

Moments later the black SUV drove out of the warehouse, Bolan at the wheel. Claire Valens sat in the passenger seat beside him.

The stormy weather closed around the SUV as the
soldier drove through the site's rusty gates, leaving Eric
Stahl and his dreams of power in a heap on the dirty
floor of a deserted warehouse. Bolan had used Stahl's
cell phone to call Brognola at the Justice Department
and arrange for a team to pick up the senator, and to tell
him Stengard was dead.

Maryland lay ahead.

And closure.

CHAPTER SIXTEEN

Valens had loaded both M-16s. She rested them against her knees as she stared out through the windshield of the SUV. One of the rear windows, shattered by Bolan's fire during the battle at the warehouse, let in the chill rain. She could feel the cold against the back of her neck. She turned to look at Bolan's profile as he drove. His face was battered and bloody, but she felt the resolve that came off him strong and undiminished. He would never give up, she realized. No matter how strong the odds against him.

"Do you think Ryan will hurt them?" she asked.

Bolan was thinking about that, too.

Joshua Riba, Saul Kaplan and Doug Buchanan.

"If he realizes there are no more options, he might use them as bargaining chips. Stengard is dead. Ryan won't know about Stahl.

"The problem is, we can't be sure who works for

who in this damned town. Ryan may call in help from someone we don't have a clue about."

"I think we have that covered," Bolan said.

He took out the cell phone he had appropriated from Stahl, along with a SAC key card. He was hoping the card might let them get inside the R&D building.

Bolan tapped in the number that would connect him with Stony Man. It was time to get the backup on stream.

Barbara Price answered.

"It's me," Bolan said, then gave her an update on the situation. "Have Stahl's files revealed anything about insiders leaking information?"

"Wait until you hear."

"Just the bare bones."

"Aaron has names our friendly senator was keeping in his files. You wouldn't believe the stuff he had on people. That man is seriously sick. The upshot is, there have been a number of arrests in Washington. Two on the White House staff. One was a woman who had access to confidential presidential databases. Senator Stahl is going to have to answer some awkward questions. Just a second. Hal's on the other line."

"Striker," Brognola said as he became part of a conference call. "The pickup team is on the way. We'll have Stahl on ice within the hour."

"It's over. Thank God."

"Not quite. I'm on my way back to the Stahl weapons facility in Maryland. Buchanan and Kaplan are still there. I need to get them out, so we're not in the clear yet. Give me a little time before you send in the troops. Hold them off. Local enforcement, as well."

"What's been going on there?"

"A little in-house upset."

"More likely a rehearsal for WWIII. I picked up on some disturbance there. I had an idea you might be involved, so we clamped down on any interference. The President made it federal business and ordered everyone to stay clear and I mean everyone. He has seriously upset a lot of people around town. I suspect the ones making the most noise are involved with Stahl and Stengard because they sense something's up. It'll be interesting to see what happens when the dust settles. Locally the story is something about possible radioactive leakage. Local cops have set a two-mile exclusion zone. The President can't expect to keep it indefinite, so finish it fast."

"Radioactive leakage. The Man has some imagination."

"They'll let you through. All you need to tell them is the code word 'Peacemaker.'"

"Who chose that? You?"

"Yeah."

"Watch it. You'll be developing a sense of humor next."

"Working with you I need one. Call me when we can come in."

THE CODE WORD got them through the police roadblock after a slight delay. There were a number of local PD vehicles ranged across the road, lights flashing through the rain. Wooden barriers had been put in place, as well.

"You look a little rough," the local police captain said when Bolan leaned out of his window to speak to him.

The cop didn't look too happy. The threat of a radiation leak, plus the miserable weather, wasn't the kind of thing to make for a happy evening. He was huddled in his waterproof jacket, a plastic cover over his peaked cap, probably wishing he were closer to retirement than he actually was.

"It's been one of those days," Bolan told him.

"I'd say. You had some unhappy clients."

Bolan touched his bruised cheek. "You know how people get grumpy."

"Tell me about it. My wife for one wasn't too happy at me having to do this tonight. Hey, this thing going to spread?"

Bolan shook his head. "No problem there, Captain. We're going to contain it. Shut the problem down for good."

Bolan surveyed the assembled patrol cars. The barriers blocking the road.

"You got the instructions? No one else comes through until I get the all-clear from my people."

"You think anyone would *want* to go in there?"

"You'd be surprised, Captain."

Bolan eased the SUV forward, taking it around the opened barrier.

The captain watched it go, and found himself wondering why a radiation containment team would have bullet holes in the back of its vehicle. He turned those thoughts away. He had his orders.

BOLAN SLOWED the SUV as they approached the service road leading to the SAC facility. He killed the lights.

"When Ryan isn't able to contact Stahl, he's going to start worrying. The guy's reckless, but I wouldn't say stupid. If he suspects things have gone bad, he'll look at his own position and what he can do to survive."

"You don't think he'll just run?"

"Possibility. Like we already agreed, I think he'll consider his options. He could walk out and find the place surrounded. But he might just see Buchanan and Kaplan as bargaining pieces. He could use them to get himself and his men clear. Use them as hostages. Or not."

"He could say to hell with it all and kill them, then take his chances."

"He could do that, too. The sooner we get in there the better. Give him something else to think about."

"Such as?"

"Who to shoot first. You or me."

"I can see you'll be great fun on a date, Mike."

Bolan reached for his M-16. Full magazine, with a couple of extras stowed in his blacksuit pockets.

"You set?"

Valens nodded, not willing to answer, because she didn't trust her voice at that point.

Bolan increased his speed along the service road.

Skirting the deserted main buildings and on toward the isolated R&D block.

"You think Ryan might have men outside keeping watch?"

"There can't be that many left," Bolan said. "But it's another possibility."

They approached the R&D building. It was shrouded in darkness except for a few isolated security lights on tall poles dotted around the area. Bolan took the SUV up to the main door and braked.

They sat and checked out the immediate area, but saw nothing, which didn't guarantee anything.

Bolan picked up his M-16, opened his door and stepped out. The chill bite of the rain hit him. He ducked his head and made for the R&D door.

"Jesus, where you guys been? You have problems or something?"

The voice came from Bolan's right. Ryan *had* placed a man outside, and the guy had recognized the SUV, thinking it was part of the team returning from Washington.

Bolan waited as the man closed in, picking up the sound of his boots on the ground. Then heard a heavy impact. A second blow followed. The sentry grunted, folding forward to drop facedown on the ground, his weapon clattering beside him.

Bolan turned to see Claire Valens standing over the guard. The back of the guy's head was red with blood and his neck had an unnatural twist to it.

"Let's hope he was the only one," Bolan said.

He checked the man's pulse. There wasn't one.

They relieved the man of his weapons, an M-16 and a sheathed knife. Bolan took the knife. He stripped the M-16 and threw the various pieces into the darkness. The magazine went into one of his pockets.

Valens kept watch as Bolan took the key card from his pocket and swiped it through the card reader on the wall. The doors slid open. They went inside, crossing to the elevator doors. The soldier used the card again, and they entered the elevator.

There were four levels to choose from.

"Level two," Valens said. "I was watching when Ryan took us down."

Bolan punched the appropriate button, and the elevator dropped.

"Ryan might have someone stationed by the elevator," Bolan said. "Don't stick your head out too fast."

"As if."

The elevator slowed and finally stopped. There was a pause before the doors slid open. Bolan and Valens stayed to the sides of the opening, waiting.

A shadow fell across the opening, and Bolan heard breathing, the soft rustle of clothing.

The muzzle of an M-16 appeared, probing, then a head and shoulders. It was one of Ryan's hardmen.

"Somebody playin' games?" the guy muttered.

He took another, hesitant step, still unsure.

It was a step too many.

Bolan hit him full face with the butt of the M-16, hard enough to put the guy down on his knees.

"Check outside," Bolan said.

Valens stepped over the man as Bolan grabbed his arm and hauled him inside the elevator.

The hardman spit blood, reaching out to resist. He got one hand across Bolan's throat, fingers digging in. His effort pushed the soldier back against the elevator wall and for seconds they struggled. Bolan let the M-16 dangle from its sling as he fought back.

He put his right palm under his adversary's chin and pushed back hard, feeling the pressure lift the guy onto his toes. He rammed his left hand into the guy's side. The knife he had taken from the sentry was in that hand. The blade slid in under the guy's ribs, the keen blade cleaving flesh and internal organs as Bolan worked it savagely. His opponent uttered a trembling moan, then stiffened, his grip on the Executioner's throat slackening as his own functions began to fail. He fell back, pulling himself off the knife, hands over the bleeding wound. As Bolan unslung his M-16, the man slid to the floor of the elevator.

Valens was crouching against the wall, her rifle covering the corridor. She glanced at Bolan, noting the bloody knife before he sheathed it. She said nothing.

"That way," Bolan said.

They walked the corridor, the soldier in the lead, Valens just behind, watching their backs.

"The office Stengard used," Bolan said.

The door was ajar, so he moved to check the interior. The office was deserted, but showed signs of having been used. There were plastic cups on the desk, and he could smell the coffee they had recently held. Something caught his eye. A flickering TV monitor.

"Stay by the door and keep watch."

Bolan moved inside the office and checked out the screen. It showed the Room, a wide-angle view.

He saw the couch with Doug Buchanan stretched out. Kaplan was at his side, talking to him.

Dr. Menard and his assistants were at the computer station.

Joshua Riba was there, too, slumped on a frame chair, under the watchful eye of a gunner. Four more were in the Room.

Bolan recognized one of them as Cal Ryan.

Ryan appeared agitated. The man had a cell phone in his hand. As Bolan observed, he punched in numbers, put the phone to his ear and listened. From his reaction it was obvious he wasn't getting any response—Bolan had turned off Stahl's cell phone. Ryan cut off the call and spoke to one of his men. The guy nodded and turned away. He went to the door and pushed it open and stepped out of the Room.

"Damn…"

Bolan spun away from the TV monitor.

"Valens." The crackle of an M-16 interrupted his

warning. As Bolan reached the office door he heard the slugs impacting against the wall. Valens expressed her anger verbally, then returned fire.

Bolan cleared the office door.

He saw Valens down on one knee, rifle to her shoulder as she traded shots with the hardman farther down the corridor.

Bolan had the extra time to aim before the gunner spotted him. He hit him with a burst to the chest, the impact driving the guy to the floor.

"You okay?" Bolan asked.

Valens nodded. "Only pissed because he took me by surprise."

"Stay that way. It'll keep you sharp."

"Comforting words."

They heard the door to the Room crash open and another gunner burst into the corridor, his weapon up and firing.

Valens gasped as a slug took her in the right shoulder. She was half turned by the impact, stumbling and going down. Bolan caught sight of the wide-eyed expression of total shock on her face.

He turned on the man and triggered a burst that hit the guy in the left hip, blowing away a chunk of flesh and bone. The guy went down, fumbling with his rifle. Bolan hit him with two more bursts, fragments of the guy's blacksuit flying as the 5.56 mm slugs cored into his chest. The guy was flung back against the wall, leaving a bloody smear as he toppled to the floor.

THE SECOND GUNNER had left the room.

The crackle of gunfire that followed stirred Cal Ryan to action.

"Time to get the hell out of here," he said.

His two surviving men exchanged glances. "Cal, what's going on?"

"Shit is going on. I can't get through to Stahl. We're stuck in this damned place with no backup. Any bright ideas?"

"We can use these as hostages?"

"And who do we negotiate with? Boys, we don't have a line to anyone."

"This is bad," one man commented.

"This is the worst fucking deal I ever signed up for," Ryan snapped. "And the first one of you hotshots who agrees I'll shoot his eyes out."

Ryan checked his M-16 and handgun. "The options have narrowed, boys. Stay and we'll end up dead. We make a run for it we might get clear. No guarantees. Personally I prefer the second choice."

"There might be a squad out there, waiting to blow our heads off."

Ryan shrugged. "Only one way to find out. I'm betting there's only that son of a bitch Belasko. The bastard outgunned Stahl and the escort. That's why I can't get through to Mr. High and Mighty Senator."

"You could be wrong, Cal."

"Everything you do has a positive and negative side. Of course I could be wrong."

"So how do we get out of this room?"

"Any stun grenades left?"

"I got one."

"Toss it down the corridor. As soon as it goes off, we vacate this place. Head to the rear door and lose ourselves in the woods beyond the perimeter fence. Then we commandeer a vehicle and get back to the safehouse. Don't forget the cash reserve the colonel kept for emergencies. Change of clothes, clean car and we can lose ourselves before anyone can locate us."

"What about this bunch?"

Ryan glanced at the captives, considering.

"What the hell. Dead or alive isn't going to make a difference to us. Leave them. We need the ammunition."

The hardman with the stun grenade slung his M-16, moved to the door and opened it wide.

Ryan and the remaining gunner stood to the side, waiting.

The guy with the stun grenade reached up to pull the pin.

JOSHUA RIBA WATCHED the proceedings with interest. He had noticed the crumbling of their resolve. Right now it was at its lowest, and he knew his chance was coming fast. Since Ryan and his men had taken control of the Room, Riba had been hoping something might offer him a chance. He had surrendered because he'd had no option. The odds were too great and the threat to Buchanan and Kaplan forced him to reach his decision. It was like Belasko had said—staying alive meant you could get another chance. Once you were dead, nothing else mattered.

As the hardmen started to arm the stun grenade, Riba slipped off his chair, braced himself and took a lunging run across the room. Before Ryan and the other hardman realized what was happening, Riba hit the guy with the grenade from the rear. The momentum of his charge took the pair out the door and into the corridor. They went to the floor, sliding across the smooth surface to crash against the far wall. The stun grenade rolled from the hardman's fingers. He struggled to free himself from Riba's embrace. The P.I. hung on, circling his adversary's neck with his left arm, bracing his right hand against the back of the guy's skull. He closed the loop, cutting off the man's air, and squeezed until sweat popped from his forehead. He felt the man struggling, making choking sounds.

"No way. This time the Apache wins."

In the background Riba heard gunfire. He half expected to feel bullets burn into his body. It didn't happen.

His adversary was still struggling. Riba increased the pressure, then jerked back against the man's neck. There was a soft crunching sound and the hardman beneath Riba stopped his struggling. He simply went limp in the P.I.'s grip.

BOLAN COULDN'T DO much for Valens. He dragged her against the wall.

"Keep your hand over the wound," he advised. "Pressure on it."

She nodded vaguely.

"Go," she said. "Don't let him get away."

Bolan snatched up his M-16.

"Let's go," Ryan snapped. He had reached the end of his patience.

Without another word to his comrade Ryan burst through the door and swung left, vanishing from sight. The man hesitated for a fraction of a second, then followed.

He saw the two men on the floor and Ryan running down the corridor, then he made the mistake of looking back along the corridor in the other direction.

And saw Belasko heading his way.

He raised his rifle into position and triggered the weapon, feeling the M-16 jerk in his hands and seeing his shots hitting the wall and floor.

Calm down, he cautioned himself, the guy's only human.

He felt something hit his left thigh. His leg went from beneath him and he started to fall. A burst of pain swelled up from his leg. He looked down and saw the ragged hole the bullets had made, blood pumping out. He was hit again. He felt himself pushed back against the wall. This time the pain was in his chest. It was suddenly difficult to breathe. He coughed. A burning sensation seared his throat, and he tasted liquid that frothed from his mouth, warm and bloody. He hung against the wall, weakening rapidly.

A dark shape moved by him. He tried to see who it

was, but he couldn't raise his head. He was sure a cold sensation swept over him as the shape moved by.

Something that left him with a chill.

It had to have been Belasko.

Or the specter of Death.

Just before he slipped into unconsciousness, he realized they were one and the same.

CAL RYAN HIT the exit door and stumbled into the rain-lashed gloom. Security lamps threw yellow streams of light across the lawned area. Ryan caught sight of the burned-out helicopter. The body of Colonel Orin Stengard was still out here, too, sprawled where he had died. As much as he had admired the man, at that moment in time, Ryan didn't give a damn about his condition.

His choices were thin: make his way around the R&D building and see if he could get a vehicle, or go for the perimeter fence and lose himself in the dense woods on the other side.

That option didn't worry him. Ryan had active experience of evasion tactics. His only concern would center around whether there were military or police units out there. He had no way of knowing whether Belasko had called in backup.

The man, whoever he was, seemed to have the knowledge to anticipate and counter opposition moves. His ability to maneuver himself out of difficult situations showed he was no novice. Far from it.

Ryan's thoughts raced through his mind as he moved

away from the door and out into the open. The ground was soft from the downpour. The rain, pushed by the ragged wind, was cold. It penetrated his blacksuit and chilled his flesh.

He raised his rifle, ready to move off, his decision to go over the perimeter fence finalized.

BOLAN SAW the open door and increased his pace. Once Ryan got into the clear he might easily slip away unnoticed.

Bolan wasn't going to let that happen.

The opening loomed in the Executioner's vision. He burst through the door and saw Ryan just ahead of him. The man was moving off.

There was no time to slow down. Bolan didn't consider it. He hit Ryan from behind, driving the man to the ground. They rolled apart, each rising quickly, no more than a couple of feet apart.

Ryan was grinning. He held his rifle across his chest, then pushed it at arm's length. He thrust and parried, butt and muzzle. Bolan used his own rifle to counter. They circled each other, testing, seeking the chance to strike.

Ryan feinted, drew back, then struck. The flat of the stock clipped Bolan's cheek, splitting the flesh. The sight of the blood brought a gleam of anticipation to Ryan's eyes. He was sensing victory. Bolan eased off, adding to his adversary's sense of superiority. He lunged, carried his feint through again. Only this time the Executioner saw it coming and countered the move.

The M-16s clashed, and the pair pushed to gain the advantage. Ryan threw a leg kick that glanced off Bolan's knee. He repeated his kick, missing as the soldier twisted to one side. He used the move to free his rifle, rolling a strike with the butt that clouted Ryan across the side of his head. The man stumbled, and Bolan kept the momentum, slashing out with the M-16. The tip of the muzzle gouged Ryan's cheek, tearing it open to the bone. Blood surged from the gash, and Bolan struck again. To the body, as well as the head.

Ryan backed off, racked with pain.

This wasn't going as well as he had anticipated. Belasko was good. Maybe too good. The game playing hadn't been intended to go against himself.

He dropped the M-16 and grabbed for the pistol holstered at his side. He closed his fingers around the butt, lifting the weapon from the holster.

Bolan slammed the M-16 across Ryan's gun hand, putting all his strength to the blow. The crack of breaking bone was audible above the driving rain. Ryan roared in agony. He lifted his hand and stared at the split flesh and the shards of bone showing through.

"Bastard," he screamed.

He saw Bolan staring at him, his own battered, bloody face glistening from the rain. The look in the man's eyes unnerved Ryan. They were cold, empty of any compassion.

"Lessons are over, Ryan."

Something snapped in Cal Ryan that drained away

every vestige of his courage. For the first time in his life he really knew what it felt to look Death in the eyes and understand what it meant.

He turned to run, but didn't take even one step before Bolan was on him.

He caught hold of Ryan around the neck, spun the man and tightened his grip. Ryan's feet left the ground as Bolan lifted him, arched his body and snapped the man's spine with a brutal jerk. A spasm rippled along Ryan's frame, from his neck down to his feet. When it had played itself out, Ryan was a deadweight in Bolan's grip. The Executioner released his burden, letting Ryan fall to the sodden ground, his open eyes staring. Seeing nothing in the living world...

"Jack. Jess. Paid in full."

TWO HOURS LATER the R&D building swarmed with people. There were teams from security agencies and the Air Force; medical and fire investigation teams. No civilian agencies were present. Bolan learned later that the local police had been dismissed and the outer security taken over by the Air Force. With their usual brusque attitudes the various teams pushed their way in and took command. Bolan didn't have the energy to resist.

He was treated with grudging respect, though sometimes with ill-concealed hostility. He realized that the President had to have passed the word down the line that Mike Belasko had special privileges. That part Bolan did like, especially if it annoyed the pain-in-the-ass types.

Bolan, Valens and Riba were given medical treatment. Before she was taken away by helicopter to have her shoulder wound seen to, he managed to snatch a few moments to wish her luck. She was a gutsy lady and losing her partner had to have been a shock. He knew she'd bounce back. Her fighting spirit would see to it.

DOUG BUCHANAN WAS surrounded by Air Force personnel, but they were having a hard time with Saul Kaplan. The man had taken on a new lease of life after his experience. He refused to be overwhelmed by the military and made it clear he was still in charge. It helped that Bolan had spoken and asked Brognola to intervene on Kaplan's behalf to the President.

"Tell him he owes me, Hal. He got what he wanted. Now let Saul Kaplan have what's rightly his."

"Tell the President he owes you?"

"Damned right he does after the last few days. Hal, we did what he wanted. Tell him if Kaplan doesn't get his, I won't vote for him when he stands for reelection."

Brognola snorted with laughter.

"Er, you're supposed to be dead. You don't get to vote."

"He doesn't know that, Hal. Come on, this is Washington. Play the game."

"HOW IS HE, Saul?" Bolan asked.

"Ask him yourself," Kaplan replied.

"He's fine, Mike," Doug Buchanan said.

The biocouch's adjustments had been activated. Now

it resembled a comfortable lounger, with Buchanan in a full sitting position. Now that the process was complete, he was able to move about on the couch, arms free with only thin membranes connecting him to the rest of the seat.

Physically Buchanan looked the same. If anything, he looked better than he had earlier.

"Hard to know what to ask," Bolan said. "This is new to me."

"Join the club," Buchanan told him. "All I can tell you is I'm feeling good."

"The process, and now the biocouch, has taken over Doug's bodily functions. He'll benefit from the continuous replenishment of daily requirements far better than he would from normal input. The couch will monitor him full-time." Kaplan smiled. "It will anticipate his needs and supply what he needs."

"And the cancer?"

"The couch will replace damaged cells and eliminate the cancerous ones on a daily basis. In other words Doug's cancer won't advance as long as he remains in symbiosis with the couch. We hope in time that the cancer may completely vanish."

"Looks like we're stuck with each other," Buchanan said.

"What about Zero?" Bolan asked.

"The Air Force is arranging transport to move Doug. As soon as everything is in place, Doug will be taken up to the Zero platform and the biocouch installed.

Once that is completed, Doug will be able to activate the sequence that will bring Zero online."

"And the rest is history," Buchanan said. "With luck."

KAPLAN HAD JOINED Bolan in one of the offices for a coffee, away from all the activity.

"I haven't thanked you for what you did," Kaplan said. "Now I do."

Bolan placed a couple of coffee mugs on the desk they were sitting at.

"Has anyone told Doug about Jess?"

Kaplan nodded. "It was the least I could do."

"How did he take it?"

"Like Doug Buchanan. He'll do his grieving in his own way. When he gets up to Zero he's going to have plenty of time for reflection."

"It won't affect his ability to do his job?"

"Doug is a remarkable man, Mr. Belasko. I realized shortly after meeting him how resilient he is. An unusually stable and coherent individual person. I believe he will cope with Zero and all it implies with ease."

"And what about you?" Bolan asked. "I thought you had thrown in the towel?"

"I deserved that, I suppose."

"It wasn't meant as a criticism, Saul."

"When I was a younger man, I was full of ideas that were going to bring about a wonderful world. I would create machines to help humankind and serve my country. But it seems the dreams of youth are easily seduced by the mistress of necessity. I allowed myself to be drawn into the creation of machines of destruction. All done in the name of national security. The defense of America. If we failed to remain strong, what hope was there for the rest of humankind? It all sounded so positive and I let myself run with the rest." Kaplan allowed a ghost of a smile cross his face. "You see there was a certain glamour attached to it all. Working with the military. Everything top secret. No expense spared. We created weapons and systems to protect America and the free world, whatever the free world is. My downfall was my own creativity. You see, I was good at my job. Perhaps too good. The military saw this and gave me a totally free hand. The jewel in my crown was Zero. When I first came up with the concept, even my military masters were doubtful it could be done. But I convinced them because the whole concept was mine and no one else's. Pride. Maybe even a certain amount of vanity. I was determined to make the thing work. It took almost six months to actually get approval to reach the design stage. By this time the Air Force project oversight committee saw the positive benefits of the project. It took two more years to realize the concept on computer simulations.

"The possible integration of man and machine was totally new territory. We did small-scale trials and the amazing thing was we got successful results from the start."

Kaplan broke off to drink his coffee. He raised his eyes and studied Bolan.

"International tensions. The Middle East troubles.

Asia. You name it. There were too many things out of our control. So it was decided to go ahead with Zero. There was a need for *something* that would enable America to remain the strongest nation, capable of having the final say when things started to slip into insanity."

"So you went ahead and built it."

Kaplan nodded. "Looking back, I suppose it was entirely presumptuous for the U.S. to make itself the ultimate decision maker, holding the fate of the world in our hands. But we became overwhelmed by the project. I mean, there we were, right at the center of this thing. We watched it being created, built, then shipped into orbit and assembled. It took another two years to complete after that.

"I can still remember the day Zero came partway online. When that floating mass of metal and electronics came to life and started to feed us data, it was an incredible moment."

"But…?"

"My doubts began almost at the same time, like your best and worst day ever all rolled into one. The total reality of what we had done started to put pressure on me. We had the subject for the bioconnection already undergoing the final implant surgery. His body was accepting the implants, and they were responding to neural stimulation. We had a way to go still. Then orders started to come through for us to progress to the final stages of the process. Something told me we were being asked to move too quickly. I tried to argue my objections. I was concerned about Doug, how this would affect him. I mean, this kind of thing was completely without precedent. We were moving into uncharted territory. Doug Buchanan was being turned into a new species almost. A man who would, if our conception worked, become as one with a machine on a level never before considered."

Kaplan took a moment to stare at one of the photographs on the wall. His reflection in the glass returned his stare, unblinking, seeming to peer deep into his own soul.

"It's hard to put into words," Kaplan said. "I mean, what we were doing was close to being a blasphemy. We were about to take a human and bond him to a machine so that his living presence would meld into the metal and plastic. Doug Buchanan would *become* the machine once the bonding process was complete. He would be the machine. A living and breathing part of Zero. There was no reversing the process. Doug would be Zero would be Doug. Total fusion. I started asking myself if we had the right to do this to another human being. Doug had agreed because he saw little else for him if he stayed as he was. There was no argument about his cancer. It would kill him. So his life would have been over in less than a year. He was given the choice and he took it, but I know without a doubt that he was helped in his decision by the hierarchy in the military. They saw Zero as the most advanced piece of hardware ever devised. You could almost see them drooling over the concept."

"And now the thing was under way the military wanted to speed the process?"

"Oh, yes. They saw their Zero platform orbiting in space, and they wanted it fully operational. I was given reasons why. The change in world views in the wake of September 11. Homeland defense. It was hard to disagree, because most of what was said rang true. So they began to push for Doug's integration sooner rather than later. When I objected, because I still had my concerns over that part of the system, they began to isolate me. They brought in their own people, took my authority away and all my research data. It wasn't long before I began to see the way it was going. It wasn't national security any longer. It had become national *superiority*. In truth the military wanted nothing more. I did my best to resist, but it's amazing to see how the people you believed were friends, suddenly turning away when you came into a room. I had become an embarrassment to them. I can't entirely blame them. They had their own lives to consider. Their jobs. But I had to air my views. Have my say. The atmosphere became terrible. I saw the futility of it all. So I resigned my position, which suited them ideally. I walked away.

"It occurred to me soon after that we haven't learned anything in the past thousand years except how to destroy each other, and there I was part of it. Look at us, Mr. Belasko. Supposedly the most advanced, intelligent species on Earth. But we maim and destroy each other. We debase and defile life as if it doesn't matter. No other species does this kind of thing to its own. Only the human species. In the end I opened my eyes. I saw the reality and I didn't like what I saw."

"There's nothing wrong with your thinking, Saul. But what alternative do we have? Sit back and let the bad guys win? By doing nothing that's exactly how they will win. We have a long way to go before we can settle global differences by the simple matter of talking. It would be nice if we could. In the meantime what do we do about the people who refuse to come to the table? Who openly defy national boundaries, or ignore any other agenda but their own and to hell with the rest of the world? Standing back and saying 'I won't listen,' and maybe it will go away doesn't work. Ignoring the bully only makes him think he's got away with it, so he keeps on doing it. Give him a bloody nose and he'll consider the options next time around. Saul, it's a sad fact, but that's the way it is."

"So you're saying we have to have our Zero platform? All our other weapons? If we want to survive?"

"Give me an instantly viable solution, Saul, and I'll be the first one out on the road tomorrow selling it."

Kaplan smiled, picking up his mug and draining his coffee.

"You make a simple, but effective argument, my friend. Too defined for me because I don't have an alternative solution. Regrettably I accept that you are right. And in that spirit I had better go and join the fray. If we have to have our ultimate weapon, I'm damned well going to make certain it's the best.

"Doug Buchanan deserves to be helped. I let him down before. I won't again. The Air Force isn't going to stop me. I'll give them their weapon, and I'll make life hell for them while I do it. I promise you that, Mike Belasko."

Stony Man Farm, two days later

"THE PRESIDENT is a happy man," Brognola said.

Bolan raised his eyes above the data sheet he was scanning.

"Is that my cue to stand up and cheer?"

"Not obligatory. You okay?"

Bolan shrugged. "This was a hell of a mess," he said. "The whole damned thing shouldn't have happened."

"Hindsight is always a bummer, Mack."

"The way Stahl and Stengard manipulated things is scary. It happened too easy. Hal, we don't need external enemies with people like that pair around. You realize how close it came to happening?"

"I know exactly how close it came. But, Mack, we stopped it. *You* stopped it."

"With the help of a few good people."

"How is Agent Valens?"

"She'll recover from the bullet wound. It might take longer for her to get over her partner being shot in front of her."

"By the way, we had a call routed in from your Apache buddy. He said to say thanks for recovering his truck and shipping it home. He says he can't recall it having a state-of-the-art CD and radio player in it. Or a digital car phone installed."

Bolan shifted in his seat.

"Should I expect billing for that anytime?" Brognola asked.

"He was a good friend to us, Hal. Small price to pay."

"The more I listen the more I'm convinced you're going soft."

Bolan held up the data sheet. "Aaron did a good job on the stuff I brought in. Traced a lot of Stengard's ex-military contacts. We can expect some arrests from those. And those Glock pistols. It appears Stahl used his company contacts to import a job lot from some dealer in Amsterdam. They were part of a stolen consignment taken from the factory in Austria. No serial numbers, markings of any kind. I guess Stahl figured they would stay anonymous and help avoid him being fingered."

"The files on Stahl's computer implicate some top people. When I met with the President yesterday, he told me there are going to be some shake-ups both in government and the military. We can expect some resignations from both camps shortly. Discreet withdrawals from the public eye and embarrassed silences all around."

Brognola leaned back in his seat, eyeing Bolan. "At the start of this, you were about to take some R&R."

"I need to go see Jack. It's time he learned about Jess."

Brognola cleared his throat. "I don't envy you that one, Mack. You want company? Say the word."

"Thanks for the offer, Hal. This is one I have to do on my own."

"Hey, take it easy, pal."

"I wasn't there when he needed me."

"That's crazy talk. How were you supposed to know? How does anyone know when things like that are going to happen? Striker, you saw to it they didn't walk free. You did that for Jack. And for Jess. And you'll be with Jack after he finds out. You couldn't do more if you wanted to."

Bolan stood. "I'll see you later."

"Hey, don't forget our date tomorrow. I hear the President is having the grass cut in honor of your visit."

"If I'm around, Hal. If I'm around."

LATER THAT DAY Hal Brognola received a message that informed him of the death of one Hank Winston. The man who had been in business with Chosan Xiang was found dead on a lonely stretch of highway near Lake Charles, Louisiana. Winston had been shot twice in the back of the head. The killing had all the signs of a professional hit.

Chosan Xiang had made good his promise to settle his score with the Winston. The killer was never found.

GENERAL TUNG SHAN was quietly removed from office a week later. He was summoned to a meeting at the winter house of his immediate superior, ostensibly to discuss his future. He entered the house at 11:05 a.m. on a crisp morning, when a sprinkling of snow had settled over the countryside.

At 11:07 his black military limousine left. It returned to Tung's HQ, where the driver was assigned to become chauffeur to Tung's successor. The new general was already in residence in Tung's former office. All of Tung's belongings had gone.

General Tung Shan was never seen again. His name was never mentioned officially, and all records of his existence in military files were deleted.

His removal went partway to appeasing the members of the Pacific Rim consortium who had been depending on China to remove the threat they believed would be posed by the Zero Option.

SHAO YEUNG and the sole survivor of Chosan Xiang's assault team were never seen again in China. Shao decided that it wouldn't be wise for them to return to Seattle, either. The pair eventually reached San Francisco, where Yeung accessed the bank account that held the money he had arranged for the mission. The substantial amount, which they divided between them over a period of time, allowed both men to take up residence in the city while they debated their futures. After three months they went their separate ways. They had both made the decision not return to China. Shao knew it would be a fatal mistake.

He decided, with the large amount of money he had, to settle in America. He found the country less of an evil place than he had been led to believe. Not perfect and with its own problems, the U.S. had much to offer. As with China it had good and bad. On the whole, America had a larger percentage of good points.

Shao had no idea how long he might get away with his new life. Maybe one day he would turn around to find one of the quiet assassins from his homeland who had been assigned to find and settle accounts with the traitor. Shao accepted that as part of the risk. In the meantime he reasoned that he might as well enjoy his stolen life.

Zero Platform One, Earth orbit

TWO MONTHS AFTER the incident at the R&D facility, Major Doug Buchanan initiated the unlock sequence code and watched Zero come alive around him. He sat in his biocouch with the spread of his control-command array in front of him and felt the platform hum into full life.

Monitors and computers clicked online. Digital displays flashed with light. Buchanan activated his couch and it slid to the left, along the smooth rail it was mounted on, allowing him to check readout panels and scan the readiness of all the weapons systems. He spent the next thirty minutes assessing the whole gamut of screens and displays, altering where something needed altering, adjusting and resetting where necessary.

Only when he was satisfied with the platform's initial performance did he open the audiovisual connection that put him through to Saul Kaplan on Earth.

"Good morning, Doug. You had us worried there for a moment. No problems?"

"No problems, Doc. We just wanted to be one hundred percent online before coming on air."

"That's good, Doug. Everything down here shows Zero is fully operational. We'll be spending quite some time running system checks and passing back anything we feel needs adjusting."

"We'll be here, Doc."

"Are you still feeling okay?"

"Yes. How else would we feel with a 24/7 health-monitoring system up and running?"

"You know how I worry, Doug."

"Any signs, you'll get the call."

The large TV monitor showing Kaplan seated at his own control desk also showed the gathered Air Force personnel standing behind him.

"Looks like you have visitors this morning, Doc."

Kaplan nodded. "Big day for us all. You're generating a lot of interest."

"Tell them not worry. We're doing fine."

On Buchanan's array a light flashed and immediately the platform's defense system powered to full alert. He scanned the array, checking readout screens and moved his couch to the far side of the main array.

"Doug?"

"We picked up a warning from one of the proximity scanners. Our first customer."

"Have you identified it?"

"Yes. It was a small piece of debris. Probably from some old satellite that's been floating around for years. I guess we'll be getting those from time to time."

"That's good, Doug. It shows Zero is working fine. I'll make a note about that debris. It's something we'll need to address."

"Don't worry, Doc. It's what we're here for. We'll handle it."

"Doug, I'll break off for now and let you carry on with diagnostic checks. Give me a call when you're ready and we'll compare notes."

"Will do. Zero Platform One signing off."

SAUL KAPLAN PUSHED his chair back from the command point, swinging around to face the Air Force personnel standing there.

"If I had a set of keys, I would hand them over and say congratulations. But no keys. Now the questions."

For the next few minutes Kaplan answered the questions thrown at him with ease. He knew how to play the game now, had enough knowledge to be able to give them what they wanted without ruffling their feathers.

"So we seem to have a success?" a senior captain said.

"Early days, Captain, but things are looking good. There's still a lot to do before we can accept Zero as completely successful. But don't worry. We'll have your Zero platform for you soon."

There was more to discuss. Kaplan dealt with it for another ten minutes before excusing himself for a break. He was tired. The past few days had been exhausting. Kaplan had only left the command point on rare occasions. He crossed the command room to the coffee station and poured himself a mug of coffee.

He only became aware of the uniformed figure after a minute or so. Looking up he recognized the lean, tanned Air Force major.

"Morning, Saul."

"Major Grant. What can I do for you? More help with the new volunteers for the program?"

"Not today. I just wanted to come and see for myself."

"And what do you think?"

"Very impressive. That platform is everything you said it would be."

"Do I detect a note of reserve?"

Major Grant smiled as he helped himself to coffee.

"No. It was just something I picked up. I don't think any of the others did. But I know you will have."

"And you are wondering if I am concerned about it?"

"Should you be?"

Kaplan shook his head. "I honestly don't think so. It proves to me that Doug Buchanan has completed his transition and is now fully integrated with Zero, which is exactly what I hoped would happen. But I understand your concern. I will be keeping an eye on Doug. You can be assured of that."

Kaplan was pleased Major Grant had picked up the item in Buchanan's speech.

Easily missed. Unless, like Grant, you were a trained psychologist. A man who spent his life analyzing what people said and did and why.

Just a small thing.

One word.

Doug Buchanan was referring to himself not as I, but as *we*. Not looking at himself as a man on an orbiting platform. Zero and Doug Buchanan were a single entity now. Not separate.

The process was complete, and Buchanan was truly home.

DEATH LANDS®

Death Hunt

*Available September 2004
at your favorite retail outlet.*

Ryan's razor-sharp edge has been dulled by the loss of his son Dean—but grief is an emotion he cannot indulge if the band is to escape the chains of sadistic Baron Ethan. Now with the group's armorer, JB Dix, imprisoned and near death, Ryan and the others are forced to join Ethan's hunt—as the hunted. But the perverse and powerful baron has changed the rules. Skilled in mind control, he ensures the warriors will not be tracked by high-paying thrill seekers. Instead, they will hunt each other—to the death.

James Axler
Outlanders®

MASK OF THE SPHINX

Harnessing the secrets of selective mutation, the psionic abilities of its nobility and benevolent rule of a fair queen, the city-kingdom of Aten remains insular, but safe. Now, Aten faces a desperate fight for survival—a battle that will lure Kane and his companions into the conflict, where a deadly alliance with the Imperator to hunt out the dark forces of treason could put the Cerberus warriors one step closer to their goal of saving humanity...or damn them, and their dreams, to the desert dust.

Available August 2004 at your favorite retail outlet.

Or order your copy now by sending your name, address, zip or postal code, along with a check or money order (please do not send cash) for $6.50 for each book ordered ($7.99 in Canada), plus 75¢ postage and handling ($1.00 in Canada), payable to Gold Eagle Books, to:

In the U.S.	In Canada
Gold Eagle Books	Gold Eagle Books
3010 Walden Avenue	P.O. Box 636
P.O. Box 9077	Fort Erie, Ontario
Buffalo, NY 14269-9077	L2A 5X3

Please specify book title with your order.
Canadian residents add applicable federal and provincial taxes.

GOLD EAGLE®

GOUT30

THE
DESTROYER
UNPOPULAR SCIENCE

A rash of perfectly executed thefts from military research facilities puts CURE in the hot seat, setting the trap for Remo and Chiun to flip the off switch of the techno-genius behind an army of remote-controlled killer machines. Nastier than a scourge of deadly titanium termites, more dangerous than the resurrection of a machine oil/microchip battle-bot called Ironhand, is the juice used to power them all up: an electromagnetic pulse that can unplug Remo and Chiun long enough to short-circuit CURE beyond repair.

Available July 2004 at your favorite retail outlet.

James Axler
Outlanders

ULURU DESTINY

Ominous rumblings in the South Pacific lead Kane and his compatriots into the heart of a secret barony ruled by a ruthless god-king planning an invasion of the sacred territory at Uluru and its aboriginals who are seemingly possessed of a power beyond all earthly origin. With total victory of hybrid over human hanging in the balance, slim hope lies with the people known as the Crew, preparing to reclaim a power so vast that in the wrong hands it could plunge humanity into an abyss of evil with no hope of redemption.

Available November 2004 at your favorite retail outlet.

Or order your copy now by sending your name, address, zip or postal code, along with a check or money order (please do not send cash) for $6.50 for each book ordered ($7.99 in Canada), plus 75¢ postage and handling ($1.00 in Canada), payable to Gold Eagle Books, to:

In the U.S.	In Canada
Gold Eagle Books	Gold Eagle Books
3010 Walden Avenue	P.O. Box 636
P.O. Box 9077	Fort Erie, Ontario
Buffalo, NY 14269-9077	L2A 5X3

Please specify book title with your order.
Canadian residents add applicable federal and provincial taxes.

GOLD EAGLE

GOUT31

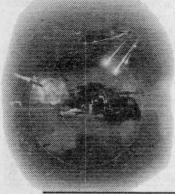